Miniplanner

A Novel

ABHA DAWESAR

CLEIS
PRESS

Published in the United States by Cleis Press Inc., P.O. Box 14684, San Francisco, California 94114.

Printed in the United States.

Cover design: Scott Idleman

Cover photo: Scott Idleman

Text design: Karen Quigg

Cleis Press logo art: Juana Alicia

First Edition.

10 9 8 7 6 5 4 3 2 1

Library of Congress Cataloging-in-Publication Data

Dawesar, Abha.
  Miniplanner: novel / Abha Dawesar. -- 1st ed.
    p. cm.
  ISBN 1-57344-115-5
  1. Manhattan (New York, N.Y.)--Fiction. I. Title.

PS3554.A9423 M5 2000
813'.54--dc21

00-064375

ACKNOWLEDGEMENTS

All the members of Jill Hoffman's workshop were very helpful during the writing of the first hundred pages of this novel. A special thanks to Robert Steward for patiently plowing through several iterations. Betty Cung, Krysztof Owerkowicz, Lisa Gordon, and Plamen Russev gave invaluable feedback. Laura DeBonis and Josh Solomon helped with the final draft. Felice and Frédérique, you both rock.

*For Mom, Dad, Chandra Aunty, Tata and
the memory of my beloved Avva.*

Miniplanner

He was my boss's boss. He came up to me and introduced himself on my first day at work.

"I'm Nathan Williams."

"André Bernard," I said, getting up to shake hands.

I had seen him once before, briefly, at my interview. We hadn't spoken.

"How are you liking it?" he asked as I sat back in my chair.

I told him I was settling in. He intruded further into my cubicle space and stroked my hair. Then he left.

I was taken aback, but then I decided it was a leftover gesture from his locker-room days. However, Tad, who had the cubicle next to mine, noticed and asked, "What was that about?"

"I don't know."

"Do you know him, André?"

"No, it's only the second time I've seen him."

"I guess you'll find out," Tad said.

Later in the afternoon, Williams called me up and invited me to a drink after work. I was surprised. My immediate boss, Yoshi Kato, had not made any such friendly gestures.

"Are you new to Manhattan?" he asked over the phone.

"Yes. I just moved last week."

"In that case, I must take you to a place you'll appreciate," he said.

I was glad that the big boss was on my side. We would become drinking buddies. I started planning my next promotion.

We met at the elevator after work. He got us into a cab and directed the driver to Sixtieth Street.

"This place is a must for everyone who works in an investment bank," he explained. The awning said "Skirts." I noticed there were only men outside on the sidewalk. The bouncers called him Nathan. We walked in.

"It's a gentleman's club," he said, gesturing to the central area, where a woman in stockings (only stockings) was hawking cigars.

We checked our coats and then Nathan meandered his way to a large sofa and sat down. There were women wearing only G-strings and sitting on men's laps. I glanced at Nathan and noticed he was wearing a wedding band. He ordered us drinks.

"So, what do you think?" he asked.

I shrugged.

"Choose a woman," he said, moving closer to me on the sofa and patting my hand.

A waitress arrived in a tight corset and stockings and handed me my scotch. I took a swig. I wasn't sure how to act. The women were attractive, but I was uncomfortable around Nathan. I didn't know what he was thinking. I made conversation about work.

"Loosen up, Bernard, let's have some fun."

I'd never been to a strip club before, but I didn't want to let on. A man sitting on a small sofa near us was watching football on the giant screen while a lap dancer sat on his lap. I watched them. He would watch the game, and during commercial breaks he'd look at her and she'd touch him.

"No touching, of course," Nathan said. He'd been able to tell that I hadn't been to a place like this before.

"Of course not," I said.

"Well, I'm going to get us a dance," he announced.

He called a bouncer and said something in the guy's ear. Soon a tall woman with straight long hair and a thin body walked up to us.

"Hello, Nathan, how are you today?"

"Good, Liz. My friend here just moved to New York. We'd like to share you."

"Hi, I'm Liz," she said, coming close to me and touching my ear.

"André Bernard is the name. Pleased to meet you."

Without any ceremony she had wiggled out of her black rayon dress and laid it on both our legs.

Nathan moved closer and whispered, "Sit like I'm sitting— her thighs will rub on your hands." I imitated him as if I were following a professional directive—which, in a way, I was.

The front of her G-string had green polka dots. She straddled our legs, putting each of her legs between each of ours and placing a cheek on each one's knee. She touched my chest with her right hand and Nathan's with her left. She knocked our heads together and then brought her breasts close to our mouths. I could smell her skin and Nathan's breath at the same time. We were both looking at her and breathing heavily.

Liz had bounced away and was jiggling her backside in our faces. She was right-on with her timing. She would move away and come back up close. She was a master. She put Nathan's hand on my knee. I had been sitting with my legs rigid and wide apart. The entire length of my right leg was now touching Nathan's left leg. Liz had her hand on Nathan's hand, which was on my knee, and she was bending down into my crotch and breathing on it. I was rock hard.

Then she did the same to Nathan. While she breathed into his trousers, he moved his hand farther up my leg till it was on my upper thigh. Liz straightened herself, removed her dress from where it was resting on our legs, and covered my crotch with it. Then she took Nathan's hand in hers and slid them both under the dress till they were practically touching my zipper.

Her face was so close to mine I thought the warm layer of air in between was going to rise and leave a vacuum, making us collide. My body was hot and bursting. She placed Nathan's hand directly on my crotch. I moaned. He was kneading me. I was utterly ablaze.

The music stopped and Liz got up to indicate her time was up.

"Stay here and help me with my friend," Nathan said hoarsely.

The music had changed, and Liz rhythmically did the grind on my legs. Then she bent her face and breathed on my zipper again and guided Nathan's hand to move quicker. I was immobile and ready to come. She pulled my hand, which had been resting on my leg, and placed it on Nathan's thigh. She was sitting in his lap now and touching his chest. I could feel his legs as tense as mine. Nathan was massaging me faster and faster. I moved my own hand farther up his leg till I could feel him. He groaned when I touched him. I placed my hand more firmly on his prick. The music picked up pace just then, and Liz switched her attentions to me. She brought her crotch close to my face. It felt as if the whole world were conspiring to give me pleasure. I ejaculated.

Liz focused on Nathan after that. I let my hand stay on his thigh but didn't do anything. I had only ever fooled around with one guy, when I was fourteen—over ten years ago. And I wasn't sure I was up for it. The song soon ended, and Nathan handed me a crisp fifty-dollar bill to slip into Liz's garter. She kissed us both on the cheek and left. We sat quietly for a while and zoned out. My boss's boss had just given me half a hand job. I was stupefied.

"Okay, let's get another," Nathan said after some time.

I was relaxed and didn't want to get into a heated state again. But I knew that he was still stiff. I smiled. He called a different girl this time. She was ethnic. Brown and luscious, but short.

"For both of us," he told her.

The new girl was shy. We didn't know her name, and she didn't get us to touch each other. But it wasn't necessary. I was completely turned on by the time she was halfway through. I could feel the heat where my leg touched Nathan's. Our thighs were pressing hard against each other. Neither of us moved. Soon the music stopped. Nathan paid her twenty.

"Want to go?" he said, standing up.

I was surprised. I got up and followed him to the coat check. I was embarrassed at the thought of stepping back into the real world with the protrusion in my pants.

"Let's get a drink next door," Nathan suggested.

Before I knew what was going on, we were inside a dark bar next to Skirts in a room full of muscular, barely clad men, and Nathan was saying "Hi" to everyone. He maneuvered us into a free space and then kissed me on the mouth. I tried to move away, but he was holding my back firmly. A part of me wondered whether this constituted sexual harassment. His legs had slid between mine, and his right leg moved all the way up. I realized it felt good and didn't resist. We French kissed by a pillar in partial public view. I embraced him. After a few minutes he took my hand and led me to a dingy room, where we started making out again. A lot of couples were doing the same thing. Nathan unzipped my pants and pulled out my penis. Then he pulled out his own. He jerked us both off. I stood balancing myself and kissing him.

"Let's go to dinner," he suggested as soon as we had come, which was more or less at the same time.

"Sure," I replied. I felt relaxed and was full of fond feeling toward him.

We got a cab and went to Karma, an Indian restaurant overlooking Central Park. It was overly romantic and terribly expensive. Nathan spoke to me gently. I was frightened.

What did he want?

"I see you have a wedding ring," I said, suddenly feeling courageous.

He laughed and then said, "She's the greatest wife on earth. We're like siblings."

I smiled. So it was merely a marriage of convenience. Mr. Head of Risk Management at Kenji Japan Bank had a wife, just like everyone else.

"We sleep together," he continued. Then he added, "She's not a lesbian or anything."

I was confused but decided to let it pass. I didn't want to poke into things that were not my business.

"I like Indian food. I'm a vegetarian," Nathan said.

I'd ordered Tandoori chicken. When the waiter placed it at my table, I felt awkward for a second. I wondered if Nathan would think me less evolved or cruel because I ate meat.

We drank Kingfisher beer. He briefed me about work, warned me about people in other departments who could prove to be cogs in the wheel for me.

"You can only go so far up in a Japanese bank. You need to leave in two years, after you've gained some experience. I'll take you with me to my next job if you want."

"How come you're so senior?" I asked. "You're not Japanese."

"Every now and then they need expertise they can only get from outside," he replied.

After dinner he flagged a cab down and said, "Can I come over to your place?"

"Sure" I replied without meaning it.

I found myself opening the door to my studio with some trepidation. First day on the job, first week in New York, and my boss's boss soon to be in my bed.

I excused myself to go to the bathroom and rummaged for condoms in the cabinet under the sink where I had put them. I put a few in my pocket and came back to the room. I was suddenly aware that he was maybe fifteen, even twenty, years older than me and had been on a half-million-a-year salary for a decade.

"I like your place, André. The little bit of your stuff that's lying around has a lot of character."

"Thank you." I could feel my face flush.

He had removed his jacket and was emptying his pockets—there was a Palm Pilot, an antique pen, two tubes of K-Y Jelly, and three Trojans in red packets. He laid them all on the floor (I still didn't have a bedside table). Then he kissed me on the mouth and slid his hand under my shirt. His hands were firm and manly, his gestures tender and womanly. When we were in bed he ran his hands on the surface of my back and I sighed with pleasure. The sight of his erection aroused me. I thought it would hurt, but with his K-Y I didn't feel bad at all. A whole hour went by in an exciting and effortless way that I had never experienced, without a single dull moment. Nathan moved me around a lot and made love with every part of his body—his hands, his tongue, his legs. I felt as if time did not exist. After we had sex, we fell asleep in each other's arms.

In the morning Nathan came up to me while I was dressing and straightened my tie. I hadn't bought a mirror yet. We went to work together.

When I was alone in my cubicle later that morning, I reeled under the shock of everything. I had no idea what would happen next. I asked myself whether I was truly attracted to men. I read all the memos on the project I'd been assigned to in an attempt to catch up. Then, Nathan called me and asked me to grab a quick lunch. I pulled on my jacket, which was hanging on my chair, and rushed to the cafeteria. I liked him.

We talked about the project that he had put me on. "It's not directly under me. That wouldn't be appropriate. But it's something that I can oversee. I'll be able to promote you."

A part of me was flattered, but the idealistic part was insulted. I was competent and could make my own mark without a sugar daddy.

"You're hating me this minute, aren't you?" Nathan asked, reading my mind.

"No," I muttered.

"Look, André. I think you bring skills to this job that no one else has, but trust me—when it comes to climbing up in this game it is partially a question of politics. I want to help you because you're bright—not because I'm sleeping with you."

I didn't say anything.

"But that's rather nice, too," he added, smiling.

I smiled back.

We were one day into what now looked like it was going to be a relationship. He spoke with a certain confidence that we were going to be together, and I found that I shared his confidence, because some things felt right. I enjoyed talking to him and reading his work-related memos to the project team. He was attentive in bed, and the sex was phenomenal.

"Don't you go home to your wife?" I asked, feeling truly comfortable for the first time.

"I do. You'll meet her. We'll talk about all that soon. Okay?"

"Good. I'd like that," I replied.

He called me late in the afternoon and asked if I'd like to spend the night with him.

"Your place, of course," he said.

"Sure."

Things were moving too fast. Two nights in a row after a six-month drought was a bit much. Moreover, I hadn't even bought myself a coffeemaker since I'd moved into my apartment. The studio needed organizing. But the idea of not being alone in bed was irresistible. I was enough at ease to ask him for a back rub; I hadn't ever had a job where I had to sit at a desk for eight hours a day. As a help desk guy in my undergraduate computer lab, I wandered among the work stations. In graduate school I was a teaching assistant. I was used to spending hours reading in the park every day. It was very unnatural to sit in front of a machine during daylight hours. Human beings were not designed for it, and hunching over the computer all day had made me sore.

Nathan recommended stores I could explore for furniture and pots and pans. He gave me a list of Thai and Indian spices to buy. He said he'd cook for me once I had my kitchen stocked. I had been ready for many lonely months in the city before I made friends, but now I already had a lover. Manhattan was as exciting as people had said—and more.

Although I had yet to buy furniture, with my signing bonus I had bought a music system. In college, I had been able to afford only a boom box and a Walkman, so all the music I had was on tapes. I still listened to my Walkman everywhere I went. It helped shut me off from the screaming police sirens in the city and the rantings of madmen. Now, I'd begun listening to Mozart and Saint-Saëns again, as I had when I was young at home and my father played a lot of classical music. I put on some Mozart for Nathan. He liked what I played.

"You know, that's quite good," he remarked, as if it were out of the ordinary that music should sound good. I could tell he hadn't recognized the piece.

In the morning, we took a shower together and dressed. He'd be wearing the same suit to work for the third day. He'd also been using my cologne. I had a bottle of Lanvin, which wasn't available in the United States. I wondered if people noticed.

"Can I see you on Saturday, André?"

It was only Wednesday, but I thought it was just as well. I needed to settle down and spend some time thinking.

I was assigned officially to the new project that Nathan had mentioned, and we had a meeting in the afternoon. There were seven people in the group. I was given responsibility for working on the new risk management system that we were building. I had to coordinate things between the quantitative group and the traders, since I was the only one who understood math, programming, and finance.

For a brief second, when I saw Nathan chew on the tip of his pencil at the head of the conference room table, I was reminded of his mouth elsewhere and felt myself getting hot. I chuckled soundlessly; I was one up on everybody in the room. But when the meeting ended Nathan bent close to my boss, Yoshi, and said something that I couldn't hear. They laughed. My boss (a handsome Japanese guy) put his hand on Nathan's shoulder. I felt a stab of jealousy that showed on my face. Nathan saw me and noticed. He stood at the door of the meeting room and let the rest of the group file out before us. He stroked my neck and whispered, "You're the only one, André. You should know."

I found myself whistling in my cubicle after I returned. My neighbor, Tad, joked and said, "You sound like a man in love, André. Who is she?"

"Yeah, right, Tad. My first week in the city. Love, indeed."

"Hey, things happen. I met my girlfriend even before I moved to New York. I was staying with a friend and looking for an apartment. We met at a bar."

"Cool, man." He was a jock. I wrote him off.

I decided on what I was going to buy for the studio. A sexy bookcase, sleek black trash cans, a glass coffee table, and a lamp. I wanted furniture that Nathan would like. Martha, the secretary on our floor, had told me that a lot of department stores were open late on Thursday evenings. I planned to leave work a bit early the next day and go shopping.

Nathan invited me to lunch again on Thursday. I looked for signs of distancing, since he'd spent the previous night at his place. But he was the same. He was consistent around me, a mix of personal and professional.

I went to Bloomingdale's in the evening and bought a bookshelf that looked like a vertical wave. I also bought straw-colored cotton curtains and steel curtain rods. By the time I got back home, I was exhausted. I wished Nathan were around. I missed his skin at night.

We met for lunch the next day; it was now a routine. After lunch I went back with him to his large office. It overlooked the river and had a view of the bridge. It was a total giveaway as to his position in the firm. There was a Bang & Olufsen music system flush with the wall. The CD rack beside it held Yanni and some other New Age music. On a bookshelf in the corner he had the complete works of Kierkagaard, Rilke, and Herder. I noticed his chairs, his desk, the coat hanger and made mental notes. His desk and credenza were unique: toffee-colored and crafted like pieces of sculpture.

On Friday night on the way home, I spotted the perfect coffee table: nonshiny steel and glass with clean lines. I bought it. It gave my apartment a clean and minimalist look. Martha, the secretary, had told me about the Chelsea flea market. I went there on Saturday morning and bought a chest of drawers and a reading lectern for my twenty-seven-pound dictionary. The pots and pans could wait till next week.

Nathan showed up for our date on Saturday afternoon with irises. They were in semi-bloom, their long petals suggestively open and longing. I looked around for something to put them in.

"I thought you might not have a vase," Nathan said, pulling out an object wrapped in newspaper from his briefcase.

He placed the vase on my table and we laughed. My coffee table and his vase looked as if they went together. Both were steel and glass. I started kissing him. It was a glorious afternoon. Sun was streaming through my window on the irises and on Nathan's skin, which glowed like gold. His buttocks were so muscular that the aesthetic pleasure alone could have given me a high. I wanted him and was aggressive and unmindful of his comfort when I took him.

Afterward, when he was drawing on my chest with his fingers, he said, "I have to go to Tokyo for two weeks. I'm leaving on Monday. The board of trustees of the bank is meeting, and I have to present a report."

I wanted to complain. What would I do in New York without him?

He traced my lips with his fingers and said, "I was wondering if we could meet for dinner Monday night before I leave. I'd like you to meet my wife."

"What?" I blurted. I was curious about her, but this was not the time. All I could think of was an empty stretch of time without Nathan's presence. I didn't want to meet his wife or know what their relationship was about.

"You'll like her. She's great at wiring people into the scene. She'll introduce you to some people."

"You said the two of you were like siblings. What did you mean?"

"We're both too grown up to think we won't be attracted to anyone else. We haven't stopped doing what we would normally do just because we're married. At the same time, at some level we know we have each other."

It sounded like a fantasy. This life was going to blow up in Nathan's face. Everyone I knew had tried the same thing in college. It never worked.

"Doesn't one person hurt when the other isn't around for them?"

"Yeah, but we're mature about it."

Nathan's world seemed like some superior plane into which the usual play of jealousy, possessiveness, and stress did not enter. My girlfriends in the past had accused me of being interfering and domineering. Nathan would have thought me a bumbling idiot.

"How many men are you sleeping with?" I asked.

"One," he replied simply.

"And women?"

"My wife. What about you?"

"You're the only person I know in Manhattan."

He smiled. I knew we had the same thoughts in our heads.

"André, I want us to be together in a relationship."

I stared at my feet. I was feeling very susceptible to injury, and I was relieved that he'd offered security.

"What do you mean by relationship?" I pushed.

"I won't sleep with another man or a woman other than my wife."

"And you won't buy irises for anybody," I said, pouting. I hadn't acted cute in front of anyone since I was a kid. Around women, I always pretended to be completely in control.

"You're so beautiful. No, I won't buy irises for anyone," he replied.

"Does your wife know about me? What's her name?" I wanted to know everything all of a sudden.

"She doesn't know. We never tell each other these things. It wouldn't work. Her name is Sybil."

"So it's the lovers who bear the brunt of all this. It's them it's hard on."

"In a way I guess you're right."

He pulled me closer to his naked torso and put his leg on mine. His calves were muscular, his knees smooth. He was entirely uninhibited, a little like my father. When I had graduated from my master's program a few months ago, my father had kissed me on the cheek and openly cried. He'd run French restaurants to put me through school. I was colder.

"Nathan, I have a lot to learn from you," I said, nuzzling up to him. It felt divine not to have to hold myself at attention all the time, to let go as I pleased and express myself. His warmth had opened me up.

He brought his lips to my nipples and brushed past them. "I'm turned on, André," he said.

"Fuck me, then."

Nathan was a masterful lover. He even managed to eroticize the opening of tubes of lube and the rolling on of condoms. He used my body any which way to please himself. Later he covered me with tender kisses and took my entire member into his mouth. I had thought that gay men were usually tops or bottoms. With Nathan, there were no rigid roles. I could be the man I'd always been, and I could be a bit of a woman, too. I never worried for a moment how I would seem to him. I was myself, and it felt good.

"I want to give you more pleasure than you've ever received," he said.

I wanted to weep. I wasn't used to such attention and such intimacy. It felt too precious.

"I hope I like Sybil," I said.

"So, are we going to have a relationship?"

"I won't sleep with anyone other than you or your wife either," I replied, poker-faced.

He laughed.

"André, you're young. I want to be fair to you. I won't ask for that much. You can sleep with others. Just don't tell me, and just don't get too involved."

"Okay," I said. I wanted to reassure him, but then I thought better of it. Nathan had said what he had for a reason. He had more experience with this sort of thing.

We went to dinner at a gay restaurant called Home Boy on Christopher Street. The entire area was gay. I had never seen that many gay men in public in my life, holding hands and kissing. This is part of my community now, I thought to myself, a little dazed.

"Nathan, are we gay?" I asked. And then felt ashamed.

"What do you think, André?" he said.

I was sure he was peeved.

"Since when have you known?" I asked, feeling idiotic at my question and trying to shape it into a normal conversation.

"Since I fell in love with a young teacher called Stephen Hart in tenth grade."

I was determined to make intelligent remarks, retrieve some dignity for myself, and understand what was going on.

"I've never understood the classification of people into gay, straight, and bisexual. Those are too discrete. Also, these distinctions ignore time," I blathered.

"You either like dick or you don't," he said, getting more upset.

"I've only liked your dick, Nathan," I replied.

"You're not serious." He looked astonished.

"Yes. I participated in some vital groping with a boy for some months in junior high. But nothing else."

"Did you like that?"

"Not much. I liked it when he serviced me. But I hated touching him."

"I was sure you were a closet case. Otherwise I'd never have done what I did."

"I'm glad you did."

"Tell me about your relationships with women, André. I want to know about you."

"Roni, Israeli. We were sixteen. Sweet. After two months it fizzled out. Samantha, summer before freshman year of college, good sex, crap everything else. Madhu, Indian, very passionate and intelligent. Her parents said she had to marry right after graduation, and I couldn't support her, so we broke it off at our commencement. It was very sad. The last was Patricia. We were graduate students. I was looking for something serious, she wasn't. Ended after a year. In the past six months...nil."

"Will you write the minutes of the project team meeting? You're good at summarizing," Nathan said. He was in a good mood again.

"Tell me about yourself."

"I will, André, in good time."

I felt cheated. He'd pried me open and backed out. I stared at the fork on my table and started playing with it.

"I'm sorry, André. I didn't mean to hurt you. It's a complicated story with Sybil."

I looked into his eyes. They were as blue as the irises he had brought me, and as longing. I reached across the table and touched his cheek. Shit! I had fallen for him. It had happened once before in my life, with Madhu. I knew the feeling.

"When did you marry Sybil?" I asked. I needed to remember this was a married and taken man.

"Last year."

"What?"

"April fourteenth last year."

"I thought you'd been married forever. You made it sound so mature."

"It is mature. We've known each other for twenty years."

I was never going to replace her. I had still been sleeping in my father's bed when Nathan and his wife had first met.

"Do you love her?" I asked.

"Yes. She's my wife."

The waiter had arrived with food, and I was saved from responding.

"Would you like some fresh pepper?" the waiter asked.

"Yes, please," I answered.

We ate in silence. I felt a little thorn in my throat. It was already starting to hurt. Pain. Nathan. Me. Pain. Why couldn't things be simple?

During dinner I eased up. Nathan and I went back to my apartment.

"Good night, André," Nathan said, sidling up to me in bed. We held hands and lay still.

"Sweet dreams," I replied.

"Are you all right?" he asked tenderly.

I moved closer to him and put my head on his chest and fell asleep.

In the morning, Nathan left after breakfast. I sat down on my bed and thought. Was I gay? Was I in love with Nathan? What did it mean?

Whenever I would pass a sexy woman, I would ask myself if I wanted her and immediately feel a rush if I did. I tried playing the same game as I thought of the most handsome men. Then I thought of Nathan. When I thought of Nathan, blood rushed to both my heads. When I thought of anyone else, it did nothing for me.

I too had had a Stephen Hart: his name was Jack, and we were in the same AP physics class. He was only a year older than me, but he seemed like a real man. He was great at physics and excelled in other things, too. He played tennis and football and always won. He was the hero of our school. I was a bit of a nerd, but when Jack took me under his wing, I moved up in everyone else's eyes. Jack's brother Danny was four years older. It was Danny I'd fooled around with.

When I first met Danny, I was eager to befriend him—after all, he was Jack's older brother. We sat together in the bleachers at Jack's football match. At half time Danny said we should go for a walk and guided me outside the stadium to a quiet corner. He kissed me hurriedly. I had never kissed before and immediately got a hard on. We made out. Whenever we met after that, Danny would rush me to an unpeopled spot and pull out his cock. He would unzip my pants and give me a blow job. He always made sure I shot all over his face. At the age of fourteen, any experience was better than no experience for me. As for Danny, he couldn't really have hoped for anything more in Gainsboro, North Carolina, in 1988.

In college I'd had a lot of friends who were gay. My best friend had been a flaming queen called John. I had asked myself then if I was attracted to men, but I'd decided that though there wasn't an ounce of homophobia in me, there also wasn't an ounce of gayness. Now this thing with Nathan was causing confusion. I didn't mind being gay, but I just needed to know, for a fact, that that's what I was. For once in my life I wanted the security of being something, of being definable and definite—in short, a word.

I decided to call John. He was taking a year off in Seattle, working in a strip club before he went back to college for a Ph.D. in math.

"John. André."

"How are you? How's the new job?"

"I slept with a man, John."

"You did? Next time I see you, there's no saying no to me."

"I'm in love with him," I said.

"Whatever happened to you?"

"He's noble. Very masculine."

"You go, bitch! How did you meet him?" John squeaked in his indubitably queeny way.

"Work."

"Aren't you working at some Japanese bank?"

"Yeah. Kenji Japan Bank."

"I gave a guy from there a blow job a few months ago. He was in Seattle on business and came to the strip club."

"When did you become a hussy?"

"He was cute, honey. So I offered it for free."

"What's his name?" I thought this was cool. Maybe all Americans at Japanese banks were gay.

"Nathan something-or-other."

A storm started in my brain, but I stemmed it.

"Fuck you, John!"

"Shit! No shit, André! Shit!"

"Yes, you cunt."

"I'm sorry. Oh! My baby, I'm sorry. If I'd known that he was ever going to be your man, I wouldn't have."

"It's okay, John. The guy's married, anyway."

"Are you cool with the gay thing and all? Have you adjusted?"

"Not quite. That's why I wanted to call you. You need to tell me something."

"Ask away, honey."

"I think I'm attracted only to Nathan, not to other men. What does that mean?"

"You're probably just not used to the idea. You'll start liking more men. It takes time. No need to rush."

"I feel like a real retard. I mean, I'm twenty-four. How was I so clueless?"

"Do you still like women?"

"I like Nathan."

"André, are you mad at me?"

"No. Honestly. It would be silly."

After that we spoke about some of our other friends. Before hanging up, John said, "All right honey, you take care. Call me if you have questions."

So Nathan was a regular at strip clubs. Not just in New York, but all over the bloody world. He'd seduced me in one, but somehow it was still really difficult to reconcile this Nathan with the Nathan in my head. I would talk to him at lunch tomorrow. He was probably going to fly to Tokyo via Seattle.

I dressed carefully for work, since I wanted to make a good impression on Sybil in the evening. I had bought a pale blue shirt and orange cuff links at Barney's to celebrate my graduation and my new job. I wore that with a dark blue suit and the blue Brooks Brothers tie my father had given me as a gift. I had my shoes shined. I wondered whether Sybil was blonde, like Nathan. Would she be tall and have straight long hair like Liz, the girl from Skirts?

"We'll meet Sybil downstairs in the lobby and then get a bite to eat," Nathan informed me over his focaccia sandwich at lunch.

"Nathan, a guy called John blew you in a strip club in Seattle. Remember?"

"Gosh! Yes." He was red with embarrassment.

"He's a friend of mine."

"It's a small world."

"Are you flying via Seattle on this trip?"

"Yes."

"Please don't go to any strip clubs." I was afraid he'd think me domineering, like all my girlfriends had, though I was practically begging.

"André, when I said relationship, I meant I won't kiss anyone, I won't let anyone blow me or touch me. Okay?"

"I'm sorry I'm so childish."

"Do you trust me, André?"

"Completely."

"You look so good. I want to fuck you. Can we go to my office?"

I smiled back. That was just what I had wanted. We finished our lunch and rushed back to the seventeenth floor, even though it was risky. He did me on his desk.

At six o'clock we took the elevator down together to meet Sybil. Nathan had brought his luggage to the office and was going to go straight to the airport after dinner. I insisted on carrying his smart leather duffel bag. He had slung his garment bag over his shoulder. As we were stepping out of the elevator, I was overcome by panic.

"Nathan. Who did you tell her I was?"

"A new guy in the firm. Someone I feel really close to. Don't worry, she won't suspect." He gripped my elbow very hard, till it hurt.

"Sybil, I want you to meet André Bernard." And then, turning to me, he said, "My wife, Sybil."

She was wearing a beige trench coat and a maroon suit under it. I took her hand, and then in a gallant gesture I brought it to my lips and kissed it. My father did that to all women.

She smiled and said nothing.

We walked out of the building and hailed a cab. I had no idea where we were going. I was trying to memorize Sybil. She was almost as tall as Nathan (he was six-foot-three) and had shoulder-length blonde hair. Was she beautiful? She may have been absolutely beautiful. I couldn't tell. All three of us were sitting in the back of the cab, and Sybil was sitting between Nathan and me. I wanted to squeeze Nathan's hand but couldn't. I looked out of the window instead and told myself I was an idiot.

We arrived at some restaurant, and I found Nathan telling me how it was their favorite restaurant and pinching my ass as we walked in through the narrow door in single file. I wondered what we were all going to talk about. Investment banking?

Nathan sat across from Sybil, and I sat next to her. They ordered toasted goat cheese salad for an appetizer, and I got mussels. Sybil said she was a vegetarian like Nathan. I wondered if it was necessary to become a vegetarian to have a long-term relationship with Nathan. I could give up red meat and even poultry, but not seafood.

It was surprisingly easy to talk to Sybil. She was a furniture and interior designer who designed the insides of offices and banks. She had been a mathematician at the Fed but had switched to design after a few years. We skipped around between light-hearted joking and serious discourse. Sybil and I shared one interest—abstract mathematics. I hadn't given Nathan any credit. I'd assumed he'd married a bimbo. But Sybil was like us. I liked her and felt very comfortable around her.

At some point, Nathan went to use the rest room. I was suddenly aware of the fact that Sybil was sitting right next to me. Our bodies were within a few inches of each other. I waited for the waiter to refill our water and used the activity around the table to move away from her.

After Nathan got back he glanced at his watch. The sight of his wrist, tempered with bulging nerve and bone, sent a tingle up my spine. He said there was time for dessert and winked at me. The waiter got us menus. Nathan read through each of the items as if we were in a recitation class in first grade and kicked me under the table when he read "Molten Chocolate Volcano."

"So what would you like to eat, André?"

"Molten Chocolate Volcano."

"Darling?" he asked, looking at Sybil.

"The sorbet."

"Do you want a whole one, André, or do you want to split it?" he asked, looking at me.

"Let's split it."

We placed our orders. When the cake arrived, it was obvious what Nathan was getting at. It sat in a rich sauce and was very crumbly. The only way to share it was for the two of us to sit next to each other.

"Sybil, maybe we should swap places," he said.

They moved around. I was getting jittery. It was time for Nathan to leave, and I hated the idea. Our legs were touching each other, and he was holding my hand under the table. I was too nervous to enjoy it or think. Sybil was smiling sweetly across the table from us, and we seemed, I gathered from their calm faces, to be having some sort of normal conversation.

"What do you think, André?" Nathan asked.

"Uh huh!"

"He wasn't listening," Sybil said indulgently.

I went beet red. Underneath the table I was playing with Nathan's wedding ring. Sybil got up to go the rest room. I was dizzy. It was like watching a high-speed movie. Nathan looked at me and asked, "Are you all right?"

"I—I love you, Nathan," I blurted.

"I love you, too," he replied, without blinking an eyelid.

My hear started thudding immediately.

We stared at each other till Sybil returned. I couldn't tell if she had caught on. Nathan looked at Sybil and said, "It's time for me to leave."

I wished Nathan had addressed me. But she was his wife. I'd better get used to the idea, I told myself.

We waited for the waiter to bring the check.

"Do you know a lot of people in the city?" Sybil asked me.

"No."

"I may go out with some friends later in the week. Would you like to join me?"

"Yes. That would be great. Thanks."

Nathan insisted in picking up the tab. When we got out of the restaurant, Nathan took the first cab we got. He put his bags in the trunk and turned to hug his wife.

"See you in two weeks, Sybil." He kissed her on the mouth. I turned away and stared at the sidewalk.

Once he was seated in the cab, he held out his hand for me. I had to bend down into the darkness of the cab to shake it. He sealed my mouth with a burning kiss and said, "I won't go to strip clubs."

"No, go and see John in Seattle," I said.

I shut the door and the cab took off. I turned to Sybil. "You'll miss him a lot."

"I'm used to this," she said. I wondered if she'd missed him when he had spent those nights with me. I felt a little sorry for her.

"Let me get you a cab," I said.

"Where do you live?"

"Twenty-ninth and Third," I replied.

"Let's share a cab. I can drop you off on the way."

"Okay."

We got a taxi. She was warm and lively. I was glad I'd met her. I almost forgot she was Nathan's wife until a little emptiness in my belly reminded me that Nathan was gone, and that reminded me she was his wife.

"Have you furnished your apartment, André?"

"Most of it. I still need a desk."

"I love furniture. I can help you buy it if you like."

"The problem is I want it to fit in this crevice by the side of my alcove, and it has to be a particular height and this specific shade of toffee."

"Nathan likes toffee-colored furniture."

"Really?" I remarked, infusing my voice with surprise. I had to watch out. Another few slips like this and she'd be on to me.

"Yeah. There's a great store in our neighborhood where you can get custom-built furniture, and they'll finish it in that color for you."

"Custom-built isn't going to work. I can explain what I want, but I could never draw it."

"I can draw. I've designed all of Nathan's pieces in the office."

"Have you really?" Was that why the side of his desk was smooth and curved and didn't hurt my stomach when I lay face-down on it? I was jealous that her love for him was embodied, ever present in his office.

"If you show me your corner now, I'll fax you a blueprint tomorrow."

"Great! Why don't you come up?" I'd spoken without think-ing and felt a tiny bit of discomfort. But then I told myself that if I hadn't been in love with Nathan, this was just the woman I'd ask for a date. I genuinely liked her—I wasn't being insincere just because she was his wife. And more than that, Nathan had wanted me to be friends with her.

I had a panic attack as Sybil and I were in the elevator rising up to my floor. I fiercely tried to remember if there might be tell-tale signs of Nathan lingering on. If he'd forgotten his fancy pen or something, that would be it. I opened my apartment door and took the whole room in. Everything seemed in order. I pointed the alcove corner to her, and then we walked into the main room of the studio.

"You're so like Nathan. He loves irises. And that's just the kind of vase he would have bought."

"Really?" I was starting to feel slimy because of all my reallys.

"Let's see, do you have a measuring tape?"

"No," I replied, smiling. I felt as if I were being difficult. I enjoyed the feeling.

She fumbled around in her purse and unfolded a piece of yellow paper torn from a legal pad. She used it to measure the area and asked me how high I wanted the desk. She asked me questions about how I wanted it to look and feel and then asked me to sit pretending the desk was in front of me so she could gauge my posture.

"I'll send you something tomorrow."

"Thank you so much; this is very nice of you. I appreciate it," I said formally. I wanted to hug her.

"André, I rarely like people instantly in the way I've taken to you. Nathan's spoken so highly of you, but more than that, I just feel like I can trust you." She was standing at the doorway ready to leave, with her arms open for a hug.

I stepped forward to hug her and kissed her on the cheek. Her cheek was warm. I felt as if I had just made a good friend. I said I'd walk her to the elevator. When the elevator door opened, we kissed quickly again, this time on the lips. She stepped into the elevator and the doors closed. I walked back to my apartment licking my lips, realizing what I was doing only after I had tasted the flavor of her lipstick on my mouth.

I went to bed feeling a twinge of longing, missing Nathan, my heart aglow with a sense of connection with Sybil. I didn't want to think about it.

Sybil called in the afternoon the next day.

"I have a few blueprints for you. Maybe we can go over them."

"Sure. I can meet you at six-thirty. I'm glad we met, Sybil," I said.

We arranged to meet in the lobby of the building just like we had the previous night. This time there was no Nathan, and I was no longer dreading meeting her. I called John in Seattle after I hung up on Sybil and told him I'd asked Nathan to call on him. I wasn't sure if he'd stop by on the way to Japan or on the way back.

Sybil was waiting for me by the fountains in the lobby, facing the large windows, her back to the elevators. I lightly touched her shoulder and called out her name. She turned and gave me a warm kiss on the cheek. I smiled and led her out of the building.

"Well, I have three plans," she said laying out sheets of white paper on the table in the café. The drawings were in fine blue ink, the lines strong and simple. I was completely blown over.

"This is brilliant, Sybil."

"Thanks."

"I want all three."

She explained which would be easier to fashion, which more practical, which more space-saving. It was like listening to a mathematician, she had such a grasp of space, and the flow of lines was crystalline. I watched her as she spoke and wanted to kiss her red lips.

An hour had passed without either of us noticing. I asked her if she'd like to get dinner. We walked from the café near my office all the way to Chelsea. The evening was warm and moist. The roads had a sheen of precipitation that made the atmosphere mysterious. I was happy walking with her.

"I wonder where Nathan is right now," I said.

"He called me in the afternoon from the airport in Seattle. He was going to take the flight to Tokyo in another hour. So he's on the plane now."

"Ah! How long have you known him?"

"Twenty years."

I had done some arithmetic in my head the previous night. Sybil looked young, in her late twenties. Some piece of the puzzle was missing.

"Were you still in a stroller when you met him?" I asked, laughing.

"Close. He was our neighbor. I was twelve when I first met him."

Sybil looked a good five or six years younger than her years. I had thought she was my age. She had a very fresh late-twenties face. I wondered if I'd look as young at thirty-two.

We had reached Chelsea, and Sybil decided on a Thai restaurant. After we'd ordered coconut milk soup, I said, "So, tell me all about Nathan and you."

"He was twenty-five. I didn't have siblings, and he was like an older brother to me. We'd go on family picnics to the countryside and Nathan would join us. Later he moved away to London for a few years. When he came back he got in touch with us. I was sixteen. I developed this huge crush on him. After that, for many years I did everything in my power to make him fall in love with me. He liked me, but for a long time he just couldn't see me that way because he'd known me before I was a teenager. He'd known me when I had braces on my teeth."

I looked at Sybil's mouth, and she flashed me a smile showing me all her teeth. They were perfect. I wondered if she'd hate me for the rest of her life if she knew I was sleeping with her husband.

"So, it's the perfect marriage," I said.

"Close. It's an open marriage."

"Open?"

"Yeah. We think monogamy can get stifling and a marriage should never get stifling."

"That's the only reason?" I asked. Was it possible she didn't know he slept with men?

"Yes."

"What if he falls madly in love with someone else?" I asked.

"It'll suck. But as long as I don't know…"

"You'd rather not know?"

"It'll be better if I don't know."

Women were complex. I was fast losing any grip on Sybil's mind. I was also asking questions that were too close for comfort.

"We shouldn't talk any more about this, André," she said.

"You're right—I don't want to."

After dinner I hailed a taxi without asking Sybil and showed her in. I didn't want to be in a situation where she'd invite herself to my place.

"André, will you come to my place for tea? You can see some of our furniture."

"Now?" I asked, my heart sinking. I couldn't say no. I wanted to see where Nathan lived.

"Yes, now."

"Okay," I said, getting into the cab.

We arrived at their apartment in the far West Village. It was a brownstone. I walked behind Sybil. She took me to Nathan's study right away. Everything in the apartment and the study was exquisite. The furniture, the paintings hanging on the wall, the smells in the room. Nathan painted. I hadn't known. His paintings were bright and abstract. They were all signed on the bottom left, his name spelled in capital letters in tiny print: NATHAN WILLIAMS. I wanted him to give me one. I wanted him to be in love enough with me to want to do it.

"Might as well give you a tour," Sybil said after she'd shown me two desks in his study.

We climbed up the stairs to the second floor and went into the bedroom. There was a huge bed with a leather base in the center of the room. Handles, shelves, and various other swiveling attachments projected from its edges. The bed was custom-made for breakfast in bed, anal sex, night reading, everything. I wanted to share all of Nathan's life with him.

We discussed Sybil's designs in the study over tea. She moved one of Nathan's desks around to show how mine would be both similar and different. She threw off her black pumps and bent down on the floor, turned the heavy desk around by its legs. When I moved to help her with it she gestured wildly.

"No, you have to sit there and look—otherwise you won't see the effect of the incline on the top."

I stood and watched. After she had made her point, I went and moved the desk back into its original position. I could feel the heat from her body. She was a little out of breath and had broken into a sweat. I stared at her.

She kissed me. On the mouth. Deliberately.

I was shocked. And hard in seconds.

She was kissing me and biting my lips. Squeezing my bum and playing with my ears. I responded without thinking. We were kicking away my shoes while we were still locked in a tight embrace, making our way together up the stairs like some clumsy bit of machinery trying to climb. We were naked by the time we reached the bed. Her skirt was at the bottom of the stairwell, her stockings hung on the railing on top. My pants were hanging with her stockings. Nathan's bed, I thought to myself as I fell on it, Sybil one with me. We landed on the soft mattress and bounced up simultaneously.

After our first animalistic fit was over, I flipped her on her stomach and looked at her back. It reminded me of the famous photograph by Man Ray of a woman's back with a violin painted on it. I was trying not to think of Nathan.

"Sybil, I have a headache."

"Lie down," she commanded and sat up herself. She gripped my forehead in her hands and pressed the sides of my head. She applied so much pressure I thought my skull would break. The headache disappeared.

"It's gone," I said.

"What were you thinking, André?"

"Nothing."

"Past love? Present love?"

"Nothing."

"Are you sure?"

"Yes." I replied, smiling. I liked her very much, and I was already lying to her and hurting her, and she didn't even know. She was humming a tune.

"Sybil, I don't want to hurt you."

"I'm the married one. How can you hurt me?"

I shrugged my shoulders.

She brought me closer to her and pulled the comforter over us. We fell asleep. I woke up a few hours later because of a bad dream, one that reminded me of dreams I'd had when I was young. I was in Nathan's bed with Sybil, and Nathan walked in. He spoke to me in the voice and tone he always used. He was upset, not by Sybil, but by me. He said I'd hurt him, and he looked sad and distant. I woke up frightened and sweating. I wanted to cry and apologize to Nathan. It would never happen again. Would he give me another chance?

I looked down at Sybil. She was sleeping calmly. I was astounded. I got angry at myself. I wasn't cheating on my wife or my husband. It was they who should feel guilty, I told myself. The emotion exhausted me. I moved close to Sybil. She stirred in her sleep and murmured. My heart stopped—I was sure she was going to say Nathan's name. She smiled, and through her closed eyes she said, "André, you're so sexy."

I gave in to the moment and let myself get drunk on the smell of her hair and her skin. I fell asleep again.

In the morning she made me eggs for breakfast and kissed me good-bye.

When I got into the office I checked my messages at home. Nathan had called from the Tokyo airport in the middle of the night New York time.

"Wanted to tell you I miss you, André," he'd said.

I got up from my desk and went to his office. I looked out his window and stared at his shelf. It helped to be in his room. There was a Post-It note on his desk that said, "Call JMF Peterson."

When Martha, the secretary, passed by I asked, "Who is JMF Peterson?"

"He's a quant."

"A what?"

"A quant."

"What's a quant?" Was I supposed to know this?

"A quantitative analyst. A mathematician."

"You call them quants?"

"Everyone calls them quants."

"Where's Nathan?"

"He went to Tokyo, did you forget?" she said, giggling.

"Oh, yeah!" I said, screwing up my forehead, and left his office.

My message light was blinking when I got back to my desk. Sybil had left me a voicemail.

I called her back. She wanted to see me. They are bloody siblings, I thought to myself, Nathan had been right. I had never met such intense people. I agreed to meet her after dinner. I needed a few hours to think. Work, sex with husband, work, sex with wife was not a good routine.

I am screwing the wife of the man I love. Do I love her? No. What do I feel for her? I like her. He loves her. She loves him. I'm a pawn. Maybe they've set me up and are having a cruel laugh at my expense, I thought.

When Sybil came to my apartment that night, the hard shell I had grown dissolved at the first sight of her. She was so gentle that it was impossible that she should plot my downfall. We talked for a while. She told me about her family and how she used to think when she was a child. She talked a lot about Nathan. I encouraged her to. I wanted to know everything I could about him. I hoped I could get a sane perspective on him by listening to someone else talk about him. But it was hopeless. Sybil worshiped him like I did. The only logical conclusion to draw was that he was perfect.

My phone rang when Sybil was talking. I assumed it was Nathan calling, so I didn't pick it up. I was afraid my voice would falter and I'd tremble for the rest of the evening.

"Let it ring. I can't be bothered," I said to Sybil.

The answering machine clicked. I held my breath. I prayed the volume was down to zero. When I realized it was, I breathed again. For minutes after that I couldn't pay attention to what Sybil was saying. Contact with Nathan could have been within reach of my hands, and I'd let it pass. I felt treacherous.

"André, can we sleep? I'm getting tired," she said after a while.

"Sure."

We both got under the covers. The phone rang again. The sound of the ringing tore through the room. We both lay still. It rang four times before my machine got it.

"Sybil, if you are so in love with Nathan, then why are we here?" I asked. I was really asking myself.

"Do I have to tell you this?" she asked, letting out a long breath.

"No. But I'd like to know."

"I was attracted to you the moment I saw you. I'm not using you," she replied. I didn't know why she had said it. But now I was sure she was using me. She had an agenda. Maybe I had an agenda, too.

"That's not enough of a reason," I egged her on.

"At some level I know I'm doing it to protect myself from Nathan."

"What do you have to protect yourself from? He doesn't seem to me the kind of person who would harm you."

"I'm obsessive about him. I don't want to talk about it. Let's drop it," she said firmly. I didn't have a choice. Everything she'd said sat around uncomfortably in the back of my head.

"Does sleeping with me help in any way?" I asked, trying a different approach.

"I think it could."

"What about me are you attracted to?" I asked, looking at the wall. I was embarrassed to be speaking about myself like this.

"Can we leave this for another day?"

"Sure. Sure."

She had come close to me, and we were breathing into each other's faces. Her hands were under my T-shirt, exploring my back. For a long time we just felt each other. It was sensuous, and it lacked the instant combustion chemistry that Nathan and I shared.

"Sybil, Sybil, Sybil," I let out when we were making love.

"André, you're the only guy other than Nathan I've slept with in a year."

"I like that."

Sybil tasted like citrus fruit. She made demands in bed that took me by surprise. And she squeezed my butt in a way that reminded me of Nathan. It was scary.

"André, I've just met you and I've seen you only three times. It's never happened so quickly before."

"We met without the usual defenses. It happened. I'm not going to hurt you," I replied. I imagined I was Nathan and said the things I thought he'd say. He'd shown me how to be sensitive, and I was following in his footsteps with his wife.

"Do you feel guilty?" I asked.

"No. Should I?"

"I don't know."

"Nathan's sleeping with God knows who," she said.

"Did he tell you?" I asked.

"No."

"Does that hurt?"

"Yes. But on the other hand, I'm the one who wanted to be able to sleep with other people if I needed to."

"Is it an emotional need or a physical one?"

"Both. I love him too much. I am so jealous this is the only way to contain it."

I was a little afraid of Sybil for a moment. She was driven by motivations that were incomprehensible to me. And to protect herself, she would do things that might hurt me.

I embraced her tightly to alleviate my fear. Then in a fit of passion I had sex with her, cleaved the cheeks of her ass, penetrated her from front and back. She liked it. I rammed into her incessantly till she was half off the bed. With her head hanging upside down from the foot of my bed and her legs flailing violently in the air, Sybil had a single, full-bodied orgasm. Just like a man.

I stared for a second in amazement at my handiwork and then realized I was in deep trouble. Not only was my sexual orientation highly dubious and my emotions for the husband-wife pair at best jumbled, but my physical desires were absurd and impossible. I wanted the same thing from her. I wanted from her what I had wanted from Nathan. I wanted from her what Nathan had given me.

I tore my sticky body from hers and sat on the bed, trying to understand my desire.

"André, do you want me to fuck you?" Sybil asked.

I was silent. How did she know?

She pushed me down on the bed and flipped me on my stomach. She lay on top of me and then with intense con-centration set to work on my backside while she bit the skin on my spine. She spread the lube and knew what she was doing. I wondered for a second if she'd ask why I had lube on my bedside table, but she hadn't noticed.

After I came my mind was blank, for a while, as usual. The first postcoital thought was André Bernard, you just got fisted by a woman. I smiled and opened my eyes. Sybil was crying silently.

"Oh God, what happened?" I kissed her face in a slight panic.

"You're exactly like him."

I wanted to say, "So are you."

"That's why you like me," I remarked. It was chillingly clear now.

She didn't respond. And her silence resounded in the room. After a few minutes she said, "André, I needed to get away from feeling those things."

She cried openly now, without stifling the sound.

Then, in a moment of anger, she started hitting my chest. The first time it was endearing, but then she used some force and I had to cross my arms in front of me.

"What are you doing?" I said sharply.

She stopped hitting me but continued crying.

"You are fucking exactly like fucking Nathan," she sobbed.

I felt tender and naked. I could have opened my soul and pulled it out and shown her. Told her everything and become complete. It took all my discipline and effort to close the doors of my heart and padlock them instead. To keep my secret.

"You're thinking too much," I said, more to myself than to her.

She laughed through her tears and said, "This is a fucking mess."

Then she settled into my shoulder. I was exhausted and fell asleep.

In the morning, when I brewed coffee in the new cappuccino maker I had bought, Sybil seemed to have regained control.

"You look good. You're going to be fine," I said, looking at her.

"I'm always fine in the morning, André."

She carried herself with a striking sort of independence. I sensed she was fighting me in some way. It made me smile and like her more.

"André, are you going to be all right around Nathan?"

"Of course." For a moment I forgot that she didn't know.

"You must never tell him," she said.

"I won't."

"I'll kill you."

I was frightened of her again. She looked like she meant it.

"Point taken," I said dryly. I withdrew from her and started to see her from the outside. Was this a psychotic woman? Nathan, I would have followed blindfolded into an abyss. Sybil, I just didn't know.

It was time for me to leave for work. Sybil came closer and gave me a hug. She tousled my hair and said, "I think I need to spend some time alone. I don't think I should see you tonight."

I nodded. I wanted to be able to speak to Nathan over the phone at night. I missed him.

Near my cubicle in the office there was a single small window. At five when the sun set, I could see the GE building in Midtown glinting like a rain of sunflowers. Everything reminded me of Nathan, the color of his skin and hair. When I got back home after work, I looked at Sybil's drawings for my desk and tried to decide which one I liked best.

I had not spent a night alone for a few days, and I felt a little lost. I went for a walk down to the Village to buy CDs at Tower Records. I put on my yellow Walkman and played it full blast as I sauntered down Third Avenue. I had been playing the *Jupiter* Symphony for the whole week over and over again on my subway ride to work. It was impossible to tire of it. It spoke directly to my body. I would jerk my head back and forth in response to some of its naughtier passages. I could feel Amadeus in my toes, and sometimes it brought an irrepressible smile to my mouth. People gave me amused looks. At Tower I bought a Grieg CD and some more Mozart. Then I came home and read an article on dreams in a scientific journal. New research had shown that Freud was wrong. Dreams weren't about one's id and ego and hidden fears but were caused by easily decipherable chemical reactions in one's brain. The brain, of course, tried to make a full story out of any information that was passed to it. Our waking minds filled in the blanks. The article concluded that just as in general we were driven by a desire to be whole, our dream interpretations were also driven by this desire. The conclusion hit me hard. It spoke to me directly—it was about me.

My dream about Nathan and my father and guilt was not a coded message in which I could find some deep truth. If the article was correct (and it was supported by twenty-three years of research on REM sleep and neurobiological studies on serotonin and norepinephrine, chemicals of the brain stem), then dreams were merely a loose mix of the thoughts I was already having. The thoughts were jumbled because the brain stem released chemicals in a different pattern when one was asleep than when one was awake. I knew for a fact that Nathan reminded me of Dad. I knew for a fact that I felt guilty. Dreams were merely distorted mirrors. There was chaos in my life in the daytime, and the same chaos was reflected at night in my dreams.

As a child I had been morbid. Most children wanted to be shielded from harsh truths and made believe in order to survive. My friend Guido, whose parents were divorced, would pretend that he was in one big happy family. I was very different. I would read the word *mother* somewhere and repeat to myself slowly, "You do not have a mother, André Bernard. Your mother is dead." I had never escaped from reality during the day or at night.

Things had changed now. I didn't deny the life I was leading, but I avoided dwelling too much on it. The first time I had avoided thinking about anything had been after my breakup with my Indian girlfriend. With the Nathan-Sybil situation, I just wasn't trying to figure it out. Was it laziness? I dismissed that idea. Any figuring out would be artificial, an attempt to understand the truth by slotting it. By subverting it and making it simple. I wasn't with Sybil because I was on a curiosity-driven fact-finding mission about Nathan. I wasn't with her because he was married and I wanted to have another person in my life for padding, like he had Sybil. I wasn't with them because I was bored, since I barely had free time to begin with. Maybe I was with them for no reason at all. Maybe life was random, and the first step to understanding it was to accept its senselessness.

Sleep and music were not senseless, though. I put on the Grieg CD I had just bought and fell asleep to his *Peer Gynt* suites. I had been sleeping a few hours when the phone rang.

"André, how are you?" It was Nathan.

"I miss you."

"Same here. You're never home. I've been calling like crazy."

"Sorry. How is Japan?" I spoke rapidly. I didn't want him to linger on that thought for long. It had been him calling last night.

"It's fine. I've been before. Have you seen Sybil again?"

My blood froze. I felt as if I'd been caught red-handed.

"Uhh. Yes."

"I was so happy we all went out. She seemed to like you a lot. What about you?"

"Yeah, great. Just great."

"I like an integrated life. I was glad the two of you met."

I had a vision of a computer image of myself breaking into a thousand pieces. A fractured existence. I wanted a single, whole life like Nathan had. I wanted peace.

"I'm glad if it makes you happy," I replied.

"André, I just spoke to Sybil and she said she was helping you with some furniture design."

"Yeah, it's rather nice of her really."

"I think she knows about us and that's why she's doing it."

"I don't think so, Nathan. She seems sincere."

"I never want her to know."

"It wouldn't be good, Nathan. I don't want her to know either."

"André, I shouldn't be dumping all my fears and concerns on you—it's not right."

"Nathan, nothing's wrong with it."

"Sweetheart, go to sleep. I know it's late."

I blew him a kiss over the phone. And got back under my sheets. He was my guardian angel. I was just drifting back into sleep when the phone rang again. I thought it was Nathan calling with an afterthought, but it was Sybil.

"I've been crying again, André," she said.

"Why?"

"Nathan called me. He's so unsuspecting."

"What do you want to do?"

"I want to see you." I thought I'd heard wrong.

"You mean you don't want to see me."

"No, I mean I want to see you. Now."

"Come, then."

"Are you sure you don't mind?"

"Sybil, you know I don't."

"I'll be right over."

She was there soon. Her London Fog trench coat tied casually over her red silk slip, her hair all over her face, and her eyes bloodshot from too much crying.

"So, tell me," I said.

"I wanted to crumble when he called."

"Do you feel bad?"

"I feel angry."

"What's Nathan done?" I wanted to go to war on his behalf.

"I'm angry at myself, André."

"For this?" I said pointing at our legs, which were touching.

"No."

"Then?"

"For wanting to crumble."

I screwed up my forehead questioningly. I wondered if Nathan understood her any more than I did. I wondered if he would act the same way I did if he were in my position.

"I've concluded, and we don't need to go into that now, that it's good for me to see you. I'm angry with myself because I wavered about that conclusion when I heard Nathan's voice. I reacted emotionally and weakly," she explained.

"What's wrong with emotion?" I asked.

"Nothing's wrong with emotion. I'm angry because I was willing to uproot my own life, and our affair, out of some soppy, childish, emotional reaction to Nathan's voice."

Each time she said "I'm angry," her eyes would become like bright pointy stars and her teeth would clench. Sybil is borderline nuts, I thought to myself and looked at her again. She smiled at me and tapped the back of my hand. It felt nourishing.

"Sybil, can I fuck you?" I asked.

"No, I want to fuck you first this time."

I played like an obedient boy and took off my clothes. Then I lay facedown on my bed, wondering if Nathan liked Sybil doing this, too. Our role reversals were complete. I was the one having multiple orgasms any which way, and she was the one coming with a shuddering stop.

The morning was clear and emotionally sparse again. I felt strong and formidable.

"Sybil, how long can we go on like this?" I asked.

"I don't know, André. Do you want to stop?"

"No." I wondered to myself why I wanted to see her. I needed to figure that out.

"We'll go on and see what happens," I added.

We left it at that. I got to work and called Nathan in his hotel room in Tokyo. I talked to him about the project. I wanted to talk to him without the emotional drain of thinking about our personal lives. At lunch I ate with Martha. I was surprised that a conservative bank had hired her. She had dreadlocks and wore bright colors. Today her dress was riding up her round ass.

At night Sybil and I were in each other's arms again. By midnight we were asleep, and at one I was awake, sweating at Nathan's presence in my dream. Apologizing, guilt-ridden, and terrified. At one-fifteen I was waking Sybil up and moving my member into the crevice between her cheeks, getting hard, and making love to her. At seven in the morning I was awake and strong again. Invulnerable. At nine I was debriefing Nathan over the phone on the project team meeting of the afternoon before and asking him for instructions on the next phase.

The routine continued for the next one and a half weeks till Nathan got back to New York. Martha the secretary was the mother I'd never had. She soothed my nervous outbreaks with her simplicity. She made me tea and brought it to my desk at moments when I most needed human contact. She played with her long brown dreadlocks and smiled as if I were special.

The night before Nathan arrived was nerve-racking. Sybil and I had been seeing each other every night. I knew that she would try to disentangle herself now. I wondered if she would be cruel.

"He's coming back," she stated after we had sex.

"Yes. I spoke to him from the office earlier and he said he'd come in straight to work."

"I won't be able to see you tomorrow night, André."

"I know. That's all right."

"Will you miss me?"

"Yes, of course," I said, and I thought how I'd miss Nathan, too.

"I can try to see you every other day."

"Sybil, can I say something?"

"Yes."

"You won't misunderstand me? You promise?"

"I'll try."

"I can't go on seeing you this way. I've become a bundle of nerves. I'm going to need some time to myself."

"What do you want?"

"I think we should meet just two times a week or so and maybe during the weekends on days or something. I have to keep myself centered. At least when Nathan is in town."

She reflected at length and then said, "That's acceptable." And looked up smiling.

I let out a long sigh in my head. If Nathan and Sybil were both to spend alternate days with me, they would never see each other, and then they'd get suspicious. I was reading a Graham Greene book in which a man got a private eye to shadow his lover. I was paranoid that they would find out and banish me from their lives.

Nathan walked into the office, scruffy and underslept, in the afternoon. He called me to his room right away. When I walked in, he shut the door and looked at me questioningly. I kissed him on the forehead. He hugged me. I was overcome with a sense of tenderness. Kissing his face and the daylong shadow on his chin aroused me.

This time I did him on his desk.

"I'm going to have to spend tonight at home, André," Nathan said as he put his belt back on.

"Yes."

"Are you okay?"

I nodded.

"Will you tell me if this ever hurts you?"

"I'll be fine, Nathan, so long as you're nice to me."

"We can manage that."

"Did you meet John in Seattle?"

"No. I was exhausted. I just slept in my hotel room."

I left his room. Then I sent him an e-mail saying he should leave without saying bye. And I sent Martha an e-mail asking if she'd like to catch a movie with me at the Angelika after work.

Martha and I were ready to step out of the office when the phone rang. It was Sybil.

"Yes," I said.

"André Bernard, don't forget me."

"I won't."

Martha and I went to dinner after the movie. It was relaxing and a lot of fun. She talked about many different things. Not in the same category as Nathan and Sybil, but bright enough. She had the most delicate hands I had ever seen, and she exuded warmth. I had felt at home with her from the first time I had spoken with her.

She threw her head back over dessert and laughed and said, "André, just what do you think of me? I'm not as tame as you think. This job is just to keep the money going."

I decided that I wanted to find out more about her. She was intriguing.

After I put her in a cab, I walked home knowing that I would sleep without nightmares. I had one last thought of Sybil and Nathan, of the two of them in bed together, as I got under my comforter. Then I was out like a light.

Nathan passed me in the corridor when I got into work the next morning.

"Tonight. Your place?" he whispered. His left eyebrow raised.

"Yes," I replied.

The afternoon meeting with the team was positive. Nathan's visit to Tokyo had generated a lot of excitement about the project with the trustees. Everyone in our office was on a high. My own role was taking shape, and my increasing importance in the enterprise was becoming obvious. After the meeting I went to get myself a cup of coffee. When I got back I made some swift calculations to see when I could hope to rise two steps up, get a promotion, and leverage off this project.

My whole short twenty-four-year-old life flashed past me in a second. I had grown up in near-penurious circumstances, and my father had worked his ass off to make sure I got a decent education. I had worked my own ass off to live up to his expectations. I'd won scholarships through school and college. I'd given every ounce of myself to my academic life so that I could make it big. Yet, now that I was practically skating on the border of success, life seemed unreal and nothing seemed to matter. Emotions that I hadn't felt before had lodged themselves in the center of my chest. Nathan's approval and affection were so much more important than moving up in life. I was lucky he was my boss's boss and that I needed to perform at work for his approval. If Nathan were a construction worker, I thought, I would have let my life go to seed with gay abandon.

I sent him an e-mail titled "Everything aside," and I wrote, "You're a great mentor."

Then I fantasized about sex with him for a few minutes.

My computer screen blinked a message that I had new mail. Nathan had written back, "Right after work. Take home burritos. Lots of action. How does that sound?"

"Smashing," I wrote back.

Sex with him was like being reunited with something larger than life. His stomach on my back and the weight of his entire body on mine made me feel a sense of inner gravity.

After he had fucked me the first time, the phone rang. I just knew it was Sybil. I leaped from the bed and turned the ringer off, and I checked that the answering machine volume was still down to zero. The machine clicked, and the sound of tape rewinding filled the room. I decided to switch to voicemail. I wanted to be mentally present with the person in whose presence I was physically. And not pine for the other, whether it was Nathan or Sybil. It was only fair. After a while the machine clicked again. It was unnerving. I leaned over and shut it off all together.

"You're trying to avoid someone," Nathan said.

"It's the great MCI-AT&T war. They're always trying to get me to switch services," I replied.

He smiled back, and I could tell he didn't believe me. We were silent for a few seconds. Then I touched him and we both returned to the present.

We had sex four times in the course of the night. I wondered if we would remain lovers after ten years, and if he would still perform as well.

In the morning at my desk, I realized I was very sore. I smiled to myself.

I was designing the new risk management system, and I had to talk to traders and quants about the new project. There were four quants, and they all sat in a room with no windows. There was a poster of Marilyn Monroe on the wall over one guy's desk. The opposite side of the wall had a poster of a Monet painting. While I was talking to the quants I forgot their names. I remembered only the name JMF Peterson, but I couldn't remember who it was. I was unable to really differentiate them. One would begin a sentence and someone else would end it. Whenever they were unsure about anything, they would look at a slow man who wore thick glasses. I dreaded him. His lenses made his eyes look like little slits, and white goop gathered at the corners of his eyes. He was from the

Midwest and spoke like an alien from a 1970s science fiction movie, opening his mouth slowly. He looked stupid, but it was clear he was the star quant. I was glad I was not a genius. In my mind I christened him "Oatmeal," because he looked as if he were eating a mouthful of oatmeal while considering my questions. When I got back to my desk, Sybil had left me a voicemail at work. Nathan stopped by my desk before I could call her back. Tad, my coworker, wasn't there, and Nathan asked, "Tonight?"

"Tomorrow night?" I asked.

"The night after?" he asked. His expression was sincere. I knew he wasn't trying to be difficult. We agreed. After Nathan left, I shuddered at the thought of the musical chairs I would have to play to keep both relationships on track. I called Sybil.

"Yeah, tonight is fine. And how about tomorrow night, too?"

"I'll come tonight, but I have to see Nathan tomorrow," she answered.

I wrote Martha an e-mail saying, "You. Me. Tomorrow."

My phone rang. It was Martha.

"André, I can see your cubicle from where I sit. What's this e-mail business?"

"Yes or no?" I asked.

"What are we going to do?"

"Why? Is your decision conditional upon that?"

"Maybe," she replied.

"My, my, are we picky. What do you want to do?"

"You suggest."

"We can walk around Central Park, then get dinner," I said.

"That sounds good."

"Done."

I opened my miniplanner, which fit into my shirt pocket, and wrote "S" under today. Then under the next day I wrote "M," and under the one after I wrote "N."

I thought about how back when Danny used to blow me, he used to tell me how experienced he was. I had wanted to be able to regale him with stories of myself, but I didn't have any. The only significant thing that had ever happened to me up until that time was shooting my load in Danny's face. I couldn't have told him that. Now I was finally living a full life.

I stopped thinking about my past and got back to work.

I had to speak to one of the traders. There were two traders on the project with me, but the senior one, a guy called Kent, pointed to the junior one and said, "He knows what I want."

"Mortimer Montgomery," the younger guy said, shaking my hand.

"André Bernard is the name."

"Well, let me tell you a little bit about portfolio management. The idea is to invest your money as widely as possible, not put all your eggs in one basket. That way you minimize risk," he said.

Mortimer was an asshole. I couldn't believe how patronizing he was. He probably understood no math and didn't know half of what I knew. And yet in the scheme of things, I had to put up with his swagger. I realized I would have to switch to being a trader at some point in my career. Having graduate degrees and knowing how to program and being a mathematician was not the way to any power job.

"I know a few things about portfolio management and risk management," I said. "Can you tell me specifically what sort of things you want in the big system we are designing? Do you have any major criticisms of the cash management module we designed on a trial basis? Specifically with the interface?"

Mortimer fiddled with his glasses, then mumbled something about the program not being too user-friendly. I pressed him for details. He let it go. I went back to my desk thinking of not putting all your eggs in one basket. Was that what I was doing with my two relationships at the moment? Was I merely hedging my bets?

I had to call Mortimer's boss, Kent, and insist on a talk to get some intelligent views from the trading side before writing up my proposal. I clarified a few points with him. After I was done, I wrote up Kent's comments and the notes from my meeting with the quants and got ready to meet Sybil.

She came to my apartment when she was done with work. Sybil was out of sorts when she met me. Eventually, she settled in. I guessed it was because it was our first meeting since Nathan's return. But we didn't talk about Nathan at all. We actively avoided the topic, and it felt unnatural.

"André, there's something wrong with your answering machine. I tried calling you all night yesterday," she said.

"Did you?"

"Were you home?"

"Yes."

"Alone?" she asked.

"Sybil."

"What?"

"That's not a fair question," I said.

"Why not?"

"Because we don't have that kind of relationship."

She stared at me quietly. Seemed very distant. Then she suddenly took my hand and bit it hard. I jumped out of bed.

"What are you doing?"

"Making sure you're for real," she said and laughed.

We didn't talk about it again. We didn't say much to each other at all. We had slow and mellow sex and fell asleep. When I woke up in the morning, I was eager to get to work. I was missing Nathan.

I stopped in the coffee shop in the lobby of my office building. Nathan was in line for coffee as well. When we caught each other's eyes, we didn't say hello or smile. He just looked at me and I did the same. It was so intimate it sent a current of electricity through my spine. We rode the elevator up together to our office on the seventeenth floor. There were half a dozen people in the elevator with us. He looked at me and mouthed the word "lunch." I nodded.

A few minutes after I got to my desk, Nathan paged me on the internal phone system.

"Will you come to the office for a second?"

"Right over."

As I walked on the plush carpets toward Nathan's office, I was suddenly nervous.

I'm sleeping with your wife. Jesus Christ! I just slept with her last night! I thought to myself. For a second I thought of Nathan not as a part of me but as a part of Sybil. It felt weird and terrifying. I was shaking slightly when I got to his office. He closed the door behind me purposefully. I was really scared now. He'd found out about Sybil and me and was going to confront me.

He indicated a chair. I sat down. He stood behind the chair and covered my face with his palm as if he were going to strangle me. I held my breath. He ran his fingers on my lips and then through my hair and pulled it hard. I sat rigid.

"I had to touch you," he finally said.

I breathed. My fear underwent a direct transformation. It precipitated into something hard and throbbing in my pants. I let my shoulders drop. I looked at him.

"André, you look completely wild."

I couldn't see my face, but I knew what he meant. I had never been that hard.

"If we take a cab now, we can be at my place in ten minutes," I whispered.

"Let's go," he replied.

He put on his jacket and we left. He tapped Martha's desk on the way out and said, "We have a meeting. We'll be back in an hour, Martha."

She nodded and gave us both the thumbs up. My mind noted that I was going to meet her for dinner. My whole body was stiff as a rod. We hailed a cab and Nathan played with my penis on the way home. I was impatient. Ready to burst. I fumbled with my keys. Then I remembered that Sybil had been with me at night. My palms started to sweat.

I slowly opened the door.

I looked around the room. I thought I could smell Sybil's perfume. I wondered if Nathan would notice. I went limp. My forehead was wet.

Nathan felt my pants.

"What's wrong?"

I felt as if I'd let him down.

"Nothing. Tension," I said, laughing.

He grabbed my tie and my starched white collar and hurled me on the bed. He bit my cheek so hard I thought my face would bleed. I could feel his erection where my thigh touched his. I got hard again. I smiled.

"Yes," he said and unzipped my pants.

We were in a frenzy. We were both undressing separately. I kicked off my shoes and removed my socks. I unbuttoned a few buttons of my shirt and pulled it off over my head as if it were a T-shirt. I wasn't sure who'd go first. Nathan lay down beside me, facing me. We jerked each other off. Then we collapsed in a heap. After a few minutes, Nathan looked at his watch.

"It's been only twenty minutes," he said.

It made me think we could do it again. And thinking that we could do it again made me want to do it again.

"Nathan, will you sit on me?" I asked.

He turned around and sat down, his back facing me, his muscles pulling my cock deep inside his ass. I loved the fact that he was totally in control of me fucking him. I jerked him off after I had come.

"We should go," he said.

We got up from different sides of the bed. My clothes were on his side. We threw our briefs across the bed to each other and put our pants and shirts in a heap on the bed while we dressed. After we tied our ties and pulled on our jackets, we kissed each other on the mouth and headed out.

I felt as if nothing could come between us. The thought of not seeing him at night didn't scare me. Our union had transcended petty concerns. He was with me all the time. I took him with me everywhere.

I was in a great mood when I met Martha in the evening. Collected and relaxed. As we walked around the skating rink in Central Park, she told me of various things that had happened to her in New York. She'd been living in the city for fifteen years.

She pointed to an office building on Fifty-ninth Street and said, "I used to work there."

Then she pointed to a building on Central Park West and said, "I lived there with a businessman who was thirty years older than me."

"How old were you then?"

"Seventeen."

"How did it end?" I asked.

"He dumped me and got a Korean girl to live with him."

"What did you do?"

"I moved into my brother's apartment and lived on his couch for six months."

"How did that end?" I asked, trying to be funny.

"Badly. I've never talked to him since."

"What happened?"

"I found out that he was a thief."

"What did he steal?"

"He was deceitful. He'd borrowed money from friends and spent it in strip clubs. He defaulted on loans. He had phone bills for nine thousand dollars."

"Strip clubs?"

"Yeah, you see, he's really fat and there was no way he could've gotten any. So he went to strip clubs to get his jollies."

We must have been walking around Central Park for over an hour. It had become dark and was getting cold. I was aware of a caving hunger in my stomach. The only restaurant I knew in the area was Karma, where Nathan had taken me after the night at Skirts. I didn't even want to suggest it.

"Martha, would you like to eat?" I asked.

"Sure."

"I don't really know of any place around here," I lied.

"Do you like Indian food?"

"I don't mind it," I said.

"Let's go to Karma. It's right there and has a great view of the Park," she said, pointing in the direction of Fifty-ninth Street.

"Okay," I replied. Life was beyond my control.

When we reached the doorway to the building, I felt sure that we would run into Sybil and Nathan in the restaurant. Luckily, that didn't happen.

"Are you happy, Martha?" I asked.

"Yes, I'm happy, André," she replied and smiled.

"Good."

The waiters had brought us our main course, and I dug in. For a few minutes I was completely focused on the food. Being a man of habit, I'd ordered Tandoori chicken again with some vegetable curry. I had an image of curry dripping through my esophagus and into my stomach. This is an experience you cannot share with anyone, I thought to myself. You eat, you digest. Only you can feel it in your belly. This and pain. Someone steps on your toe and you hurt. There was so much one couldn't share with anyone. But there were things one could share. If I cooked for Nathan, his mouth, his tongue, his stomach would feel and know and grind the food. He might even have dreams influenced by what I'd cooked. The idea of cooking for Nathan emerged. It was a sexy idea. I had to learn. Now! I decided to go to Barnes & Noble and buy a cookbook.

"What kind of food do you like, André?"

"Mexican. Italian. Everything, really."

Our conversation was flagging. I wanted to leave and go home. Think in peace about Nathan for a little while and go to sleep. I had plowed through all the food that had been put in front of me and was suddenly full and shivering.

"I always feel cold after dinner," I said.

"It's because blood rushes to your stomach to help you digest the food."

I nodded.

The waiter came to take away our plates and asked if we wanted dessert. I looked at Martha.

"No, not for me."

"The check, please," I said.

"So, who are you bringing to the office party next week?" Martha asked.

"Which office party?"

"You didn't know?"

"No."

"There's a firmwide party next Thursday in the Park Plaza Hotel."

"Oh!"

"Everyone goes, pretty much. And you can bring a date."

"Is it a sit-down dinner with speeches?" I asked.

"No, just plenty of food and booze. A dance floor and a live band."

Nathan would no doubt bring Sybil. I knew I should ask Martha. That's why she'd brought it up.

"Do you already have a date, Martha?" I asked, looking at her earnestly.

"No."

"Can we go together?"

"You got it," she said.

We got the check. I was unsure what to do. I didn't see why I had to take Martha out for a hundred-dollar dinner. She gestured for the bill.

"I got it," I said. I noticed I had mimicked her words. They had probably stuck on the outer surface of my brain and skidded right off my tongue. I was reminded once again that men were creatures driven by chemical reactions, biology, and physics.

"Sure?" she asked.

"Yeah, sure."

We took the elevator down. I hailed a cab for her and opened the door.

"That was nice, André," she said, coming close to give me a kiss.

I turned my face so that her half-opened lips grazed past my cheek.

"I'll see you tomorrow," I said.

I got home and tried to make sense of the day as I undressed for bed. I switched on my radio so that its noise could fill the room. There was a talk show about the onset of spring. The announcer was asking people whether they had suffered yet from a bout of spring fever. Most of the people had, even though the temperature in New York was in the low thirties and it had been raining off and on all week.

The announcer asked a lesbian in Park Slope how she felt about spring.

"I was walking to the subway the other day and wanted to grab this girl's titties."

I visualized a large, pendulous woman, the dimensions of a road roller, wanting to grab Sybil's breasts.

The next person to be asked was an old man who worked for the MTA.

"I can see that the young ladies have taken out their shorter skirts. Women's legs were always my favorite," he croaked.

The announcer said that a lab in Florida had made a pheromone scent that was odorless and tasteless. The scent worked on the olfactory nerves of the members of the opposite sex and made them want to sleep with you. He raised some pointed questions on whether finding a boyfriend or girlfriend that way was legit and asked listeners to phone in with their responses.

I shut the radio off and got into bed. Attraction was about pheromones, love and dreams were about serotonin, happiness was about some other chemical. The modern world of biochemistry had sullied my idealism and my vision. I yearned for an earlier age when one could believe that love was about the soul. I wondered if Nathan ever thought about these things. I pulled an extra pillow near my chest for comfort and played with the hair on my chest, wishing that he were there to play with it. I was restless. I got back out of bed and went to my CD rack. I pulled out *Downward Spiral* by Nine Inch Nails and put it on. Then I got back into bed and masturbated. Suddenly I felt it was a good thing that the body could release chemicals even in the absence of a loved one. I fell asleep.

I woke up in the middle of the night squeezing my pillow. It was wet, and so was my chest. I must have had a nightmare. It was four in the morning and I couldn't go back to sleep. I wondered if Nathan was sleeping. I wanted to call him but then thought better of it.

I switched on the light and wrote a letter to my father telling him how I liked New York. I wrote the letter on the back of one of Sybil's drawings, since I had no paper in the house. Then I pulled out my miniplanner and opened it. Where I had written "S," I put two check marks. Next to "M" I put a single check mark, and then next to "N" I put four check marks, in anticipation. I knew I wouldn't be disappointed. I went back to bed.

In the morning I thought of Nathan as soon as my eyes opened. I was going to spend the evening with him. The thought filled my veins with blood. I dressed for work. I chose a colorful purple tie with splotches of yellow. It was not conservative, but it reflected my mood.

I went to a shoe repair store in the subway station to get my shoes shined. I was becoming a regular there. The store had four Hispanic boys who shined shoes. One was particularly good-looking, and he always took me on if he was free. I would sit on top of the high red chair and look down on him. He would look up and into my eyes. Then he would fold up my pants so they wouldn't get dirty and get to work. Today I was spaced out. I didn't watch him or read the paper. I looked out of the store window and registered nothing. Every now and then he would forcefully rub his cloth on my shoes and I would have to tighten my foot's grip on the foot stand so that my foot wouldn't slip. He sprayed some liquid on my shoes and then buffed them again. A curly lock of hair fell on his forehead, and I wanted to pull it and jerk his head up. I sat still feeling the stiffness of my cock in my pants. When he was done shining my shoes, he tugged down the fold of my pants and they slithered on both sides past my erection. I maneuvered myself out of my seat, handed him a buck as a tip, paid the cashier at the shop a dollar fifty, and took the uptown six train to Grand Central, telling myself that I was a putrid pervert and a sex maniac.

I had to sort myself and get a grip on life. But how was I ever going to control the chemicals that were inextricably linked not just to my emotions and my sex drive but also to my thoughts? It was known that serotonin and norepinephrine were responsible for judgment and memory. If only my damned brain stem had shot a little more of both when I had met Sybil. Maybe I'd eaten the wrong dinner. Maybe coconut milk soup had some other chemical that prevented the brain stem from firing out the right stuff. I was standing on the subway platform. I knew my limitations. I wasn't going to solve the mind–body problem that had haunted intellectuals for generations while waiting for the rush-hour train. I pulled out my Walkman and turned up the volume. Saint-Saëns infiltrated into the folds of my brain. His Bacchanale from *Samson and Delilah* released chemicals in my head that made me feel like one unified free spirit, alive with joy.

I bought a double-strength espresso from the coffee shop in the lobby and went straight to my desk. There were no voicemail messages from anyone. Sybil and Nathan had entirely forgotten about me, I thought to myself. I switched on my computer and got to work. There was another meeting in the afternoon, and I had to report back on a few things. I felt I was doing remarkably well on all the duties I had. I wrote up a report on the basis of the notes I had taken in my meetings the day before. I worked straight through till eleven-thirty without a break. Then I went to the men's room. When I got back I passed Martha's desk.

"Hi!" I said.

"Hey, how are you?"

"I'm alright. Yourself?"

"Oh! I forgot Nathan was looking for you just now."

"I'd better find him. See you later."

I walked to Nathan's office. He was on the phone. I popped my head through the door. He waved. I tried mouthing the words, "I'll be back," but he waved again, indicating that I should come into the room and sit down.

"I thought we'd been very clear on this. We knew that it would never be mutually convenient. We both know that we can't always coordinate our absences from each other in a way that always suits the other," Nathan said into the mouthpiece.

My heart started beating loudly. Sybil and he were fighting. I could imagine Sybil crying on the other end of the phone line, saying that Nathan must spend the night with her tonight. Be realistic, André, I thought to myself, they are going to find out pretty soon that it's you. Prepare yourself for it.

I looked in Nathan's direction again, and he looked at me and winked. Then he scowled into the mouthpiece and rolled his eyes. Sybil dropped in my esteem when Nathan did that.

I took a Post-It from Nathan's desk and wrote, "I'll understand if you need to cancel on me tonight." I pushed the yellow paper under him. He read it and then turned to look at me. He had this look in his eyes that said, "Are you nuts?"

Nathan said, "Look, Sybs, André is here to finish up work on his deadline for this afternoon. I have to call you back."

I felt color rise to my cheeks. Nathan mentioning me to Sybil to get out of an argument, him calling her Sybs in that intimate way, her calling me immediately (as I was sure she would) after to see if she could spend the night with me tonight, me squirming out of it with a pathetic excuse so I could sleep with her husband—it was all comical.

"She was being a real pain. She can be very demanding," he said after he had put the phone down.

"Hope everything is okay," I muttered.

"It'll be fine. Don't worry."

"I feel bad," I said.

"No, don't. Please," Nathan said.

"Did you think of me last night, Nathan? I woke up in the middle of the night thinking about you," I said.

"I missed you. I sat in my study for a few hours and tried to paint."

I could imagine Nathan dabbing a thick brush in purple paint and another in yellow paint and covering a canvas in the kind of pattern I had on my tie. I could see his study in my mind, its wooden easel in the corner. I remembered that Nathan didn't know I had been to his place. I wasn't supposed to have seen his paintings or know that he painted.

"You paint?" I asked.

"Yes."

I didn't want to pretend any more with him. I changed the subject.

"Nathan, this damn meeting today. What's expected of me?"

"Just the write-up on what you think the needs are on both sides."

"I was working on a draft proposal."

"Actually, that's a good idea. Maybe you can bring that in next time. Let's do it verbally today. It'll give you more time."

"Okay."

"What do you want to do tonight?" Nathan asked.

"I'd like to talk to you."

"Done. We'll go to dinner," he said.

"I have to get back to work."

I went back to my desk and noticed the voicemail light flashing. I picked up the handset reluctantly and punched all the numbers in.

"This is Sybil. If you still remember me, then call."

I called her at work.

"André here," I said.

"Hi, how are things?"

"How are you?"

"I thought you'd forgotten me," she said.

"And why is that?"

"No calls, no messages."

"I can't really call you at home, can I?" I said.

"I guess not."

"Are you doing all right?"

"Yes. Will you see me tonight? Please," she said.

I was filled with a sense of dread. She'd mounted the pressure on me. My neck got tense.

"I can't tonight. How's tomorrow?" I said, trying to sound neither too casual nor too guilty.

"Why? Who are you seeing tonight?"

"Just friends."

"Which friends? Nathan had told me you didn't have friends in Manhattan."

She was turning unpleasant, and her voice was irritable. I wanted to yell at her. I felt ugly.

"I'm sorry I can't do tonight. And I don't feel obliged to tell you why," I said.

Silence.

"Sybil."

"I'm sorry, André. I had no right to talk to you that way. I'll come by tomorrow."

"I'll look forward to it," I said.

I felt thoroughly drained. This was too burdensome. I considered confessing to Nathan that night. I stepped out of my cubicle and went downstairs to get soup. I came back and ate lunch at my computer, surfing the Net. I did a word search on Nine Inch Nails and it came up with 9,073 matches. I looked at the top ten. Someone had posted a survey on the Net that concluded that 75 percent of all women and 43 percent of all men found Trent Reznor's music highly sexual. Sixty percent of both men and women had wanked off to *Downward Spiral*. The statistics got me thinking: there were men who wanked off to it who didn't find it sexual, and there were women who did find it sexual who didn't wank to it. There was a fundamental difference between men and women. I wanted to understand it one day. At any rate, it gave me comfort to think that I was a mainstream kind of guy in my masturbatory tastes.

After this, I did a word search on "Haydn, masturbation." There was a single retrieval from the Lycos search engine. I tried a couple of other search engines, and they came up with nothing. So I went back to the Lycos site. The article summary said that

14 percent of the students in Oberlin College had wanked to Haydn's music. I double-clicked on the article and got the message "URL not found."

People thought about such things; they conducted surveys and wrote up results in HTML format and posted them on the Web. Other people like me looked up these things while drinking spoons of potato-leek soup in front of their computers at lunchtime. The world was absurd. Entirely.

I thought of the kind of sex I had been having. I had never been fisted by anyone, man or woman, till Sybil had put her hand in and up. I had just let her do it without thinking too much. She had coated her fingers with the Eros Concentrated Bodyglide that Nathan had left at my place. I was surprised she hadn't been more suspicious.

I did a word search on Lycos for "fisting." It came up with 24,983 matches. The first ten were from *Susie Sexpert's Lesbian Sex World*. I double-clicked on it. It was a summary of a sex manual for lesbians. I had never known any lesbians, and I decided I should meet some. Maybe I could learn a thing or two from them. I typed in, "gay, lesbian, New York" and hit the search button. I came upon a list of resources, including the Gay and Lesbian Center on Thirteenth Street. I scribbled their phone number on a Post-It.

Then I had an uneasy feeling that someone was behind me. I hurriedly double-clicked on the X in the window to shut down the browser and turned around. Martha was squinting behind my desk. Luckily, there was a harsh glare from the sun on my computer monitor, and from where she was standing she couldn't have read much.

"What are you up to, André?"

"Oh! Nothing," I replied.

I wanted her to leave so that I could call the Gay and Lesbian Center. But she came closer to my chair and eventually parked her flanks on my desk. She was wearing a thin cream–colored blouse and a brown skirt. There was an uneasy crease on her shirt where her left nipple was. I tried to look discreetly without staring and concluded it wasn't a stiffy. It could have been a nipple ring but somehow she didn't seem the type to me.

"I wanted to thank you for dinner last night."

"You're welcome."

"I'd like to have you over for dinner sometime," she said.

"You cook?"

"I'm rather fond of cooking."

"Will you teach me?"

"Sure. What kind of food would you like to learn to cook?"

"How about vegetarian Thai or Indian?"

"Absolutely. Maybe this weekend?" she asked.

"Can I get back to you on it? I need to check on a few things. By when do you need to know?"

"By tomorrow."

"Great."

She wandered out of my cubicle, hovered around the window for a second, and stared at the GE building, as if waiting for me to say something more. Then she left.

I called the Gay and Lesbian Center.

"How can I help?" a low male voice asked.

"Where are you located?"

"Thirteenth between Seventh and Eighth."

"Are you open on the weekends?"

"Yeah. Will this be your first time here?"

"Just moved to New York. What sort of activities do you have?"

"There are support groups, health groups, counseling, safe-sex workshops, reading groups, dykes on bikes—which you can't participate in—dances. What are you interested in?"

"I just want to check it out. I'm kinda new."

"New to the scene?"

"Yeah, really new."

"Welcome. Join us. When are you thinking of coming in?"

"Saturday afternoon, maybe. What's your name?"

"Richard Murphy. I'll be here on Saturday. Look me up."

"Will do."

"Bye."

I hung up the phone and looked around outside the cubicle into the corridor. There was no one. I reviewed the conversation in my head to see if anyone could have caught on. Then I got out my miniplanner and under Saturday, March 7, I wrote "Richard Murphy." Then I crossed it out and wrote "R.M."

The last two spoons of my soup were cold, so I threw the carton into the trash and looked at the clock on my phone. It was almost two. I got back to work. I had half an hour to decide on what I was going to say in the meeting.

Nathan was not in his element at the meeting. He wasn't very articulate. My boss, Yoshi Kato, noticed and took over. Nathan doodled a little on a notepad. I could tell that every now and then he would make an effort to focus on the discussion, but he would get distracted. I assumed he was feeling hassled because of Sybil. I was getting nervous. It was my turn to speak. All the people whom I had consulted were there: the four quants and Mortimer Montgomery and his boss Kent. They needed to agree with my views. I wished Nathan would listen and help.

He looked at me while I spoke. He stared. I could tell he wasn't listening to a thing, but he seemed pleased. I forgot what I was saying, but I kept talking. A part of me had slipped away from the moment and was trying to imagine what Nathan was imagining. I had an image of Nathan having an image of my thighs tensing as I was about to ejaculate. I looked at him and made my concluding remark, "Of course all these suggestions are subject to approval on both sides. Any questions?"

Yoshi Kato opened his mouth to speak. But Nathan gestured to him and started speaking instead.

"That's impressive, André. Unless someone has major objections to any of your points, I think it's best that you just keep working on it and have us take a look when it's done. What do you all think?" he said, looking from person to person.

There was a faint mumble in the room.

Oatmeal spoke up. "Mr. Bernard, you haven't told us how we will ever be able to modify the payoff formulas to accommodate new structures."

I forgot his real name and was actually tempted to say, "Mr. So and So." But I caught myself in time. "I haven't reached that part yet, but I was thinking of having user-defined payoffs in one section of the program. The traders can use the GUI, but you'll be able to define payoffs as you please. There will be a predefined syntax to assist you."

He nodded. Nathan jumped right into the silence, "Good. I guess that's it. Let's reconvene in two days. Will you be able to complete the draft by then?"

"Yes," I said.

Nathan picked up his jacket from the back of the chair and moved briskly toward the door. Everyone else got up from their chairs. I walked back to my cubicle with Yoshi Kato. When we reached my desk he said, "Well done, André, I was impressed by that."

"Thanks, boss," I said.

There was an e-mail waiting for me. It was from Nathan.

"Can't wait for this day to end," it read.

I wanted to call Sybil and tell her to stay out of his hair. I wondered if Nathan would ask to spend tomorrow night with me. What would I tell him? I was supposed to see Sybil tomorrow night. I promised myself that I would play clean with Nathan. I would answer "Yes" or "No." I wouldn't make bad excuses or tell too many lies.

At six o'clock sharp Nathan called me.

"Ready to get outta here?"

I wanted to work for another hour so I wouldn't have to kill myself on the project the next day, but I said yes to him.

I pulled on my jacket and overcoat and walked to the elevator.

We didn't speak till we were out of the building and on the street.

"So, how are you?" we both asked, looking at each other, at the same time.

"She's been chewing my head off today."

"I'm sorry. It must be PMS," I said, laughing.

"I thought so. Then I calculated. She isn't due till the week after."

"You mean the fourteenth?" I asked, making a mental note and hoping he wouldn't wonder why I was so interested in Sybil's period.

"No, the twentieth."

"Should we go to some health store and look for a bio-rhythms chart? I could read my girlfriend in college like a book with one of those," I said.

"No, I don't want to think about her any more."

"What would make you feel better, Nathan? Would you like to go to Skirts?"

"Hmmm," he said, looking up at the sky as if the weather were going to play a role in the decision.

"Hmmm," he repeated, then added, "I guess that's an idea."

I felt upset. He had me in the flesh. I would do anything for him. But he wanted Liz breathing on his crotch. I was suddenly overwhelmed with emotion and close to tears.

"Do you want to go to Skirts, André?"

"No," I managed.

"What do you want to do?" he asked.

"I'd like to give you a full-body massage and relax you," I said.

He turned around to look at me. I was wearing my heart on my sleeve, in my eyes.

"Oh, André!" he said, "Let's go to your place."

As soon as I walked into my apartment I picked up the phone and turned the ringer off. Then I looked through my bathroom closet and brought out a bottle of massage oil that I had bought a year ago. I pulled off all of Nathan's clothes, his shoes, his socks. I made him lie facedown on my bed and kneaded his neck and back. I massaged his butt and his calves, his ankles, his toes, and the insides of his thighs.

"Turn around," I said when I was done.

I put oil on his temples and pressed them. His forehead and his face needed work. I was glad I'd learned something in my time with women. I'd always been happy to do whatever my girlfriends had wanted, and now I was putting it to use. I made my way down to his penis and worked on it till it was stiff. Then I worked some more on it till he shot out and went limp. Nathan remained still through all of it. I could tell that he was completely immersed in the moment. I wanted him to be addicted to me. I wanted him to miss this even if he didn't miss me.

When I was done, I pulled a sheet over him and dimmed the light in my studio. I sat on the chair by the window and stared at his silhouette.

After fifteen minutes, Nathan stirred and said, "I've never felt so relaxed in my whole life."

"Good."

"Take off your clothes and come close, will you?"

I took my clothes off and got into bed with him. He hugged me. He turned on his side, faced me in a fetal position, and buried his elbows and knees into my flesh. Nathan seemed vulnerable all of a sudden. I felt waves of protectiveness and tenderness course through my heart. It must be like this to be a father, I thought to myself. We fell asleep.

We slept for a few hours, then Nathan got up from the bed. I woke up as soon as he moved. He went to the bathroom. He didn't turn on any lights, and he peed with the bathroom door open. Then he flushed the toilet and came back to bed. When he got back in bed he lightly kissed my head.

"Are you hungry?" I asked.

"You're awake."

"I just got up."

"I'm sorry I woke you up."

"No."

"Do you want to eat?" he asked.

"Only if you do."

"André, are you hungry?"

"I could swing both ways."

"I could do with a small bite."

"What would you like?" I asked. I'd collected menus from some restaurants in the neighborhood that delivered.

"What time is it?" asked Nathan then proceeded to feel the floor for his watch. He brought it up close to his face and said, "It's only ten."

"What do you want to eat?" I asked.

"Let me take you to Royal Siam in Chelsea. It's good."

I had been with Sybil to a Thai restaurant in Chelsea. I wasn't sure it was the same one, but I wasn't going to take a chance. I couldn't believe he was willing to risk it. It was almost as if he wanted Sybil to know.

"No, let me take you to Mugsy's Chow Chow in the East Village," I said.

"Sure," he replied, smiling. He had the kind of look my father used to have when I would announce that I had made a great discovery. I'd come home once and told him, "Guido's parents are divorced." I was four years old then, and he hadn't yet told me what being divorced meant.

Nathan kissed me and got out of bed. He hunted around for his clothes and put them on slowly. We hadn't turned the lights on in the room. Light from outside lit the room faintly. I started getting dressed. Nathan was wearing his shirt.

"Do you want to wear something more comfortable, like my jeans?"

"Hmmm," Nathan said, holding up his suit jacket and contemplating it, "Yeah, that would be nice. Can we hang this stuff up?"

I took his jacket and pants and hung them in my closet. I pulled out my longest pairs of jeans and passed them to Nathan. He was a few inches taller than I, and I wasn't sure they would fit. I gave him a hemp shirt that my girlfriend in graduate school, Patricia, had given me for my birthday. I wore another pair of jeans and a shirt. I pulled out two sweaters for the two of us. It was in the low twenties outside, so we'd need more than overcoats.

Nathan looked cool in my hemp shirt. I looked through a small box of stuff I had and found a necklace of beads. I put them around his neck. He smiled.

"That's how Indians get married," I said. "They put garlands around each other. My ex-girlfriend Madhu was always trying to get me to do it."

Nathan put his arm around my shoulders and we both walked out of my studio. I felt silly because of the comment I'd just made. I felt like a stupid twelve-year-old around his first crush.

There was a twenty-minute wait at Mugsy's Chow Chow. We got Sierras and sat at the bar. I put my hand on Nathan's thigh.

Neither of us said anything. I was content being with him. The waitress hovered around us before she told us our table was ready. She fidgeted and looked uncomfortable, as though she felt embarrassed to intrude. I smiled at her and held Nathan's hand on the way to the table. She saw and smiled at me.

"Ready to order?" she asked, putting olive oil and bread in front of us.

We ordered the specials. Nathan poured the oil on a saucer and added salt to it. We broke off pieces of bread and dipped it in. I realized I was hungry. Nathan started talking when the bread got into his system. He talked a lot, about nothing in particular. I hung on every word. His favorite books in high school, his father's illness, his years living in London.

"Nathan, I don't have a mother. She died when I was four and a half," I said when he paused.

"I'm sorry," he said. Then added, "Mine died when I was ten."

"Are you close to your dad?" I asked.

"I was till he died a few years ago. And you?"

"You remind me of my father, Nathan."

"Do I look like him?"

"No. But things you do remind me of him. I slept in the same bed as him till I was ten. After that we moved and I had my own room, but sometimes I would still go and get into his bed if I was having bad dreams."

"When was the last time you did that?"

"I was around fourteen."

"Pumpkin ravioli in a butter sage sauce," said the waitress, coming up to our table. I pointed in Nathan's direction.

"Your pasta with shrimp," she said, putting a plate in front of me. I stared into her face. She smiled.

"Thanks," I said, continuing to stare. She lowered her eyes and smiled again. She was wearing a thin white ribbed cotton undershirt over a dark black athletic bra. That woman has to be a lesbian, I thought to myself.

"Do you think she's a dyke, Nathan?" I whispered.

She had her back toward us. Nathan looked in her direction for a moment, and I followed his gaze. He looked at her hair, then her back, her ass, her shoes. He looked back at me.

"I'd say so," he said.

"Bon appetit," I said, and I dug the fork into my plate of shrimp. My father always said it to the clients in his restaurant and to his friends when we had them over for dinner. I thought to myself that I would invite my father to visit me and I would learn how to cook the best French food in the world. And I'd have Nathan and Sybil over for dinner and get them to meet my father. He'd love Sybil.

"André, can I tell you something?"

"Of course."

"Sybil has been acting rather strange ever since I got back from Tokyo."

"She has? In what way?"

"She was always very demanding, but she's gotten even more so. She's cranky a lot. It's clear to me she's having an affair with someone, and I don't mind, but she's unable to handle it."

"What makes you think so?"

"First of all, she's always a little bitter when she says things. She said the other day 'you and those like you.' I asked her what she meant by those like me, and she said that I wasn't as unique as I thought."

"That could mean anything, Nathan."

"I know. I could be wrong. She could just be upset that I'm having an affair."

"Does she know for a fact?"

"I'm only spending every other night with her."

"That's true."

"And she's spending every other night with someone else."

"So you never see her?" I asked innocently.

"No, I'm exaggerating. I see her a little less than I see you."

"Less?"

"Less," Nathan repeated.

I wanted to ask him if open marriages worked. I wanted to ask him if he would be involved only with me if he could. But I could feel my armpits itch with sweat.

"How is your ravioli?"

"Pretty good."

We ate in silence for a few minutes. It felt awkward to me. I had to return to what we had been talking about.

"What are you going to do about your wife?" I asked, trying to sound as normal as I could.

"I guess I'll try talking to her. I've been trying, but she's been really uncommunicative."

"What will you say?"

"I'll ask her flat out if she's in love with someone else. I'll ask her if she's still in love with me."

"Surely you don't doubt that?"

"I don't know, André. She's never been so abrupt and bitter with me."

"Ever since you got back?"

"Yeah. Spending time at home with her has been hell. We fight about what we'll do in the evening, what we'll eat. I keep trying to be friendly, and she just gets more impossible."

So, the night Martha and I had gone to Karma they'd fought. They had spent only two nights together since Nathan returned from Tokyo. I couldn't believe I was affecting their life. I wondered if they'd had sex—and if they had, whether it was like the sex I had with Nathan or the sex I had with Sybil.

"Is it an equitable relationship?"

"Sort of. I've known her since she was very young. She's more your age, André, than mine."

"She looks very young," I said.

"We were neighbors. I always liked her but never really thought very much about it. Then I left for London. When I got back, Sybil had gone from being a teenager to being a woman. I was friendly with her parents. They were living in Westchester then, and she was going to school at NYU. We'd meet quite often in the city. Then somehow I decided I wanted to get married, and she proposed."

"She proposed?"

"Yes on the twenty-ninth of February. It was a leap year. She got on her knees and proposed. I said yes. She gave me a tie."

"Then you married?"

"Yeah."

"You never thought about living your life with a man?"

"I had crushes on men I respected. But I never met a man whom I actually had an affair with. It was just sex in the back rooms with men. Blow jobs by the parking lots of clubs. Bath houses. The sort of thing that doesn't happen as much any more."

"You've never had a relationship with a man?" I asked. I couldn't quite believe him.

"Never before, André."

I just stared at him. I didn't know what to say. I didn't know what to think.

"Why not?"

"I never met the right man. The men I really liked were straight."

"Hmmm," I said.

Nathan got up to go to the bathroom, and the waitress came to clear our table while he was gone.

"Been working here long?" I asked.

"Just a month."

"Like it?"

"It's cool. I like the art," she said, raising her eyebrows in the direction of a large painting of a woman with asymmetric breasts.

I looked at her. I didn't want to smile, so I just held her gaze.

She left with our plates. When Nathan got back, she came back to our table and asked if we wanted dessert. Nathan didn't, and I passed up as well.

I said I'd pick up the tab. I paid by credit card, and when the waitress gave me the yellow slip to sign, I wrote my number on the bill with my name. I wondered if she'd call me. I was just playing.

We went back home.

I let my jeans slip to the floor and got into bed. Nathan did the same. We went to sleep. Our bodies touched all night. In the morning, we must have woken up at the same time. I was aware of him as soon as I woke up.

"Good morning," I said.

"Good morning," he said, yawning languorously, "been up long?"

"Just woke up."

"Me too."

I ruffled his blonde hair and rubbed his forehead. He looked young in the morning light. I climbed out of bed and went to brew some coffee and shower. While soaping myself, I remembered I was going to spend the night with Sybil. I felt as if I hadn't seen her for years. A part of me wanted to see her, but all of me wanted to see Nathan again. I got out of the shower with my white towel wrapped around my waist and got the coffee ready. Nathan had gone right back to sleep. I shook him and sat down on the side of the bed.

"Lazy bones, we have work to do. And someone has a major deadline tomorrow."

"Yeah, yeah," Nathan said, turning to face me. Then he took forever to prop himself up on his elbow in bed and take his mug from me.

We sat and sipped our coffees. Nathan's eyes looked startlingly blue. He tugged slowly at my towel till it came off my waist. Then he rubbed my stomach with his hand.

"Stop it, you're turning me on," I said.

"Do you want me to stop?"

"If you don't, you won't like what follows," I said.

"What makes you think I won't like it?"

"You're half asleep," I said in a high-pitched drag queen kind of voice.

"This is helping me wake up," he said.

Coffee was now spilling on my bed. I barely managed to get both mugs on the floor in time. The pillows fell off and Nathan threw the comforter on the floor. By the time we were done it was twenty to nine.

"You can afford to go in late, big boss, but I have to get to work now," I said, jumping out and running to my closet.

Nathan laughed and got out of bed.

"For you, only for you, would I go to work without a shower," he said and started getting dressed.

I threw the comforter on the bed and smoothed it out.

"We're going to wake up early from now on so that we can have a boom and a bang without being late," I said as we got into the elevator on my floor.

"From tomorrow morning?" he asked, looking at me.

My heart skipped a beat. God knows I want to see you tonight, Nathan, I thought to myself. I reached out for his hand and squeezed it.

"Tomorrow night work for you, love?" I asked softly.

He looked away for a second and then said, "Sure."

Unspoken feelings hung around in the space between us all the way to work. We made conversation about the project meeting, Yoshi Kato's future, and maybe getting a bite at lunch together. I felt guilt hanging like a dagger ready to drop on my head.

When I got to my desk I wrote Nathan an e-mail, saying, "Nathan, do you understand and will you forgive me?"

He wrote back instantly, "Don't think about it. Don't worry."

I felt more at ease after he'd consoled me. I dug into work. I called Sybil and made arrangements for that night. I e-mailed Nathan to ask if he was free the night of the day after. He wrote back saying, "No."

I went over to Martha's desk and told her I could do dinner Saturday night. Then I walked to Nathan's office and asked him if he wanted to go get lunch. We talked about work.

"How well do you know Martha?" I asked.

"Pretty well. I met her when she had a scrap with her brother. I got her the job here."

"She seems nice. Something about her is very calming."

We finished lunch and I went back to my desk and got to work. I ordered voicemail for my home. As evening approached, I started to stress a little about Sybil. I was anxious because of what Nathan had told me about her being emotionally demanding. I felt as if a monster were about to clamp its jaws on me.

I left the office and got into the elevator. Nathan had been right behind me and jumped in as the doors were about to shut. We were alone in the car. He smiled and said, "Fun night planned?"

I shrugged my shoulders.

I was supposed to meet Sybil at my apartment. Nathan got a cab on the street.

"Can I give you a ride somewhere, André?" he asked.

"No thanks. I'm taking the subway," I replied.

I walked to the subway station feeling false and empty. I was sleeping with the man and was sharing every sort of intimacy with him. Yet there was this great façade I had to maintain. I wanted to tell Nathan. At the very least, I thought, I had to stop the affair with Sybil. I didn't love, her so why was I going on? Because she was sexy. And it was perfectly enjoyable. I knew that wasn't a sufficient explanation.

Sybil was waiting for me outside my building. I gave her a quick kiss and we took the elevator up. She hugged me warmly. I was tired. I wanted to let my briefcase drop off my shoulder and give up all responsibility for life.

"I missed you, André," she said.

"How have you been?" I asked.

"Pulling along."

When we were in front of my door I remembered Nathan had spent the night. I opened the door slowly and went in first. I turned on the light and looked at the room. There was nothing of his on the bed or the coffee table. I stepped into the bathroom and took a look. Clean.

"So, Sybil. What do you want to do tonight?"

"Let's rent a movie."

"What would you like to watch?"

"Something light and comic."

"Like?"

"A Fish Called Wanda."

"I haven't rented a movie since I moved here."

"There's a Blockbuster around the block. I noticed it when I came by."

"Good, let's go get me a card. What will I need?"

"ID and credit card, that's all."

We picked up the movie and got falafel sandwiches from the shop next door. Then we watched the movie lying on my bed. The movie made me laugh very hard. At one point I shook my head while laughing and noticed the two coffee mugs from the morning on the side of the bed. They screamed of decadence and early-morning love. When Sybil went to the bathroom, I immediately shoved them under the bed. My heart split in two thinking of Nathan.

As the movie went on, Sybil moved closer and closer. It was cozy, and I wished Nathan were there. She was light and long. I felt as if she'd draped herself around me. I couldn't tell anymore which part of my body was mine and separate from her. After the movie, we both slumped farther down on the bed and played with each other's hands. I made silly cooing noises and Sybil let out a series of long moans. I felt completely at ease, as if I'd been living my whole life with her. The thought of Nathan would float into my consciousness and I would miss him, but then the reality of Sybil would seep back in and displace the thought. I would enjoy her.

"You're like a cat, Sybs," I said. As soon as I had said it I felt blood coursing through my body and a thousand knives digging into my back.

"Did you just call me Sybs? Nathan calls me Sybs."

"I heard him call you Sybs. I was in the room."

"That's right. He told me you were there to discuss something. It felt weird to know he could see you right then."

"Hmmm," I said and buried my head into her. I wanted to go back to feeling easy and comfortable.

"Should we sleep?" she asked.

"Yes. Did you have a rough day?"

"No. Just trying to get the interiors finished for this bank downtown. Spent most of the day on site."

"Do you do a lot of that? Coordinating people and looking over workers' shoulders?"

"Sometimes. You have to do it. Otherwise, no matter how good the contractors are, they'll do something different from what you meant."

"I think it's just so cool that you can build furniture and the insides of buildings."

"Thanks. Did you decide which desk you wanted?"

"Oh! Yes." I got out of bed and went to my coffee table to get the sheet of paper with the design I'd chosen.

"Good choice. It'll look nice there," she said, pointing to the alcove.

"What next?" I asked.

"We go on Saturday to the furniture store and order it."

"Cool. What time?"

"It'll have to be afternoon."

I thought for a moment. I could visualize my miniplanner, in which I had written "RM." Richard Murphy would have to wait another week.

"Afternoon then, around two?" I asked.

"Two's good."

I got back into bed and crawled closer to her.

"André, why are we both wearing all these clothes?"

"Huh! Good point."

I stood on my bed and removed everything.

"What about your clothes?" I whined, trying to be funny.

"You can take those off, too," she said.

I sat down on the bed cross-legged and naked in a Buddha pose and undid the buttons of her blouse. Then I lost my patience and removed the rest quickly, throwing everything all over the place. She was wearing white lace underwear.

"Nice panties," I said.

"Nathan got me these."

"From where?"

"Victoria's Secret."

"Cool." My mind's film studio played the image of Nathan in his brown leather hunting jacket strolling through Victoria's Secret, flirting with the saleswomen, touching women's lingerie with his fingers, choosing white lace for Sybil. When would he do these things for me? I felt more romantic toward Nathan than I had anyone else. I had loved my girlfriend in college, but I hadn't been very romantic then. With Nathan, I wanted to go to candlelit dinners and get roses.

"Good though they look, they're coming off," I said to her and unclasped the bra. Something inside me had dried up because of thinking of Nathan. I wished I could come back to the moment, be here and now with Sybil.

I ran my lower lip on her skin. I ran my lips up and down her arm and then all over her forehead. I licked my lips again and again so that they would not chafe her. I did it till my lips tingled and were mesmerized by the feel of her skin. Then we made love. When I ejaculated, I thought I would never be able to ejaculate again in my life. The muscles of her vagina contracted and almost hurt my penis.

I fell asleep within minutes after that but woke up in a few hours. I was sweating and my heart was beating fast. As soon as I opened my eyes, I thought of Nathan. I picked up my phone. I had voicemail. Nathan had called.

"Hope you're having a nice night. I just wanted to tell you that I was missing you."

I replaced the handset and didn't even try to sleep. I raised my pillow and let it rest against the headrest of my bed and half sat. I watched the patterns made by the light coming from the street through the blinds on my window. After what seemed like many hours, I lay down again and went to sleep. When the alarm went off in the morning I was too sleepy to turn it off. Eventually, the sheets rustled and Sybil moved. She shut the alarm off. I went back into a deeper sleep. Then she was waking me up.

"André, I have to go to work. Don't you?"

"Huh?"

"It's eight-forty, André."

"Oh! Shit." I sat up in bed and rubbed my eyes. She sat down beside me and kissed my forehead.

"I have to go."

I waved at her.

"God, you can be cute," she said and came closer and nibbled at my lips. Then she was gone.

I lumbered out of bed and considered putting on my suit. I had to shower to wake up. I got into the bathroom and let the hot water flow. After a few minutes I was awake. I made it to work at nine-thirty.

"Late night, André?" Martha asked as I walked in.

"Couldn't fall asleep," I replied.

My draft proposal was due. It was almost done, but I had to revise it. I booted up my computer and checked my office voice-mail. Nathan had left me a message at nine.

"Where are you?" he'd said very quietly.

I buzzed him on the internal system.

"Sorry, I overslept."

"Want to show me the proposal before the meeting?"

"Yes. That'll be great. In half an hour?"

"Yes, come by."

"Thanks."

I read over my draft and made some changes. Then I went to his office. He wasn't there, so I left the draft on his desk and went back to my cubicle. I had an e-mail from mkt1499@cede.net. I had no idea who that could be.

The text of the message cleared up my confusion. It read, "Is this André Bernard? This is Madhu Kapoor (née Tandon)."

I replied immediately. "Yes, where are you? I'm working for a Japanese bank. How did you get my address? Ever in NY? Let's meet." And I added my work and home numbers and addresses at the bottom of the e-mail.

Madhu had been my most serious involvement ever. I hadn't stayed in touch after we broke up, because she was going to get married and I didn't have the courage to deal with it. She had agreed to let her parents find a man for her. I had received her wedding invitation during my first week of graduate school:

"Mrs. & Mr. Tandon request the pleasure of your company on the occasion of the marriage of their daughter Madhu to Srini Kapoor (son of Mrs. and Mr. Kapoor)."

I had thrown it in the trash can and walked around that day in a daze, locked myself in the bedroom and cried. After that I'd gone to a bar, watched a Rangers game, and gotten drunk. A fat woman had picked me up. I'd gone to her apartment and banged her. The next morning I'd woken up with a huge hangover and sworn I would never think about Madhu again. I couldn't remember the fat woman's name now. I tried to jog my memory. I thought John might remember since I had mentioned it to him.

Nathan buzzed me on the phone.

"Just read your proposal. Will you come here a moment to discuss it?"

"Yes."

I walked to Nathan's office, still trying to recall the name of the fat woman. She could have been an Amy or a Julia. I gave up. It was rattling to think that there were people I'd slept with whose names I couldn't recall. I should make a list to keep track from now on, I thought. Nathan was standing behind his desk and staring at a painting on his wall. I realized I hadn't seen him since the previous day. I felt happy just looking at him.

"Hi! Is the draft okay?"

"It's great."

"I don't want to disappoint you."

"No, this is very good."

"Anything I should add?"

"One tiny thing."

"What?"

"How much time will it take to design and implement this system. Testing time. Debugging time. How many people will be needed? How much money?"

"I don't know. I have no idea."

Nathan smiled at me, then said, "Of course you have no idea. Make it up."

"Make it up?"

"André, this is real life. We need estimates, resource allocation. I'll have to ask you to go and hire people. How many will you hire, and how much will you pay them? You're going to be captain of this ship."

"Oh! God!"

"It's a lot of responsibility," he said, squinting. Then he added, "You can do it."

"I'll be working my ass off."

He moved his head up and down a few times.

"Will I ever have time to hang out with you?" I asked.

"Yeah, you will. Choose some good people you can rely on."

"How should I make estimates? Time allocation I can. But money?"

"Talk to David Botolph in MIS. He does this sort of thing all the time. You can use him. I didn't officially put him on the project because he would have walked all over you."

"Did he handle the last one? The prototype cash management module?"

"Yeah. He doesn't know all that much. He's a systems guy but doesn't have a quantitative background. We need someone who speaks our language. Like you."

"All right, I'll get hold of him."

There was another e-mail from Madhu when I got back. She was going to be in New York over the weekend with her husband, Srini. She wanted to know if I'd like to get together. I wrote back saying yes and asking if they were free for Sunday brunch. Then I called David Botolph and asked him if he'd meet me for lunch in the cafeteria.

David Botolph was a mildly overweight man of medium height, with black hair that fell flatly on his head. His shirt was so tight it looked as if the buttons would pop any minute. His pants were as tight.

"Thank you for taking the time to meet with me," I said.

"It's okay," he said in a flat, toneless voice, without smiling.

"I'm working on the new risk management project."

"I know."

"Nathan said you would have a good idea of how to estimate resource allocation for the project."

"Nathan who?"

"Nathan Williams, the Head of Risk Management."

"Yes."

"What's the best way to estimate these things?"

"Once you've estimated the amount of man hours, you can simply use a chart in the personnel office."

"Which chart?"

"The work allocation chart. It lists the amount of money you can expect to spend per man hour by level of education."

I couldn't believe my ears. One would think we were pushing paper in a bureaucratic socialist regime. In my mind, the world of finance was the opposite. It was sleek and sharp and efficient.

David Botolph had no intention of helping me in any way. I couldn't see the sense in breaking my head against the wall asking him more questions. So I swallowed my lunch as fast as I could, thanked him for his time, and left. At my desk I made some random assumptions about how long it would take me to program a small portion of the risk management system and extrapolated those projections. I used my base salary as the salary level we could expect to pay the average programmer and came up with estimates. I e-mailed the spreadsheet to Nathan with a cover note explaining how I'd made my calculations.

He wrote back, "It'll do. P.S. What did you think of DB?"

I wrote back, "Asshole."

He wrote back, "He's the only one in the bank who knows about me."

I wrote back, "Why, is he one too?"

"Yes." Nathan wrote.

I wondered for a moment if Nathan had done anything with DB. The thought was revolting. He was hideous, plus his personality sucked. I had, against my will, an image of DB naked. I wanted to gouge out my eyes.

The computer blinked. I had more e-mail. It was from Madhu, saying that Sunday was fine, she'd call me at ten. And she was really looking forward to it.

It was time for the meeting. I made eight copies of my final draft proposal and headed to the meeting room. Nathan was already there, but no one else had arrived.

"Are these rooms bugged?" I asked.

"I know for a fact they aren't," he said.

"Did you ever do anything with DB?"

"No. Surely you didn't think..."

"No, I didn't but I wanted to be sure."

"I'm moderately discriminating, André."

"How do you know about him?"

"Ran into him in a bar in Chelsea once. He came on to me. He even said he was a virgin."

"Yuck!"

"Let's not waste any more time talking about him."

Yoshi Kato walked in. He waved at us both and sat down. I had to ask Nathan what the deal with Yoshi was. He was, after all, my boss. In a few minutes the room was full. Oatmeal was the last to join. I could feel the atmosphere become charged and battle-like when he walked in. He made me tense.

Nathan convened the meeting. My proposal was the first and last point on the agenda. I was the youngest in the room, the least experienced, and the one responsible. I realized at that moment that promotions, salary, and ego were at stake. My affair with Nathan might have a lot of consequences.

For once, I forgot all about Nathan being my lover. I was aware only of what I was saying, completely absorbed and focused on work. I passed around copies of the proposal and highlighted the main points in my presentation. I impressed myself. I was succinct, and everybody nodded a lot. Even Oatmeal looked at me without a sneer, Nathan made check marks on the proposal, and Yoshi smiled a few times. I ended by asking if anyone had any questions.

"This is pretty thorough," Oatmeal said, raising his head to look me in the eyes. From where I was standing, he looked particularly puffy-eyed and malignant. I waited for him to hurl a real blow, but he didn't.

Yoshi said, "André, this is very good. I don't see why we can't start implementing it right away. We should start looking for some programmers and get on with it."

"I agree with Yoshi," Nathan said, adding, "Can anyone see any problems with anything?"

I thought Mortimer the asshole junior trader might try to score some points over me, but apparently he knew when to keep his mouth shut. There was all-around silence.

"Great. Well done, André," Nathan said.

"Thanks. I'll e-mail everyone with the next step, and let's tentatively plan on meeting next Thursday to see where we stand," I said, making eye contact with all eight people in the room. I felt as if I'd just snatched away authority from someone, but no one seemed to mind. They slowly got up. I walked out with Yoshi and Nathan, and we went down to the coffee shop in the lobby to get espressos. It was already four-thirty. Another couple of hours and I'd be alone with Nathan. One of the best things about fucking a man was that there were no days when he could say, "I have my period, my back hurts."

I pulled out my planner when I was back at my desk and wrote "S" in the Saturday afternoon slot and "M" in the Saturday night slot. Then I wrote "Madhu + hubby" in the Sunday morning slot. It had been almost two years since I'd seen her.

Madhu and I had met during freshman orientation week in college. I had gone to see Buñuel's *Tristana* in the student film center. Madhu had sat beside me by chance. She was wearing a red sari with a white border. It was exotic. To a boy who had grown up in many small towns, it was absolutely enchanting.

"I like your outfit," I had said.

She'd leaned close to me and whispered in my ear, "I'm feeling really out of place. I just came from an international student reception for freshmen."

"Where are you from?" I asked.

"I'm from California. I thought I'd go in a sari so that the freshmen from India would feel good, but they all showed up in jeans."

I laughed.

When the movie started, Madhu let out chuckles every now and then. When one of the characters in the movie made one-line statements about love existing only in freedom and outside of marriage, Madhu clapped and look at me, saying, "He's so right."

After the movie was over, I asked her if she'd like to get a cup of coffee with me.

"I'd love to, but I told my roommate I'd meet up with her. Why don't we trade numbers?"

I'd written my number on the back of a Seattle's Best Coffee Frequent Cupper Card.

"André Bernard is the name. It was nice to meet you."

"Great," she said, taking the card and looking around distractedly. She didn't have a purse and was carrying her room keys and college ID in her hand.

"You don't have a place to put it," I observed.

"Well, I was in India this summer, and I'm going to do what they'd do over there." She slid the card into her blouse and smiled.

"Right next to your chest," I said.

"Safe."

I'd gone home turned on by the thought of an Indian woman cradling my phone number in her blouse, the paper of the card touching her soft brown breasts.

I hadn't thought of Madhu since our breakup at commencement. I had blocked her from my mind and just gone on with life. I hadn't kept in touch. And now, thinking back on the relationship brought warm memories devoid of pain. I was glad I was meeting her. I was curious to see what sort of man she had married. If she was happy. If we still got along as well as we had in college, maybe we could be friends. She'd be tickled to know I was sleeping with a guy. Or maybe not. I suddenly wasn't sure I could rely on Madhu's open-mindedness.

My miniplanner had a blank after the Sunday brunch date with Madhu. I e-mailed Nathan to see if he would see me Sunday afternoon or night. I also had a half-thought that I should spend a little bit of time alone.

I opened a blank Excel spreadsheet and made a timetable for myself. Tomorrow I would decide on a hiring process for new programmers and on deadlines and inform the team. I made some notes about the kind of expertise we'd need on the project.

Then I opened a new Excel spreadsheet and tried to compare different things in my life. I dealt with all my emotions that way. Even my deepest fears and greatest joys I would put into a spreadsheet in my mind and weigh against something else. People always said not to compare apples and oranges. I was going to experiment. Most experiences in life took time. Time wasn't experienced evenly at an internal level, but from the outside it was even and objective.

In one column I wrote "Allegro molto from Mozart's Symphony No.1, K.16 in E-flat major." I closed my eyes and played it in my head. I remembered how it made me feel. The very first second would take me into its fold. It had complete hold over me for its full length. It made the muscles of my leg move up and down when I was sitting. For entire seconds, my heart would jump and be on edge. After five minutes and fifty seconds, it stopped in my head. I thought of five minutes and fifty seconds with Nathan when we had sipped Sierras at the bar at Mugsy's. My body hadn't moved, but I had been completely there. I wrote "=" beside the cell in which I had written Mozart and wrote "Sierras with Nathan."

It was a seductive idea that one could reduce everything to time. I decided to play with the idea for a while. Maybe I'd learn a few things. I looked at my spreadsheet again and closed my eyes. This time I played the Allegro molto again in my head and thought of Nathan at the same time. In a minute I discovered the problem. I'd chosen two experiences that were both outside time. Both absorbed me fully. Whether they took twenty minutes or three, they had the same effect. Comparing waiting in line for coffee to having dinner with Martha would be more accurate for the purpose of the experiment. But also less meaningful. I closed down the spreadsheet after saving it as "Time warp." Then I buzzed Nathan.

We went to get a drink after work. Nathan told me that Yoshi was merely paying his dues in the New York office before he joined the Tokyo office as an official of great consequence.

"How come?" I asked.

"He's the oldest son of the most senior trustee of the bank."

"Holy cow! Why didn't you tell me that before?"

"I'm telling you now. He likes you, by the way."

"How old is he?"

"Thirty. He's worked in every major office—Buenos Aires, Paris, London, Hong Kong, and Sydney."

"He's different from the others. I mean from the other Japanese guys."

"He studied here. He's got a rebellious streak I find rather endearing."

"Do you know him well?"

"The two of us went on a vacation to Machu Picchu when he was working in Argentina. We talked a lot then."

"Nothing else? Just talked?"

Nathan started laughing. "André, do you think everyone is gay?"

"Sorry."

"It's charming, your borderline jealousy."

"Stop patronizing me."

"You can be so young," he teased.

My confidence bit the dust. I felt thoroughly immature. I sipped my pint of lager in silence, while Nathan talked about the bank and how well it had done in the past few years. When he was done expounding, I declined another drink and we headed out of the bar. It wasn't clear to me what we were going to do next, and I made no effort to find out. I was still feeling upset.

"Dinner?" Nathan asked.

"Sure."

"What are you in the mood for?"

"Anything."

"Stop sulking."

"I'm not sulking." I was feeling less and less good about myself. I just couldn't pull myself out of it.

"You're acting like a woman," Nathan said irritably.

We were walking through Bryant Park toward Fifth Avenue. It was a cold but clear night.

"I'm not a woman," I said.

"You're more woman than many I've known," he said.

I grabbed his neck and his left arm and twisted them hard. Then I thought it might hurt him, so I threw my entire body on his and made him fall on the grass. He looked furious. I couldn't stop. I was afraid I'd gone too far and I had to pull him back. I started tickling him. He wiggled and thrashed his knees and giggled. I got closer to him and gripped his waist tightly in my arms, then I tickled his back and said, "Are you going to forgive me or not?"

"Yes yes yes."

I stopped tickling him. The adrenaline flow had put me in a better mood. We got up. I dusted the grass off his black overcoat, and he straightened my tie.

"You weren't just being like a woman, you were being exactly like Sybil," he said.

"Shhh," I said.

A bum was sitting on a bench and a couple was necking by the fountain. The couple looked up when we walked past them. The woman said, "Just the kind of night for this."

"Yeah," I said. Then I raised Nathan's hand to my lips and kissed it.

She waved at me. Her boyfriend glared.

Nathan said, "Let's go down to your place and find something to eat near there."

"Yes. Can we walk? It's a nice night, and I miss fresh air."

"This is hardly fresh air. But I know what you mean. We're cooped up in the office all day."

"It depresses me."

"Aaaw," he said, in a sudden gesture of warmth, and patted my hair. I felt like a toy. I loved the feeling.

We walked to Third Avenue and then down to Twenty-ninth Street. I linked my arm in his as we walked. Two men in business suits and black overcoats, I couldn't help thinking to myself. It reminded me of the homosexual affair in E. M. Forster's *Maurice*—a contemporary version.

"Nathan, have you read *Maurice*?"

"Of course. In fact, my high school teacher who I had a crush on assigned it to us."

"Did you have an affair with him?"

"I wanted to, but he was too moral."

Over dinner, Nathan talked about the upcoming office party. He was worried because Sybil had been acting funny and we'd all be meeting again. I was much more worried than he ever could be, but I soothed him with all sorts of assurances.

"She'll never know, Nathan. I'll avoid you. I'll talk to Yoshi and Martha."

"She'll find that even weirder. We all had dinner together," he agonized.

"Look, I'm on perfectly good terms with her. She's designing my desk."

"That's right. How is it?"

"She's brilliant. I've chosen a design."

"You're not going to get upset, André, are you?"

"No, Nathan. I'm not. Don't you trust me?"

"I do. Okay. We can stop talking about this."

I slept fitfully that night, dreaming in the background about a loud room of people dancing. In my dream, Yoshi, Sybil, and Martha had a ménage à trois while Nathan and I were bouncers freezing outside the club. Then I heard something and woke up. Nathan was talking in his sleep. His language was garbled. Not a word was discernible, but he was talking rapidly and jerking his head. I wondered what chemical his brain stem was secreting. I held his head in my hand and moved my own head closer to his. He got still, and I felt his head growing heavier against mine. Then I felt mine get heavier and his get lighter, as if there were some sort of physical transference. Were chemical reactions within bodies interchangeable? My last conscious sensation was of my head rolling off my pillow. Then it was morning.

We sipped coffee in bed and Nathan rubbed my back.

"What are your plans for the weekend, André?"

"Bunch of stuff. This ex of mine, Madhu, will be in town with her husband. I've promised to meet them. Haven't seen her since graduation."

He grunted.

My mind went into a tailspin. What if Sybil had mentioned that we were meeting to go over the desk design? I should have told him that the night before, but it hadn't occurred to me. He'd get suspicious if I didn't mention it at all. If she hadn't spoken to him, I could always tell her first thing this morning and she could bring it up with him. I had to choose my words carefully so that neither of us would get implicated.

"I'm also supposed to coordinate on the desk with Sybil," I said.

"I can do Sunday night. I got your e-mail. I forgot to mention it earlier."

"Thank you," I said and leaned closer on the bed to kiss him.

"Let's shower together," Nathan said.

Friday passed quickly. I left a message on Sybil's voicemail at work telling her that I had mentioned to Nathan that I might meet her about the desk, and that we could talk tomorrow morning about it. I hadn't arranged with either Sybil or Nathan to meet them that night. They hadn't seen each other for three nights. I didn't want to ask Martha again, since I was going to eat dinner at her place on Saturday. For some reason, I was scared of being alone. I decided that for that same reason I had to do it.

I put in an honest day's work, short but intense. At six I left without looking Nathan up. I went straight home after I picked up two slices of pizza and a can of coke from Tommy's Pizza Parlor at the base of my building.

There were serious things in the business of living I hadn't done in ages. I put on some Mozart and pulled out a book I had been meaning to read for a while on theories of intelligence. I began by flipping to a section on the Emotional Quotient test. I didn't really need to ascertain for the fourth time that I was an emotional retard, but I took the test anyway. My score had gone up. Now, I was among the top 10 percent of emotionally intelligent people in the world. I decided this was because, as with every other standardized test that one could master by practice, I'd learned to take this one. I didn't feel emotionally average, let alone intelligent. I was going down a path that could only end in tears for all parties involved. I lost interest in the book and put it away.

I opened my miniplanner. I turned to the last page, where I was in the habit of jotting down names of good movies, books, CDs, and restaurants. Time and again people had mentioned Ingmar Bergman's *Seventh Seal*. I ran down to Blockbuster to get it.

The movie left me trembling. It made me think about useless things like death and old age, which I had already wasted my adolescence on. It made me feel terrifyingly alone. It also made me think of Nathan. I wanted to have him close to my chest when I died. I certainly didn't want him to die before me, but he was so much older that it was likely to happen. My poor dad had been so lonely after Mom died. He'd lived on only for me. I called my dad.

"Papa."

"André. I would have called you next week if you hadn't called."

"How are you?"

"The arthritis is very bad because of the cold weather."

"Are you taking any medicine?"

"Yes, Dr. Werner has given me painkillers."

My dad was still working, cooking in his restaurant till eleven every night. I had to make some money quickly so that I could convince him to retire and take it easy. He was the reason I was working at an investment bank. He was the reason I wanted to get rich. He'd lived his life only for me, and I wanted to be a good son and pay him back.

"Papa, as soon as it gets warmer I want you to come and visit me for a couple of weeks."

"I have to run the restaurant, André."

"I know—just take a week off. I want to show you New York. I want you to meet my friends."

"All right, maybe I can come in April before the tourist season begins in May. I can't be away then."

"That leaves us only a few weeks. Do you want to come the first weekend of April and then stay till the end of the next weekend?"

"Let me check the calendar, André."

I could hear him shuffle around the room and groan. Finally, his heavy breathing was audible over the phone and he spoke again.

"I can come, but I want to leave on Saturday so that I can rest on Sunday before starting work again on Monday."

"Great, Papa. I'll book the tickets for you."

"You don't have to book tickets. I can buy them here. Shirley will arrange it for me."

Shirley was a neighbor of ours who watched out for my dad. She was younger than him but divorced, and she had moved into the apartment next door when I had moved to college. I didn't know her very well, but she and my father went for walks once a week, and they always took care of each other. Knowing that Shirley was around gave me a sense of reassurance about my father.

"Papa, I'll send you the tickets."

"I can pay for my tickets, André. I'm coming because I want to see New York."

"Papa. Please. We'll talk about it later," I said.

"How is the bank? Do they give you health and retirement benefits?"

"Yes, everything is going well."

"André, I have to go because I told Shirley I would ask her if she wanted anything from the market tomorrow."

"Bye."

"God bless."

I put the phone down. My chest felt heavy and empty at the same time. Calling my dad hadn't helped. I felt sick. There was a time I'd slept in his bed, played with his moustache every day. Now I thought of him a few times a day, but I didn't miss him. He was getting older and would die one day. Maybe all alone in his apartment or in the restaurant while he was working. Shirley would call me. I'd feel sad. Then it would be over. One day I would die. Nathan would die. We'd all be dead. It was pointless to drudge through another forty years of life only to slowly wither away and pass out. I wanted to die now. In the prime of my youth. When I was screwing attractive people.

My thoughts were stifling. I decided to go for a walk.

I put on a pair of worn-out sneakers and my old canvas jacket and walked toward the East River. The river was desolate and industrial. It reeked of urban decay. Twisted metal wires and broken porcelain toilet bowls were scattered on the concrete walk by the river. Three identical high-rises jutted out from the earth. The view of Queens was uninspiring.

My jacket was not warm enough for the March evening. The wind was blowing quite hard, and my fingers were numb. I started walking back home. As soon as I reached First Avenue, buses blared their horns and taxicabs flashed by. Shin Lee take-out, with its flashing red neon lights and its solitary customer, stood on the street corner. I'd been living in New York City for less than a month, but already I knew I'd never leave. I couldn't imagine living anywhere else. I could see the owner inside laughing and talking to someone on his phone. I wondered if he had a son. Maybe the son went to Harvard and Shin Lee was a proud man. Maybe I will be hiring the son for a programming job next week, I thought.

I was going to spend a few hours programming every week and many hours supervising others who were programming. I was spending hours and hours slaving for a bunch of Japanese aristocrats so that I could earn money that I would then spend in restaurants, eating food I'd digest badly, thinking troubling thoughts that would make me more miserable. What was the point? So what if I ate in restaurants with Nathan? So what if all these questions were pointless and not worth asking when Nathan's cock was stiff and inside my ass? Those moments were brief. The rest of the time, life was futile. Maximizing sex was hardly an escape from this kind of existential angst.

When I was fourteen and reading big books, it had felt grown-up to have such attacks. It was merely childish now. Everyone knew about death, and everyone lived. Nathan was wise. He'd surely had all these doubts. My father had lived through more loneliness than I'd ever faced. Both of them still got some joy from life. They were warm, and they made others happy. I decided not to watch any more Bergman movies. Or spend any more nights alone. It wasn't a solution, but till I figured out the solution there was no point in giving myself a hard time and wandering around New York City feeling alienated and purposeless.

I got back home, turned on the stereo, took off my clothes, and lay on my bed. K22 in B-flat started playing. It was the first piece on the CD I had bought the other day. I fiddled with my member. Quite against my wishes, I had this image of an eight-year-old Wolfgang tiptoeing up to a curtain behind the stage to take a peak at an audience and then turn back, take a peak again and turn back. The first movement in K22 was mischievous. I was alarmed that I was turning myself on with it. Mozart had written it when he was eight or nine, prepubescent. I dived across my bed for the remote and shut it off. Then I made my way to the CD rack and put in another CD in the dark. It was Haydn. He was not easy to wank to, and it took a long time. At the end I felt one with 14 percent of the Oberlin class and slept.

When I woke up in the morning, the angst had passed. Like some strange skin allergy, it had afflicted me briefly and then disappeared without a trace. I couldn't relate to my thoughts from the night before. I got out of bed and made myself a cup of coffee. I walked around my apartment naked, stretching as I walked. The phone rang.

"André, this is Sybil. Are we still on for this afternoon?"

"Yes."

"Meet me at the furniture store at two. I'll come back with you to your place for a few hours."

"Great. When do you have to be back?"

"By six."

"Okay. Give me the address of the store again."

I wrote down the address and hung up. Then I called Martha and asked her when I should meet her. I arranged to go to her apartment at seven-thirty. I still had a few hours to myself before meeting Sybil. I was feeling lazy. I got back into my bed and slept a little more. The phone rang after some time and woke me up.

"Nathan here."

"Hello!" I replied, stretching and yawning into the phone. I could feel the entire length of my leg. It felt delicious. Nathan's voice draped over my bare skin.

"Just wanted to see if you might be free in the afternoon?"

"Oh, no! Sorry. I have to see Sybil about the desk."

"I know that. I meant after that."

"I just made plans. We're still on for tomorrow night, aren't we?" I felt guilty saying no, and it made me angry that I felt guilty.

"Yeah, I can even meet you in the afternoon. Anytime after four." He didn't sound disapproving that I had made plans. I was glad Nathan never played on my guilt.

"Let's meet at four. Do you want to just come over?"

"Yes. I'll do that."

After I put the phone down I hopped into the shower and decided to get a bite to eat. I walked to Chelsea and went to the Big Cup. The man at the cash register flirted with me. I picked up a gay newspaper that was lying in a corner and sat on one of the couches. I opened the newspaper in front of me and used it as a cover to scope the guys out. There were a couple of good-looking guys. I stared at the classifieds distractedly. Husky men were looking for passionate relationships. Tops for bottoms. I wondered if I had another half, floating around somewhere, someone who'd complete my puzzle, as Plato's *Symposium* would have one believe. Was Nathan the one? When I finished my cup of coffee and my bagel I decided there was no point cruising for guys—I didn't need any more lovers. I left.

Sybil was waiting for me outside the furniture store when I got there. She was wearing a tight leather skirt and high-heeled shoes. Her blonde hair was flapping in the air, and her lipstick was redder than usual. She was in an adventurous mood. She grabbed my arm and led me into the store. We went into the manager's room, and Sybil explained what we were looking for. We showed him the design, and he said it would cost me fourteen hundred dollars. I had two thousand dollars in my bank account. I agreed. In my mind, it was not just a desk. It was something Sybil had designed and a twin of what Nathan had. If there was one piece of furniture I'd keep all my life, it was this.

In half an hour we were done and in a cab on our way to my apartment. Sybil sat close to me in the cab, her right hand innocently tucked in the space where my legs joined. I felt a rush of happiness at being with her.

At home, I made her some tea and we sat at the table sipping it.

"André, can I blindfold you?" she asked.

"Why?"

"Can I or can't I?"

"Go ahead," I said.

She loosened the leopard-print scarf from her neck and tied it around my head. Everything got dark for me.

"Is this too tight?"

"No."

Then there was only silence in the room. I couldn't hear her or feel her presence at all. I couldn't even hear her breathe. Everything was still for what seemed like a long time.

"Sybil, what's going on?" I asked after a while.

Silence.

"Sybil?"

Silence.

"Sybs, answer me."

I felt her finger on my lip. Then her lip on my lip. Then her tongue on my lip. Then her pubic hair on my lip. Then her labia on my lip.

I started licking her. I was aware only of my lips and the taste of her excitement. She pulled my cock out of my pants and sat on it. Sucked it inside her vagina. She moved back and forth on it.

"My briefs are hurting me, Sybs," I said.

She undid the button on my pants and got up from my lap. I stood up. She pulled my briefs down and pushed me back on the chair. She positioned herself on my penis again and started moving. Then she groaned, and I could feel her muscles clamp. My briefs and pants were dangling around my ankles. I spurted into her. No condom, nothing.

"Can I see you now?" I asked.

"No."

"What next?"

She got up from on top of me and said, "Get up."

My pants were twisted around my ankles on the floor.

"Want to help me with my pants?"

She steadied me as I lifted one leg and then another. Then she led me to my bed. I imagined myself walking across my room, blindfolded with a woman's leopard-print silk scarf and wearing only my straw-colored hemp shirt. My knee knocked into the edge of the bed. I doubled over.

"Are you okay?"

"I'm fine," I said, rubbing my kneecap.

"Lie down."

She licked my legs and then my stomach. She gave me little love bites on my neck. I was still exhausted by the last orgasm. I didn't think I could get hard again. She removed my shirt and made me turn on my stomach. She sat on my butt and breathed on the back of my neck. I could feel her wetness on my butt. She was rubbing against it. Sybil is an animal, I thought to myself. Suddenly sex seemed base. Sybil was in heat, there was nothing mental or psychological about her desire. I felt the beginnings of disgust bubble in my stomach. I wanted it to end. I felt impatient. Time hung. In my mind I opened my spreadsheet and wrote "Sex with Sybil first time = timelessness" "Sybil on my butt = waiting in line for coffee." Her voice interrupted my analysis.

"Turn around," she said.

I turned on my back. She took my penis in her mouth. And got it hard. I was no longer impatient. The disgust died.

"I want to be on top of you and fuck you," I said.

She rolled on the bed and pulled me on top. She wrapped her legs around me and thrust her hips toward me. We climaxed. The beat of my own heart and Sybil's filled the room. We were sweating so much that the areas where our skins touched stuck together. I pulled off my blindfold and buried my face in her hair. After a while, I stopped sweating and felt cold.

"Should we get under the covers?"

"What time is it?"

We both turned to look at my alarm clock on the side of the bed. It was five-thirty.

"Wow! I need to get going."

I looked at Sybil. For a second, I wanted to hug her close.

"Oh, André! I don't want to leave," she said.

She flopped on me and hugged me. We kissed each other furiously. Then she started getting dressed. I lay naked in bed and watched her. When she was ready, I walked her to the door. We kissed again. Bit each other's lips.

"Soon again, please. Don't say no," she said urgently.

"Monday night?"

"Okay."

She opened the door and left. I locked it shut behind her and got dressed myself. Sex with Sybil had left me feeling whole. I didn't feel like taking a shower.

Martha lived on the Upper East Side. I decided to walk there, even though it was drizzling. I wore my headphones and carried an umbrella. Mozart's *Prague* sounded splendorous when I was surrounded by tall lit buildings and walking by myself. The evening air felt good against my skin. Then the rain started to come down furiously. But the music had taken me to a different place, away from my immediate environment. I was in a court in Salzburg with a kiddywink playing the piano in a little red coat and a white powdered wig, finishing his performance amid applause and then talking urgently to his young sister. My heart was bursting with happiness. I bought a bottle of Merlot for Martha when I was near her apartment.

"André, good to see you!" Martha exclaimed, as if she hadn't been expecting me.

I gave her the wine and removed my jacket as I walked in. My pants were soaking wet at the base. She put my jacket on a hanger and hung it on the doorknob.

"Nice place," I said. It was a cookie-cutter apartment, but the insides were distinctive. Rugs and African prints hung from all the walls.

"Thanks."

"What are you going to teach me to cook?" I asked.

"Do you like eggplant?"

"Yes."

"Get to work, then," she said, indicating six small, freshly washed eggplants on her cutting board.

"What do I do?"

"Cut them."

"How?"

"Into thin and even slices."

I felt stupid. I was nervous. I needed her to demonstrate, but I didn't want to seem like a fool. So I closed my eyes for a second and tried to remember how my father cut vegetables in his restaurant. Then I started slicing.

"Is that all right?"

"Not bad."

Martha lectured me on the basics of Indian cooking. She explained that one used cumin seeds for seasoning in North Indian cooking and mustard seeds in South Indian cooking. Turmeric was essential to both. The aroma of mustard seeds splattering in a tablespoon of oil filled her apartment. It made me hungry. She had made steamed white rice and dal.

"How did you learn to cook Indian food?" I asked.

"I taught myself. Someone I had a crush on liked Indian food," she said.

I chuckled to myself. I was learning so I could cook for Nathan. Martha had learned so that she could cook for someone else. Humans were herd animals. We were all driven by the same motivations. We needed to feel close to other people and express that closeness in similar ways.

After dinner, we sat on Martha's couch and sipped more Merlot. She sat close to me and told me stories about her delinquent brother. She asked about my life. I spoke about my ex, Madhu.

"You know, André, it doesn't seem to me like you ever really dealt with it."

"Yeah. And I would have just gone on not dealing with it, too, if she hadn't e-mailed me the other day."

"Sometimes you need to get events and people and other lovers between yourself and the other person before you can go back and think about it."

"I'm just wondering what will happen if I feel anything for her tomorrow at brunch."

"Of course you're going to feel a lot. You haven't seen this woman in two years, and when you last saw her you loved her."

"Yeah," I said. I was glad I didn't have conversations like this with Nathan and Sybil. It was boring discussing myself. But I'd been the one to start it in the first place—Martha was not to blame.

"It's late. I'm going to go home," I said, getting up. I didn't care that she'd think me abrupt.

She looked at me funnily. I knew I was expected to stay and make the moves, but I wasn't interested. I was still carrying Sybil's juices on my skin. I'd had two fantastic and meaningful orgasms in the past five hours. I didn't feel the need to touch Martha. She was nice-looking but not fatally attractive. She was easy to resist. I put on my jacket and thanked her for dinner. At her door, I gave her a quick kiss on the cheek and turned around and left.

At home, I thought of meeting Madhu the next morning. I remembered all the significant times we'd had together. Our walk by the beach in Nantucket one summer when she first told me she loved me. The first time we had sex after she went on birth control pills. I slept deeply and well, waking up in the morning only when she called.

We met for brunch in Union Square. I reached the restaurant before them and sat reading the *New York Times*. They made a grand entrance. She looked the same as when I'd last seen her. Almost.

"André, hello. This is my husband, Srini."

"Nice to meet you, Srini. André Bernard is the name."

"Hi, André."

I turned to Madhu and said, "Hi."

We all sat down. Srini and Madhu sat facing me. I felt I was in front of an execution squad. I also felt a sense of déjà vu. Then

I remembered I knew another husband–wife pair. I wondered what it would be like to do with Srini the kind of things I was up to with Nathan. I looked at Srini and smiled. He looked startled. He was stuffy. I couldn't imagine it seriously with him.

"Excuse me, I'll be right back," he said, getting up from his chair. I flashed my teeth at him again.

As soon as he was out of earshot, Madhu leaned across the table and whispered, "André, he doesn't know about us. He thinks I was a virgin when we married."

"Right," I said, smiling stupidly. I felt great.

"How are you liking your job? You just started, didn't you?"

"I'm sleeping with a man," I said by way of response.

She looked shell-shocked. I was suddenly uncomfortable. Maybe she wasn't all that cool. I looked at the bottle of ketchup on the table.

"Were you interested in men when we were together?"

"No. Never," I replied.

We both saw Srini emerge from the corridor that led to the men's room. He was still out of earshot.

"I want to know all about it. But we can't talk now," Madhu said. She looked excited.

"We'll e-mail," I said.

After Srini joined us, I was aware of a different dynamic. Madhu was clearly not very much at home with him. The ease one sees between happy couples was missing. I didn't know how she'd met him or how they'd married. But when she smiled and spoke, I felt as if she still liked me, was still a little in love with me.

I made conversation with Srini. He was a C++ programmer for the Fed in D.C. Madhu was a consultant. She was now on a project that brought her to Newark several times a month for short periods. In the back of my head, I realized this meant we could see each other without him knowing.

My heart felt warm. It was like seeing a cousin from your childhood you'd always loved. I couldn't wait to talk to Madhu in private again and tell her all about my new life. She knew me well. She'd help me figure out what I felt for Nathan and Sybil. She'd unearth my motives. Madhu didn't look too happy, but Srini seemed all right, if boring. He didn't look as if he beat her.

It was time for us to leave.

"Well, it was certainly nice to see you again, Madhu," I said, feigning formality. Then I turned to Srini and said, "Good to finally see you."

He shook hands with me with a self-important air. He believed that I was glad to see him. I wanted to punch him in the face and wake him up. I wanted to tell him he was a dildo and his wife was still in love with me. He thought too highly of himself. His tight-set, shiny white teeth protruded from under his dark skin and thick lips. I wished I could rescue Madhu. I looked at my reflection in the glass door of the diner. My heart ached at the thought that she had to copulate with this man after having had me. I was frightened by the violence of my own emotions toward the guy. Did this mean I was still in love with her? And was I very mean?

The evening with Nathan was easy. I told him about Madhu. All my uneasiness had passed from the night when I had walked around alone. Nathan said that Sybil had had a minor outburst the previous night. It must have been after she had gone home from my place. I tried imagining myself as Sybil, blindfolding a guy in a leopard-print scarf, having sex two times in a row, and then going home to Nathan. It seemed like the perfect life in my imagination.

Nathan didn't tell me details of their fight. I made discreet inquiries but got nowhere.

"Does she know you're having an affair?" I asked.

"Not for a fact."

"Then?"

"I don't know what's bothering her."

But I assumed this meant that she would throw tantrums around me as well. I would have to prepare myself for tomorrow night. He said, "She's getting very difficult to handle, André. I don't know what to do."

"Are you still bringing her to the office party?" I asked.

"Yes. I'm sorry, André. I shouldn't be putting you through that."

"It's fine," I said, looking at him seriously.

"If you say so."

Monday mornings at work were always intense but inefficient. I put a lot of pressure on myself to get things done and somehow never accomplished enough. By Tuesday I would warm up, and then on Wednesday and Thursday I would be in full swing without even noticing that I was working. On Fridays I'd wait for the weekend.

I asked Martha to put me in touch with somebody in personnel who might be of more help than David Botolph had been. I was going to hire four programmers within two weeks. For a second I was tempted to ask Madhu's husband, Srini. He was happy at his job with the Fed, but I knew I could lure him away with money. He'd work for me and under me. I dismissed the idea. I had to get Madhu's side of the story first, before planning a childish and idiotic revenge.

The idea of wielding authority over four grown men sent a tingle through my spine. I wondered how power made Nathan feel. I would be able to lord it over competent professionals. I felt like a man-eating tiger anticipating the taste of human flesh.

Martha introduced me to David Botolph's sworn enemy, Hans Horfmeister. Unlike Botolph, he didn't act as if he had a ruler stuck up his ass, and he helped me put together a team. There would be no David Botolph in the hiring process I was initiating. His advice to look at charts in the personnel office had left me feeling insulted. Did he think I was that stupid? I was vain about my intelligence, and I couldn't forgive him. I'd make sure that DB was done for in another few months. I e-mailed the members of my project team my self-inflicted deadlines for the next two weeks.

At the end of the day, when I left to meet Sybil at a restaurant in East Midtown, I felt that life was in equilibrium. Work and play were both going perfectly. But then I saw Sybil's puffy eyes. She looked angry.

"Hey, Sybs, are you all right?" I asked.

"Don't call me Sybs," she said through clenched teeth.

"Relax, man."

"I'm not a man."

"What's the matter?"

"We have to talk."

"All right, talk."

"Not here."

"Then let's leave," I said. I was irritated at Sybil for having ruined a perfectly good day. I could feel my whole body recoil with tension. We got up and left the restaurant. The waiter who had shown us to the table looked perplexed.

"We changed our mind," I said.

We took a cab and went straight to my place. She sat quietly in the cab. For a while she was aloof, but then she moved closer to me and sat like a schoolgirl in need of security. I couldn't be angry when she did that.

When we got to my apartment, she said, "I feel like crap around Nathan. I can't be normal."

"What do you want to do? Would it be better for you if we stopped seeing each other?"

"No," she said sadly.

"Then?"

"Then nothing."

"What am I supposed to do?" I asked.

"Listen."

"I'm listening."

"Nathan has escaped from me. There is a part of him that I could never grip. I thought having an affair with you would distract me from the fact that I couldn't hold his whole soul in my hands."

"But it hasn't distracted you?"

"It did work for a while. But not any more. I've reached the same situation with you. There is a part of you that I can't grip."

I didn't know what she meant exactly, but I knew she was right. There was a part of me that was only for Nathan. I was glad there was a part of him only for me. Or maybe it wasn't that simple. I couldn't know how she felt things.

"And you've been so upset about it?" I asked, looking at her face.

"Yes."

"Sybil, everything is in your imagination."

"No it isn't." She looked as if she might cry. I thought for a moment that it was like looking up at the clouds, wondering if it would rain. I felt humble and at her mercy. If she decided to gush now, I would be like a man stranded without an umbrella in inclement weather.

"What precipitated your getting upset?"

"I left you the other night and went back to Nathan. On the way I felt sick and sad. It was a feeling in the stomach. A feeling of being torn away from something. As soon as I reached home I wanted to be joined again. I had sex with Nathan. After that we went to dinner. I had the same feeling of being torn away from him. I felt even more sick and sad."

I couldn't follow what she was saying. I felt protective toward her. I wanted to consult with Nathan so that we could both take care of her.

"So now?" I asked.

"So now you have to forcefully take me so that this vicious emptiness passes."

"It'll pass?" I asked.

"André, I'm miserable."

She started crying. She was sitting on my bed. I went close to her and started patting her hair. It was soft and long. I liked the way it slipped between my fingers. I kissed her on the forehead. I could smell her hair. It smelled like apples. I kissed her hair.

"Don't cry baby, I care," I cooed. I felt as if I were floating, not as if I were next to someone who was upset and hurting. Everything seemed unreal and intangible.

She was now crying into my shirt and my tie. I looked down to see which one I was wearing. It was my red striped tie, my least favorite one. She could cry into it. I loosened my tie and opened my collar. Her tears were seeping through my shirt. My skin was wet. A starched white shirt anointed with a woman's tears, I thought to myself. This was what being responsible and being a man was about. I felt like I was a strong buff man in a movie.

"Sybil, darling, don't cry."

"Then fuck me, dammit," she said through her sobs. She had a hard edge I recognized. It sent a shiver down my back.

I slipped off her pumps and her stockings. I made gentle slow love to her. I licked her moist parted lips before I took off my pants and slid myself into her. I rocked back and forth gently for a long time.

"Force, André. I want to feel hammered."

I felt angry that she wanted something other than what I was giving. But I got more forceful. She was happy.

It had left me exhausted. I wanted to eat.

"Are you hungry?"

"You want to leave me and eat?" she asked.

"I'm not leaving you anywhere," I said.

"Wanting to eat is leaving me," she said. Her eyes welled up with tears.

"What on earth gave you that idea?"

"You're just like every other fucking guy, André Bernard. You don't understand these things."

"We won't eat," I said, placating her. I was drained. I couldn't keep trying to make her happy. It was thankless and impossible.

She didn't reply. I moved closer to her. I was breathing into her neck, and she was breathing into my shoulders. I was aware of sweat and the smell of sex in the room. Her head was on my shoulder. I remembered being depressed after the Bergman movie and walking around alone. Sybil was feeling that way, I thought, as I drifted to sleep.

Before I knew it, it was the next morning. Sybil woke up in a good mood, and we said good-bye on kissing terms.

On Tuesday I booked my father's tickets and called him. I e-mailed Madhu but did not hear back. I saw Nathan in the evening. On Wednesday I saw Sybil again, this time without any emotional drama. On Thursday I wore my blue fish tie in anticipation of the company party in the evening.

Thursday was the high point of the week. I got e-mail from Madhu saying that she had been traveling on a consulting assignment but she'd love to meet me for dinner next time she was in Newark, which would be next week. I e-mailed her a "YES," bold and italicized for emphasis. At the afternoon project meeting, I told the group that I was talking to Horfmeister about hiring. We had posted an ad on the company Web site and informed two head-hunting companies that we needed to hire. I was already beginning to get résumés. I would start interviewing by the beginning of next week.

"After the first round, I will need guidance for the final selection. I've never hired before," I said.

"I'll do it with you," Nathan said.

It just didn't feel like it was my first month at work (however that was supposed to feel). I felt responsible for the project team meeting, and Nathan, the senior chief, seemed happy to let me take over. Since Yoshi's personal success in the company did not depend on looking good in front of the team, he was pretty laid back too. I was a child whose parents had agreed to let him play with expensive toys without supervision.

After the meeting ended, I asked Martha to come downstairs with me for a cup of coffee. I had ignored her for most of the week and wanted to make sure she was not too unhappy before the party. She was wearing a shade of bright red nail polish that turned me off.

I called Sybil when I got back to my desk. This would be the second time all three of us would be in the same room—and the first time since I had started sleeping with Sybil. There was plenty of potential for a comedy of errors. I was playing my cards close to my chest. I knew that seeing me with Martha would get Sybil upset. Nathan would be fine.

"Sybil, what are you wearing tonight?" I whispered over the phone as soon as she picked up. I knew women liked to be asked questions like this, and I wanted her to be well disposed toward me that evening.

"The maroon suit I wore when we first met. I'm afraid Nathan will know as soon as he sees us talking."

"He won't. I made sure to get a date so that he doesn't suspect."

"You have a date?"

"Yes."

"Who?"

"Martha. She's a secretary here. She's pretty cool—you'll like her."

"I've met her before. I don't like her," she grumbled.

"Sybil, stop being upset. You're going with Nathan."

Silence.

"Sybil," I whispered. I was afraid of raising my voice in case Tad walked in.

Silence.

"Please say something."

"Why do you have to fucking protect yourself from me?"

"I'm not protecting myself. I'm protecting us," I said, glancing over my shoulder to make sure that Martha was not hovering around.

"Whatever."

"Whatever," I repeated, losing my patience. Why did I always have to be the one assuaging hurt egos? Why did I always have to be the grown-up?

I heard someone talk to Sybil and ask her for instructions on a design.

"I have to go, André," she said.

I hung up, partially relieved but mostly irritated. I was worried that she'd have another one of her attacks and Nathan and I would have to hold her and kiss her while she cried. I remembered that I hadn't told Nathan I was going with Martha.

I e-mailed him.

He wrote back, "Good. I was going to suggest you take someone. Less suspicious that way."

I stared out my window and thought of Nathan. He was so confident and sensible and kind. He didn't assume the worst of me and wasn't insecure. I trusted him, and I didn't feel insecure around him. At least not often. I wanted to spend my life with a man or woman like him. But no woman could be like Nathan. It would have to be a man. Where would I find another man like Nathan?

I opened my miniplanner to see what the previous week had been like. I noticed the scratched-out "RM" under Saturday, so I called the Gay and Lesbian Center on a whim and asked for Richard Murphy.

"This is Richard Murphy."

"Hi! I'd called last week to get the address of the Center. I was wondering if you'd be there this Saturday."

"Yeah, I will. Who is this?"

"André Bernard is the name. I'm new to New York," I said.

"Yeah, great. Come along anytime—we'll be glad to talk to you."

"I realize it's odd I should call you again. You just had a great voice," I said, laughing nervously.

"Hey, don't worry, André."

I wondered what he looked like.

I opened my spreadsheet called "Time warp" and wrote "Five minutes with Richard Murphy" in one column. Next to it I put an equal sign, and then in the column beside it a question mark. Then on another row I wrote "Night with Sybil when she is cranky." Was it worth as much as listening to Ravel's *Pavane for a Dead Princess?* The answer was no. A cranky Sybil didn't even equal some ten-odd minutes on a tape—she burdened me. Pavane, on the other hand, always moved me. It was so terribly sad and beautiful, it made my soul weep. I looked at the spreadsheet. I couldn't compare dead French composers with people here and now, people with skin and flesh and weight. I wrote "Twenty good minutes with Sybil" and thought for a second. I'd give up even the sad beauty of Albinoni's trumpet concertos for that, I thought. I had based my spreadsheet on reducing all experience to time spent, but I had ignored the medium of the experience altogether. Then I was angry with myself for indulging in childish exercises. No Excel columns and rows were going to help me figure out why I was doing what I was doing. What do you want from your life? I asked myself.

Just before it was time to leave for the office party, I called Sybil and said, "Please don't be mad at me."

"I'm not," she said. She'd cooled off.

Martha, Nathan, and I took a cab to the Park Plaza together. Sybil was supposed to meet Nathan there. We all sat in the backseat, and I was in the middle. I casually threw my overcoat over my leg and Nathan's so that we could touch.

Nathan stayed back in the lobby while Martha and I went to the ballroom. She linked her arm in mine, and I was suddenly aware of how stupid it was to go to an office party with the seventeenth-floor secretary as my date.

Martha and I went to greet Yoshi, who was alone.

"You're all alone here?" I asked.

"Yes."

"Are you married, Yoshi? I've never asked you."

"No."

"Would you like drinks?" I asked, looking at Martha and then at Yoshi.

They both did, so I left them talking to each other. Martha chatted warmly with him, but I could see he was maintaining his distance. He talked like that to everybody, from a bit far away. He'd broken the ice and been friendly to me a couple of times. He was always friendly to Nathan.

The ballroom was filling up. I saw David Botolph walk in all by himself and look around the room sneakily, as if he were planning a heist. "Faggot," I thought and then got alarmed at myself. Oatmeal was picking hors d'oeuvres from a plate a waitress was carrying. His eyes followed the waitress after she walked away from him. His mouth was slightly open, and I could see spittle forming on the side of his sloppy lips.

I got a martini for Yoshi and red wine for Martha and walked back to where they were standing. I wanted to talk to Yoshi alone. Not to further my career, though it might do that, but because he was good-looking and intelligent. I handed them their glasses and excused myself to get a drink.

I couldn't figure out what was taking Nathan and Sybil so long. I got myself a virgin piña colada. I was so tense at the three of us meeting eye-to-eye that I wanted to be sober. I turned around from the bar and saw them walk in. Sybil looked ravishing. I went up to them both.

"Hello, Sybil, nice to see you again," I said, leaning forward and kissing her cheek formally.

"Hello, André, how have you been?"

"Good, thank you. Yourself?"

The corners of Sybil's mouth were turning up, threatening to break into laughter. Nathan's forehead was tense. I could see tiny beads of sweat gather in the ridges of his worry lines. I was swaying on my feet and getting dizzy. I felt drunk.

We all walked toward Yoshi. He had stopped talking to Martha, and they were both staring at the three of us. Yoshi looked at Sybil without blinking. Oatmeal had gravitated toward us and was also staring indiscreetly at Sybil. I wanted to punch Oatmeal in his stomach. DB observed the spectacle for a second and walked away with his nose turned up.

"Yoshi, you've met Sybil," Nathan said, holding Sybil's hand and virtually clasping it into Yoshi's. I was confused. I was sure Nathan could see what I could. It was plain that Yoshi wanted her. He'd lost it.

Sybil said hi to Yoshi and then to Martha. Oatmeal introduced himself to Sybil as well. He wore thick glasses that magnified his eyes. They looked large and hideous. Oatmeal was standing without a drink. Nathan offered to get drinks for him and Sybil, and I said I'd go help him. He pretended not to see the bar close to where we were and went to the one at the far end of the room.

"Did you see what I saw?" I asked.

"You mean Yoshi?"

"Aren't you upset?" I asked.

"No. Relieved."

"You're kidding," I said, doubly relieved. I knew what he meant. Sybil was an emotional weight. Draining. It might have been different if one was in love with her. If Nathan felt relieved, then maybe it meant he felt the same way about her as I did.

We went back to the group with drinks. Yoshi was looking at Sybil, his eyes ablaze. Sybil was laughing and glowing but not looking him back in the eye. Martha looked at one, then the other, and then at Nathan, as if to ask, "What's going on—aren't you going to do something about your wife?"

I nudged Martha with my elbow. I wanted to get away for a few minutes. She followed me. We walked around the room saying hello to a few other people. Martha had been working with Kenji Japan Bank for over six years and knew almost everyone. We ran into Hans Horfmeister from personnel, who told us a few jokes and made an ass of himself just to get us to laugh. I decided that he was a good soul, a kindhearted clown. When we walked way from him Martha said, "Poor guy, his wife and daughter died in a car crash some years back. He asked me out last year."

"Did you date?" I asked.

She smiled and said, "No. He's too big for me."

Horfmeister must have been at least seven feet tall. He was a giant. He also looked completely asexual.

A string quartet started playing Brahms at one end of the ballroom, and a couple in their late fifties started dancing. The man was wearing tails, and the woman, who looked like Sophia Loren, was wearing a tiny lace dress with spaghetti straps.

"Who are they?" I asked Martha, throwing my head in their direction.

"Mr. and Mrs. Pusey," she said.

"And?"

"He came on the board of trustees a year ago when his bank merged with Kenji Japan Bank."

"Does he sit in the New York office?"

"He comes in once a week. He's a full-time philanthropist."

"I can't dance to this music. Is there going to be a real band?"

"This is good music," Martha said icily. I immediately had an urge to prove myself and tell her everything I knew about the piece, but I stopped myself.

"I didn't say it wasn't good," I said.

I wanted to leave her and go back to Nathan. But I couldn't leave her. It must be like this to be married, I thought.

"I want to go back to the group," I said.

"Why don't you go? I want to say hello to a few more people in the room—then I'll join you."

"Are you sure?"

"Yes."

I was relieved she'd released me. I went to the bar, got myself tomato juice, and went back to where they were all standing. Sybil was clearly holding court. Yoshi and Oatmeal were rooted to the spot looking at her, and Nathan was fidgeting. I went up from behind him and touched his back.

"Are you having fun yet?" he asked.

"I want to dance. I wish they'd play real music."

Sybil looked at me and said, "You sound like you're fond of dancing. Can I have the first dance, André?"

"It will be my pleasure," I said.

Yoshi and Oatmeal gave me positively vicious looks. Nathan smiled to himself. I was dismayed that he was smiling. He wasn't on to the truth at all.

I wanted to talk to Nathan and help him escape from the drudgery of conversing with straight men who were after his wife. I wanted to dance with Nathan. We would dance along with the old Pusey couple. I could imagine Nathan in tails, leading me. I'd wear a silk shirt and a cravat. I'd look like a faggot. At the end of the number we'd kiss dramatically. With Nathan, I could dance to anything, I thought.

"Would you like another drink, Nathan?" I asked. "I'm thinking of getting one."

"I'll come with you."

We asked the others and then made our way to the bar. On the way I said, "Can't we go to the men's room for a second?"

"Of course."

We turned off to the right and discreetly went into the men's room. I bent down and checked all the stalls to make sure there was no one else. Nathan grabbed my butt while I was bending. I stood up and kissed him.

"This party is so boring, André, I'm gonna die," he said.

"Are you truly not upset by her?" I asked.

"No, I'm not. I wish she'd lighten up a bit. She likes attention and all, but the only person she's responded to in any way is you."

"What are you saying?"

"André, I want her to have an affair with someone like Yoshi, who'll always be around, so she'll get off my back."

"Don't you love her?" I asked. Did I just not know Nathan at all? I asked myself.

"Look, it was all okay earlier. I'm very fond of her. But I was never madly in love. I thought I'd marry because I'd started to get lonely. She was in love with me, but we talked about it and she said she could handle the inequity if she could have affairs. If we had an open marriage."

"Then?"

"Then you came along, André Bernard."

I kissed his lips.

"Let's go, André, they'll wonder."

"Come," I said, holding his hand.

"No, you go first. I'll follow in a few minutes."

"I'll see you at the bar."

I found Martha alone, so I went up to her and chatted. I looked at my watch. It was only eight-thirty. This was going to go on for another couple of hours. I was still charged with nervous energy, but it was dissipating. The string quartet was now playing Broadway show tunes. A group of young men in torn jeans and yellow and blue hair were standing in the corner unpacking a set of drums.

"Is that the band?" I asked Martha.

"How should I know?"

"Let's go ask."

We walked over to them. One of the guys was black. He was well-built and wore a tight black T-shirt. He was the only one who didn't look like a punk. I was sure he was gay.

"We go on in about half an hour," he told me.

"What will you play?"

"Whatever you want."

"I want something I can dance to," I said.

"Ma'am, you want to dance, too?" he asked, looking at Martha.

He thought we were an item. I was appalled. Martha said something to him, and then we walked away. I turned back to look at him. He was still looking in our direction. I caught his eye and winked at him. Then I saw Nathan at the bar and went over to him. At the bar, I turned around again to see the black guy. He was fiddling with his saxophone. He looked at me again. I stared back. Then the three of us got drinks and went back to the group. I decided to finish with the virgin drinks and got a glass of wine.

Dinner was served. Yoshi's gaze was still clasped on Sybil, but he was now looking at her whole body bit by bit instead of just staring at her face and shoulders. When she walked ahead of us to the buffet section, he quickly darted his eyes up and down her frame, the curves of her hips and the length of her legs. I felt sorry for him. I was sure he had never fallen for anyone before. I wondered if Sybil found him attractive. He stood ahead of me while we got dinner, and I looked him up and down. He was tall for a Japanese man. His features were delicate and precise, his eyes intense and fierce. I concluded I'd do him. And I'd do the black sax player. I would never do Oatmeal or DB or the gentle giant Horfmeister. It had become second nature to me now, as soon as I saw someone, to ask myself if I'd do them.

"Martha, what would you like to eat?" I asked. I had forgotten all about her and was standing ahead of her in the buffet line. I pretended I had done it on purpose so that I could serve her first.

"That pasta would be nice," she said.

I made my way along the table, tossing greens and garlic bread on her plate, skipping the beef and giving her a double portion of wild rice.

Nathan had located a large circular table that would fit us all and had put his napkin on the seat to his left. Sybil was on his right. I sat beside Nathan with Martha on my left. I couldn't even see all of Sybil from where I was sitting. Yoshi sat next to her. I could see him. Oatmeal sat across from me, his pasta sauce trickling down the side of his chin as he gaped open-mouthed at Sybil.

"That man is disgusting," I whispered, leaning close to Nathan.

"He's a genius."

"He's still disgusting."

"He's still a genius," Nathan persisted.

"Does being a genius make up for the fact he's disgusting?"

"Sure. It redeems him."

"Would you sleep with him because he's a genius?" I asked. Did Nathan measure people up and weigh their different qualities like I did?

"No. Intelligence is a necessary but not sufficient condition for an affair," he said.

"I was talking about sex, Nathan, not an affair."

He smiled. "No sex with JMF Peterson—never."

I was startled to hear that Oatmeal had a real name. I had forgotten it.

Nathan had pulled the long tablecloth over our legs and firmly established his hand on my knee. Martha chatted pleasantly with Oatmeal and commented on the flavor of the rice. I ate with a sense of lightness. The wine had reached my head. As soon as I was done with my first serving, the band came onstage. The black guy introduced the band. His name was Bobby.

Sybil leaned across Nathan and said, "André, shall we?"

"Sure," I said. Everyone looked at me. I was embarrassed. Sybil had made such a production of it that no one would ever think anything. It was under their very noses. But I didn't think it was a smart idea. Martha would not be happy. Nathan might get upset. Bobby would think I was straight, and Yoshi would have me thrown out of my job.

I gave Sybil my arm, and we went to the floor. No one else was dancing. The Puseys were sitting at a table by the dance floor and clapped as we stepped out.

I looked over my shoulder and said to them, "Join us."

"Soon," Mr. Pusey said.

The band played quick music. I was thankful. Sybs hung on to my whole frame nonetheless and whispered rubbish in my ears.

She was drunk and in a very good mood. She asked me if I felt good that she'd chosen me out of all the men who wanted her. I was angry with her. She was immature. I could imagine how hassled Nathan must feel.

The first number was short, and it ended soon. Everyone was clapping. I held Sybil's arm to lead her off the floor and back to the table.

"One more, André," she said.

We stayed. The band started to play again. The old Pusey couple got up and came to the floor. I disentangled my arm from Sybil's and applauded them. Someone's eyes were boring into my back. It was Bobby the sax player. His face was inflated as he blew into the sax. His eyes were fixed on me. I winked at him and felt a rush of blood. I started dancing with Sybil.

She swept me up with her completely. I had gone river rafting once when I was in college. The raft had rolled up and down with the rapids. I was a part of Sybil's ebb and flow; she was the river. I was a child in a mother's womb swishing around in amniotic fluid.

The music stopped. I was dizzy and so was she. I gripped her under her arms to steady her. I kissed her on the cheek. Then we both walked back to the table. I realized everyone, including Nathan, was staring at us. It was plain and obvious for the world to see if they wanted to see it. I had acted on the spur of the moment, without thinking. Thought had been impossible. Now I had to face the consequences.

Yoshi looked deeply upset. He wasn't even glaring at me any more. Martha looked pissed. Oatmeal just stared. Nathan was silent. He looked quiet, as if he'd retreated into a space without sound.

I sat down in my chair, trying not to look sheepish. I placed my hand on Nathan's knee. I moved it up his thigh as far as it would go without becoming visible. He sat without reciprocating.

He didn't bring his legs closer or put his hand under the table to touch me. Martha and Sybil got up from the table to get seconds, and Yoshi and Oatmeal followed them. I glanced around quickly to make sure no one was watching us and then squeezed Nathan's balls. I wanted him to come back to me.

He looked at me, his emotions nakedly visible. I'd hurt him.

"You are upset," I said and immediately felt stupid.

"I'll be fine."

"Can we talk about this sometime?" I asked.

"Yes, tomorrow. If you're available?" he said.

"Of course I am," I replied.

"There's no of course about it."

The others were coming back to our table. I asked Nathan if he wanted seconds. He didn't. I went alone for a refill of chicken and penne alla vodka.

I hoped Sybil would not want to dance again. I noticed Martha while I walked back to the table and resolved to have a conversation with her. She was my date, after all. I hadn't treated her well. I wanted to make amends.

"Martha, what are your plans for this weekend?" I asked, sitting down.

"Watching a movie with a girlfriend, doing laundry, jogging in the park. And you?"

"Reading. Calling my father. He's going to visit me."

"Where does he live?"

"North Carolina."

When I spoke to Martha, I felt my creative juices dwindling. Life lost some of its luster. If I was in pain, she distracted me and made me less unhappy. But if I was doing okay, she tired me. I was wasting my time with her.

A lot of people were walking around and talking to each other after they finished dinner. A few couples were dancing. I looked at Martha and Yoshi and Nathan and said, "How about we all go and dance?"

"Yes," Yoshi said, his eyes lighting up a little.

"Sure," replied Martha.

Nathan got up from his seat and said, "Come."

He pulled back Sybil's chair for her. We all made our way to the dance floor. I wanted to dance with Nathan. Sybil looked over her shoulder at me. Yoshi wanted to dance with Sybil. We all swayed our bodies to the beat of the music. Every now and then I'd look up and make eye contact with Bobby the sax player, who was very hot.

Yoshi was dancing as close to Sybil as he could. I pretended that I was paying attention to Martha. Nathan simply danced. I wished he'd look at me and send a meaningful glance my way. But the dance floor was crowded and there was too much bad energy because of Yoshi.

I felt a need to escape. I excused myself and stepped off the floor to go to the john. I stared at my reflection in the mirror. I was uneasy. When I was young I used to have nightmares about not getting my homework done on time and the teachers complaining to my father. This was the same kind of feeling. I was afraid that everything would blow up in my face.

When I got back to the ballroom, the band was playing a slow number. Martha was standing on the edge of the dance floor by herself. Yoshi was standing and staring at Nathan and Sybil, who were dancing together. I was glad they were dancing together. It gave me a sense of domestic peace that I needed. I went up to Martha and held out my hand and led her to the floor. I danced close to her. It didn't turn me on, but it set my mind at rest. I wanted to sleep on her shoulder and wake up in a world devoid of the monsters of my own making.

Bobby announced that the band would take a fifteen-minute break and that dessert was being served. We all went back to our table. Martha and Sybil sat down while I went to get them dessert. Yoshi sat down at the table, but Oatmeal came with me. Nathan had excused himself.

I put two cups of chocolate mousse in front of the women and then noticed that the band members were getting a bite to eat from the buffet table. I wandered over, trying to think of a pickup line.

"Just talk to him, André, don't worry about picking him up at this stage," I told myself.

"You guys played really well," I said, walking up to Bobby.

He gestured to the guitar player and the drummer, both of whom were standing beside him. He didn't say a word.

"I've wanted to learn the sax all my life," I said.

"You have?"

"Yeah. Do you give lessons?"

"Not really."

"Would you?"

"I can think about it."

"Why don't you do that and give me a call," I said, smiling.

I pulled out my wallet and found a business card. I wrote my home number on top of it and added "DO CALL!"

I offered it to him. He was holding his plate in one hand and serving himself chicken with the other.

"Mind putting it in my shirt?"

I craned in front of the table and slowly pushed the card into his shirt pocket, letting it graze past his nipple. I looked at him while I did it. He smiled.

When I was done, I looked up and saw Nathan staring at me from the other end of the room. He had seen it all.

I wanted to die of shame. I felt guilty and superficial. I walked back to the table and sat down next to Martha. This behavior hurt Nathan—I had to stop. Then I saw Sybil sitting on my right. She was his wife. He had no right to get upset with me when I couldn't have him fully. I was justified in trying to pick up men like Bobby. The only thing that was wrong was my having an affair with his wife. But even that wasn't wrong, because he had said at the beginning of our relationship that I could sleep with others. I wasn't, strictly speaking, violating any rules. I still felt like shit. All the justification was useless.

Martha had finished her chocolate mousse. I decided to take her home. The last thing I needed now was to feel lonely. But you can't mess up someone else's life just because you're feeling weak, a voice inside me said. Oh just stop being so miserable—everyone uses everyone else, another voice said.

"Martha, are you done with dessert? Would you like to leave?" I wanted to leave before everybody else did.

"So early? They're going to play some more," she said, pointing to the table where the band was sitting and eating.

"I was thinking we could go back to my place and have some hot chocolate," I said in a low voice.

She looked at me and said, "I'd be up for that."

We both got up. I said good-bye to everyone at the table at the same time and left without making eye contact with Nathan or Sybil. On the cab ride back, I felt alone and disconnected. I was grateful that Martha was there. Without her, I would have wanted to fling myself into the murky East River. It was my turn to be nice and pay some attention to her.

"Did you enjoy yourself, Martha?"

"It was fun, don't you think?"

"Yeah. What was going on with Yoshi, though? "

"I think he's fallen for Sybil."

"In a big way, don't you think?"

"He's like that," she said.

"You mean he's behaved this way before?"

"Yeah. At the office party two years ago he made a pass at the ninth-floor secretary. Poor girl—she'd come without a date. He hounded her."

"He's a good-looking guy. Why didn't she go for him?"

"Good-looking? You should go to an eye doctor, André."

"You're kidding. I thought he was so handsome." I thought of his fiercely intelligent eyes. How could anyone not think so?

"Not from a woman's point of view."

This was news to me. I had thought my taste was like everybody else's. I wondered if Nathan wasn't good-looking.

"Do you think Nathan is handsome?" I asked.

"Of course."

I wanted to ask her what she thought of Bobby, but I didn't want her to get suspicious, so I left it at that.

When we got home, I decided not to bother offering her hot chocolate. I needed human skin and some kind of joining, however base, with someone else. There was no point in spending time on useless things. I kissed her on the mouth. Her lips were chapped, and her lipstick tasted like medicine. I kissed her mouth till there was no flavor of anything left on it. I was in a strange state of not being aroused but wanting bodily warmth. I spent a lot of time kissing her neck and licking her ears before I started undressing her.

I unhooked her bra and removed her shirt and made my way to her nipples. My tongue felt something cold and round.

"Oh! I should have warned you I'm pierced," she said.

There was a metal ring that went right through the tip of her nipple. I like cocks in my ass, I thought to myself, so why can't she like metal in her skin? I had to talk myself into being open about it. I wasn't as cool as I had thought.

"I don't want to hurt you," I said, pulling my face out of her bosom.

"It doesn't hurt," she said, laughing.

"Are you sure?"

"Look." She gripped her ring between her fingers and twirled it around till it did a full circle inside her nipple.

"Stop," I said squeamishly.

"I can't even feel it, I swear," she said and tugged at it till it pulled her entire breast in one direction. I was horrified.

"I believe you," I said and removed her hand from the ring. I wasn't prepared for this.

I felt her stomach with my tongue and continued to work my way down. When I was removing her skirt I looked at her and said, "Is there anywhere else you're pierced?"

"Yeah, you'll see," she said.

I groaned to myself. I didn't want to do this anymore. I removed her stockings and, sure enough, dangling from her labia was another piece of round metal. I couldn't imagine letting my dick rub past that. I was afraid that the smooth surface of the curved barbell ring (as she told me it was called) would get hooked into the skin of my penis and tear me. I needed some time with this one. I flipped her on her stomach and kissed her back. I made my way down her back and opened my eyes only to stare into the terrified eyes of a large mouse tattooed on her left cheek. I wanted to ask her why why why.

I turned her around again and let my body rest on hers for a second.

"Am I crushing you?" I asked.

"No."

I was limp. I didn't know what to do. I didn't have the energy to close my eyes and think of Nathan till it got me hard.

"Can you hang on a second?" I said.

"Sure."

I walked over to my stereo and put on Ravel's *Bolero*. Then I came back to her. Martha started kissing me. She put my member in her mouth. That took care of it. I thanked God I was only twenty-four. I'd kill myself the day I couldn't get it up.

I pulled out a condom from the side table and put it on. "Guide me, will you?" I said to her.

She held my penis in her hand and slid it in. I could feel it rub past the barbell ring. It didn't feel half bad. It took an endless amount of grinding, swaying, and hammering to reach satisfaction, but she seemed to have a good time because of it. I was exhausted when I finally shot. I pulled myself out.

"I'm feeling wet. I think it burst," Martha said.

I looked down. She was right.

"Oh, shit!"

"Well, nothing to be done about it now."

"Will you take a morning-after pill tomorrow?" I asked. She nodded.

We were quiet for a few seconds. Then I forced myself to kiss her with a great show of affection and say "Good night."

I fell asleep. I don't know if she slept.

I woke up at five in the morning sweating and thinking of Nathan. I wanted Martha to disappear. Events from the previous night flashed in my head at rapid speed. My dance with Sybil and the scene with Bobby only seemed worse in the clear light of day. I had to apologize before it was too late. I got out of bed and showered. Then I made coffee and prodded Martha up.

"Sorry, Martha, I need to go to work really early today."

She woke up looking cross. But then she sat up in bed and nursed the coffee mug between her hands. She got up and started dressing. She rolled her black stockings into her purse and slipped on her pumps. I saw her off at the door with a quick kiss.

"Don't forget the morning-after pill."

She looked at me with some disgust but then covered it up with a smile. I had thrown the broken rubber on the side of my bed. I picked it up, wrapped it in some toilet paper, and threw it in the trash. Then I left for the office. It was seven in the morning on Friday. The shoeshine shop was just opening.

"Want a shine?" my favorite boy asked.

"Yes," I said.

"Come sit," he said, pointing to the high red chair. I climbed up. He brushed my shoes and rubbed them with a cloth.

As soon as I got into work I called Nathan at home. I knew that he wouldn't normally come into the office for another hour. Sybil picked up.

"Sybil, this is André. Can I talk to Nathan?"

"He's in the shower."

"Can you please ask him to call me at the office? I have a few urgent questions for him."

"Sure."

"Thanks."

"André."

"Yes?"

"Are you all right?"

"Yes, and you?" I asked.

"I'm fine."

"Good."

There was an awkward silence; then I said bye and hung up. Nathan called me back in minutes.

"Can you come to work early? I need to talk to you in private."

"Yes," he said wearily.

I waited for him nervously and looked at my watch every two minutes. I remembered Yoshi—one more thing on the list of things that had to be dealt with. I wanted to escape into some other world, far away from all this. I thought of Madhu and e-mailed her asking when she would be in Newark. I opened and shut my desk drawer as I waited for Nathan. Finally, after what seemed like years, he arrived.

We went to a diner across from the building and ordered breakfast.

"Nathan, I'm sorry and ashamed about last night," I said, getting straight to the point.

"About what exactly?"

"Everything."

"Like what?"

"I made you upset—that's what I'm sorry about."

"I thought about it. I'm not upset anymore."

"Well, I'm upset. I shouldn't have acted that way. I shouldn't have danced with Sybil."

"André, life's complicated. You're both free agents. I had no right getting upset. Plus, she asked you."

I looked down. And I'm sleeping with her, I said to him in my head. I wished I could tell him and then ask him to forgive me. I didn't want any secrets between us. The Sybil secret was too much to carry.

"I have something to say about Martha," I said.

"So do I," he said.

"What?" I asked.

"I slept with her a few times before I married Sybil."

"I slept with her last night," I said.

"I figured you had and decided I should tell you about it."

"You're angry?" I asked.

"No."

"I was lonely, Nathan." I felt like I needed to justify myself to him.

"I understand that only too well. I wish I could be with you more."

He was honest and clean and good. He wouldn't hurt a fly and had the most tender heart I had ever seen, other than my father's. I wanted to pray on my knees to him and weep. I wasn't as good as him. In my mind I opened another spreadsheet. One that compared the worth of people. André ≠ Nathan.

"I don't deserve you, Nathan."

"Shh! Let's not say anything more." He took my hand across the table and gripped it. The diner was full of the Midtown office crowd, but I didn't care if anyone saw us at this point, even Yoshi. I wanted to ask Nathan if all was right on the Sybil front, but I didn't want to interrupt the new sense of flow and acceptance I was experiencing. Everything was forgiven now, because everything was understood. We trusted each other.

We got back to work and I tried to wrap up a few things before the weekend. Madhu called me and said she'd be in Newark on Monday, would I want to meet for dinner around eight? I gave her instructions on taking the PATH train to the World Trade Center and made reservations at an Ethiopian restaurant in Tribeca. There was light at the end of the tunnel—Madhu would open my eyes to it. I pinned all my hopes on her. She'd help me understand myself.

"Nathan, are we meeting tonight?" I buzzed and asked him.

"Yes. I can't tomorrow, though."

"Night with Sybil, eh?"

"Yeah."

I called Sybil and arranged to spend Sunday with her during the day. She sounded peeved. She wanted to spend Sunday night with me, but I was hoping to rope Nathan in for Sunday night on the pretext that I couldn't see him on Monday because of Madhu.

"Can you never just change your plans because I want to see you?" Sybil demanded.

I couldn't tell her that I would never be able to do that. Having affairs with a husband and a wife was terribly inconvenient.

"Sorry, Sybil. You shouldn't always exert so much pressure on me," I said. I wanted to seem stubborn, because making excuses wouldn't work—she'd catch on.

"Fine, André Bernard, but I may just get another date."

"Enjoy yourself, Sybil."

I pulled out my miniplanner and wrote "N" under Friday and "S" on the top half of Sunday. I was free on Saturday night. I decided I would not see Martha, come what may. I'd check out Richard Murphy during the day and then maybe go to a gay bar at night.

That evening, Nathan didn't talk about Sybil at all. He talked a lot about himself. He was worn out and tired of finance. He wanted to spend some time doing more creative things. He was sick of sitting in an office, managing people and pretending it was important.

"Actually, I had the most fun when I first started working in my twenties. I didn't spend any of my time on useless politics. I was too junior to deal with people. I got instructions from senior quants and wrote models."

"All day long?"

"I love math. It was the best time. But with you, we're half skipping that step so that you can move up."

"I like dealing with people."

"It's funny, this world. It's not technical skills and sheer intelligence that are rewarded the most. It's managing people that gets the most money."

"Well if you are to be believed, that's the most boring, and it's only fair that the most boring work should make the most money since there's no joy in it."

"Okay, André, so you're right as usual," he said wryly.

He made me feel pigheaded and young. I had no idea what I was talking about.

"Nathan, what does painting mean to you?" I asked, determined to learn a few things from him.

"It's like math. It's like being able to solve a problem. The same kind of liberating feeling accompanies every brush stroke."

"I've never done anything creative."

"Math is creative."

"Well then, I've done nothing else that's creative."

"Making love is creative."

I wanted to make love to him. I did. The feeling of being with him was almost immeasurable. I could see two columns clearly: one said "Two years in the life of André Bernard" and the other said "Feeling Nathan's skin on March 13, the Year of Our Lord 1998." There was an equal sign between them.

On Saturday morning, Nathan left early. He agreed to meet me again on Sunday night at seven. I got dressed after he left and made my way to the Gay and Lesbian Center to seek Richard Murphy.

"Hi, I'm looking for Richard Murphy," I said to the man at the desk.

"You've found him," the guy said.

Richard Murphy was not quite a two-toothed septuagenarian, but he was close. He had a short crew cut and wore a red-checked flannel shirt. His dark blue indigo jeans were pressed, and I could see a sharp crease on the front of them. His sneakers were large and white, his teeth entirely black. He reeked of alcohol and cheap cologne. I was speechless.

"Are you the guy who called?" he asked.

"Yes."

He shook my hand.

"I was looking for information."

"I thought you were looking for something more," he said.

I felt my ears getting hot.

He laughed in a braying sort of way and handed me several flyers. He made a few cross marks around certain sections to highlight events and explained how some of the support groups at the center worked. I stood and stared at him in disbelief. The voice and the body just didn't go together. Then I thanked him and left in a daze.

A wind was blowing, and it helped clear my head. I took a cab back to my apartment. Bobby had left me voicemail. I noted down his number, made some tea, and sat down at my table to look through the literature I had picked up. There was a magazine called HX with a list of gay cafés and lounges. It also had classified ads and articles. I scanned through a list of clubs and circled the ones that sounded interesting. Depending on my conversation with Bobby, maybe I'd ask him to go clubbing with me.

It was one-thirty and I hadn't eaten. I decided to try my hand at cooking. I went to a grocery store down the street and bought some potatoes and spices and a bag of rice. The potatoes took forever to peel and slice. I poured some olive oil in a pan and put the potatoes in. I added basil leaves and salt. The potatoes stuck together, and white starch covered my stirring ladle, making it impossible to move the potatoes in the pot. The congealed glob was like nothing I had ever seen or wanted to see again. I turned off the stove and threw the contents of the pot into the trash. Then I left the pot in the sink and turned on the hot water faucet. I left it running and went downstairs to Tommy's to get a slice of pizza and a coke. When I got back I turned off the faucet and drained the pot. It would be a while before I could cook for Nathan. I went to the table and ate my pizza. I called my dad.

"Papa."

"André, how are you?"

"Great. Just great. I wanted to tell you to pack some warm clothes. New York is cold."

"I will."

"Are you excited about coming here?"

"At my age, what excitement, André? I'm happy I will be seeing you."

We chatted some more. His wheezing was getting worse, and he said the pain in his joints made it hard to get out of bed in the mornings. I wished I could do something about it. I made a note in my miniplanner to buy a heater, since my studio got cold at night. I hadn't quite decided what to do about the sleeping arrangements. My futon was big enough for both of us, and he wouldn't think it weird. I'd like it too, I thought. But the idea made me uncomfortable. I'd decide when the time came.

After I talked to my father, I called Bobby. He said he didn't have time to teach me to play the sax.

"Do you have time to go clubbing?" I asked flat out.

"Sure," he replied.

"Tonight?" I asked, feeling particularly bold.

"No, can't tonight. I have other plans."

"Next week, then?"

"That sounds good."

"I'll call you during the week," I said.

You could pick anyone up as long as you just asked what you wanted of them. It was all a matter of how confident you were. Before I had met Nathan, I would never have had the nerve to proposition people this way. But both Nathan and Sybil were so sassy. And their directness had worked for me. I was sure mine would also work on anybody. I decided to go clubbing by myself. I rummaged through my closet to decide on what to wear. New Age hemp was out. I found a relatively tight black T-shirt and black jeans and put them on a chair. The pizza had made me sleepy. I put on some Celtic music and took a nap.

I got to the club at ten. I was the only soul there. The doors were not open. I walked around the neighborhood till I found a bar and went in. The bar was full of gay men. I got myself a kamikaze and watched TV for a while. A few other guys were hanging around. A couple was making out. No one looked promising. There was a slight flutter at the door, and a transvestite walked in. She had thick false hair and false eyelashes. She had shaved her legs. The bartender gave her a kiss on the mouth, and the couple who had been making out encircled her in their arms and fussed over her. She was wearing a small fur stole, and they petted it. She was a piece of work, a character. But I couldn't see her as a good lay. I felt sad. I was sure that she never got any.

At eleven I tried the club again. People were trickling in. I got a drink and sat at the bar. When the DJ played his first good number, I got up and danced. Another guy started dancing with me. The dance floor was empty, but he danced close to me and made eye contact. He was average-looking, but he seemed to have a good body. I smiled. He caught on. He locked his legs in mine and danced. He held my butt in his hands and rubbed his crotch on mine. When the music changed he said, "Would you like to go downstairs?"

"Sure," I said. We went down the steps of the club. The basement was dark. I was expecting mattresses, but there weren't any.

"Do you want to have sex?" he asked.

"Here?" I said, pointing to the floor.

"Yeah."

The floor had never seen the light of day. I was sure it was dusty and crawling with lower forms of life.

"I don't think so. Why don't you come back to my apartment?" I suggested.

"Cool."

We got out of the club. The guy asked the bouncer to stamp the back of his hand so that he could get back into the club without paying a cover charge.

In the cab home, I wondered what the hell I was thinking. Even if someone asked me for a cup of coffee, I'd usually have thought before saying yes. He was fondling my dick. So I fondled his.

When we got home, he took off his pants without ceremony. He must have been the same age as me. He had amazing arms and a six-pack stomach. I took my clothes off. He was pushing his naked cock into my anus. I gave him lube and a condom. He fucked me. Then he rolled over on his stomach and stuck his ass up in the air. I fucked him. As soon as I had ejaculated, I wanted him to leave. I could see no reason to hide that from him. There were no feelings involved. We hadn't even kissed. I didn't know his name.

"I want to be alone," I said.

He got up and pulled on his jeans and shirt.

"See ya around," he said, waving as he left my studio. I didn't get out of the bed to see him to the door. I waited till I heard the door bang shut and rolled over and buried my head in my pillow.

Nathan had spent twenty years having this kind of sex. What sort of person did that make him? The sex had made me feel hard and cold, but I still felt warm and tender toward Nathan. If I had anonymous sex for over a decade, would I still be able to feel warm and tender toward anybody? I fell asleep and woke up only with Sybil's call the next morning.

When we met, Sybil was relaxed and in a great mood. She seemed to have forgotten all about our bristly conversation the previous day. We didn't talk about the office party. I wanted to ask her what she thought of Yoshi, but I stopped myself.

We walked around Central Park and got lunch at a café. Then we went to my studio and made love. It was around five in the evening, and I was getting nervous. Nathan was supposed to show at seven. I had to get Sybil out of my apartment. It was clear that she had no intention of leaving.

"Sybil, I need to go and visit a friend."

"Now?"

"Yeah, an old friend from school. He's in town just tonight, and I'm supposed to pick him up at his hotel in half an hour."

"Can I come with you?" she asked simply. It hurt me to reject her.

"I can't, Sybs, I'm sorry. I haven't seen him in ages, and it's just not appropriate. You're another man's wife."

I hated this sort of prevarication. If Sybs had been any other man's wife, I would gladly have shown her off to my imaginary friends.

Sybil started crying.

"André, you knew what you were getting into before we did this. You knew I was another man's wife," she said.

"I didn't say I didn't know."

"Then why can't I come with you?"

"It's just that certain things aren't possible for us. Being a regular couple is one of them."

I kissed her forehead and clasped her bra. I felt a little ruthless. No weeping wives were going to come between Nathan and me.

"Sweetheart, I don't want this to be a burden," I said. I felt my heart soften a little. I cared for her. "Sybil, think about this. If this hurts you, we are going to stop," I added.

"I'll think about it," she said.

I dressed as she dressed and then walked out with her. I put her in a cab and walked around my block. Then I came back to my studio and waited for Nathan.

The evening with Nathan was slightly depressing. He was facing a midlife crisis. He was not happy with his professional life at all. From everything he said, it became clear to me that his only goal in his working life now was to play my mentor. He saw me as an heir apparent. He didn't want to see his twenty years as an investment banker go to waste. He wanted to push me forward and further my career. He wanted to make sure I avoided any mistakes he had made. He thought I was worthy of it. All that was flattering, but the truth that stood out for me was that he was unhappy professionally. And with his married life as well, it seemed.

"Nathan, would you marry Sybil today, knowing me?"

"No," he said, shaking his head and looking at the floor.

I had always needed great demonstrations of love and affection from my ex-girlfriends. For the first time ever, I felt I didn't need proof that someone loved me. I kissed his forehead.

"Nathan, there is something that I need to tell you, but I can't right now. I have to prepare myself to tell you."

"Will it change everything?" he asked intuitively.

"I don't know," I said.

I expected Nathan to have all the answers. I realized now that he was as vulnerable as I was. I was an equal partner in the enterprise. On the work front, I hadn't disappointed him. I knew I could deliver what was expected. But I didn't know if I had the strength to provide him with what he needed in the relationship. I wondered if he would ever forgive me about Sybil.

"Let's not talk about all these things right now. I'm tired."

"Did Sybil make you tired?" I asked.

He nodded yes.

"Nathan, it's none of my business, but I'd like to know more about your relationship with her. Will you tell me some day?"

He nodded again.

"Thanks."

We went to sleep. The way he put his face into my chest and let his shoulders slack, I knew that he needed rest and looked to me to shield him from the world. I lay still as he slept, and I spent most of the night thinking. Each time he breathed, I felt as if my responsibilities were increasing. A seriousness descended upon me and settled on my shoulders. My mind softly played Satie's sober and purposeful Gymnopédie No. 1, 2, and 3.

Monday was a new day. The beginning of a new week. I felt hopeful leaving for work in the morning with Nathan by my side. I took him to the shoeshine store near the subway and asked my favorite boy to shine Nathan's shoes. I saw him look up at Nathan the same way he looked up at me. Nathan smiled at him. It made me glad. Another guy shined my shoes. On the way to work, I told Nathan about the random erection and the shoe shine boy. I wanted Nathan to know me. There was no point in him being in love with something that I wasn't. It seemed to me that we were similar. Both of us needed warmth and security, and both of us were sexually driven. Moreover, we were mathematicians. I was sure that mattered in some way, though I wasn't sure exactly how. We'd also slept with two of the same women, and I was rapidly coming to believe that my feelings for Sybil were similar to Nathan's. I had so much in common with him.

At the office, I avoided the logistical work related to the recruitment of the new programmers. I put it off till Tuesday and threw the ball in giant Horfmeister's court, while I focused my attention on a prototype database for the risk management system. Intellectually, it was more challenging and satisfying to design programs than to inform brilliant students with strong accents that they had been granted interviews the following week.

In the back of my head I was constantly anticipating meeting Madhu. I was looking forward to the emotions that would fill me and take me by surprise. At five-thirty I went to Nathan's office and told him I was leaving. In a particularly reckless moment, I went behind his desk and gave him a kiss. His office door was wide open.

"I hope it's not too hard with Sybil tonight," I said to him.

"I hope so, too. Enjoy your dinner."

The subway ride down to the World Trade Center was gruesome. I was listening to Satie; I had put the tape into my Walkman because I thought I'd want to replay it for real once. But my own head played Saint-Saëns, and I had to shut off the Walkman to end the dissonance. The cars on the express train I was taking were packed. I stood without hanging on to the metal railing, my face caught in a draft of air caused by the exhalations of a white construction worker and an Indian businessman. The construction worker was wearing his orange hard hat; his breath smelled of metal and asbestos, and his sweat was pungent. The Indian guy looked like Madhu's husband, Srini. He was wearing a badly cut suit and carrying a shiny imitation leather briefcase. I stood within millimeters of these men for a good ten minutes. When I stepped out on the platform at my station, it felt more liberating than my high school graduation had. I went to the PATH train platform and waited for the train from New Jersey.

Madhu got off the train and opened her arms to hug me. She smiled, and a huge dimple appeared on her cheek. I had missed her. For two years I'd not had any contact with one of the most important persons in my life. I felt a sudden rush of emotion. I put my arm around her and we got out of the station. The night was slightly nippy but pleasant. We decided to walk to Tribeca. We walked close to each other, my arm on her shoulder. I felt like an elder brother. I felt only affection and fondness. I reminded myself that this was my ex-lover. I used to sleep with her. But I just couldn't see her that way.

At the restaurant we sat on little wooden stools. People at a nearby table were eating off one plate. The waitress told us it was an Ethiopian tradition.

"You'll have to order vegetarian, André," Madhu said.

"Vegetarian? Since when have you turned vegetarian?"

"Since I married Srini."

"Wow!" In college, she'd take a blasphemous delight in eating beef.

"Yeah, things change," she said.

"Is it for love?" I asked.

"No. I didn't have a choice. He's really strict."

"He's not here. And I won't tell," I said.

"If I taste flesh again, I'll crave it all the time," she said.

I ordered vegetarian food. Nathan, Sybil, and Madhu were conspiring to turn me into some sort of leaf-eating herbivore. But they couldn't. My father's special recipe for monkfish was just too perfect to pass up.

The food arrived on a large round plate. We broke pieces of the bread and dipped it in various lentils. Madhu smiled and told me about her job. After the first glass of wine, she also told me about her husband.

"Have you been happy, darling?" I asked, my voice imitating John the queen's. When we were in college together, I would often talk like John when I was alone with Madhu. She found it hilarious that a straight man like me could do such a great flaming queen routine. She started cracking up again.

"André, he's all right to me, but he's not exciting."

"There's something to be said for stability."

"He's nasty in bed. He doesn't believe in foreplay or female orgasm."

I was surprised at her frankness. She had always been frank with me, but with the rest of the world she was reserved. She was the kind of person who was close to one person at a time. She had had a best friend all through her junior high and high school years. After she met me, she transferred all her confidences to me. We had a joined and combined existence in college. We were each other's best friends. After the breakup I had been sure she would transfer everything over to her husband. Her being frank with me told me she had either changed in this regard, which was highly unlikely, or she had never let him in. That was chilling.

"Madhu, are you in love with him?"

"No."

"You've been married two years, and you're not in love with him?"

"No. He's different, André. He's closed-minded, and I can't be myself around him. I tried when we went on our honeymoon, but I realized that he preferred his own image of who I was to the real me. He didn't want to discover me."

"But that's an awful marriage."

"Yup," she said matter-of-factly.

"Are you going to do anything about it?"

"I may. I was young then. I could only think about the fact that I was breaking up with you when I married him. If I had had any sense, I wouldn't have done it. I thought that my parents would leave me with no choice, but in retrospect I know I underestimated them."

"Madhu, this makes me sad," I said, patting her hand.

"Tell me, what's going on with you?"

I told her how Nathan had seduced me at Skirts. Then I told her about Sybil. I was surprised that I told her. It was a relief. I hadn't realized that I had not spoken about it to anyone on earth. I even told her about Martha and the anonymous guy, though I worried that she might think less of me after hearing about those two.

"You've become such a slut, André," she said, smiling indulgently.

I smiled. I liked Madhu calling me a slut. I didn't like being slutty, but I liked her accepting that side of me.

"I like being penetrated, Madhu," I said.

"By Nathan?"

"Even Sybil," I said, blushing.

"Will you like it from me, you think?" She was being perfectly serious. And she was being herself, unflirtatious and direct.

I looked into her eyes and stared silently at her.

She'd set me thinking. I often felt as if Nathan were my father or my son, and that had never stopped me. So I knew there'd be no problem getting it on with Madhu, my brotherly feelings notwithstanding. On the one hand, I really wanted to make it up to her for having a lousy husband. I wanted to give her the kind of multiple orgasms she'd had in college. For hours after, her skin would be radiant. On the other hand, I was scared that it would hurt her. Madhu and I had had deep feelings for each other. Everything would explode in our faces. It would be easier for me knowing that she wasn't in love with her husband; it would be tougher for her. I was in love with Nathan at least as much as I had been with her.

"Will you like it from me?" she asked again, in a hushed whisper.

"I don't know, Madhu," I replied honestly. Our dynamic had never been like that. Our relationship had been very heterosexual and straightforward. I would more or less take charge everywhere we went. She was nourishing and loving but not dominating.

We left the restaurant, and it was clear that at the very least she would spend the night with me, whether or not we did anything. The flow of conversation between us was comfortable. A warm fire was kindling in every cell of my body. I love this woman so much, I was thinking to myself. After all these years, it still feels good. It had ended without any bitterness, and it had ended when it was still passionate. We had spent the last month before graduation crying every night in each other's arms. She had said that her parents would arrange her marriage very soon. I could not take on the responsibility of being married at twenty-one. I owed my father money. I needed another degree so that I could get a good job. Her father was very ill. They weren't sure he'd live very long, and he said that he wanted to see her married and settled before he died. We both understood the position we were in. I couldn't blame her, and she couldn't blame me. We loved our fathers and we had no choice. Her father had recovered after the marriage and was now hale and hearty.

Madhu and I walked uptown for a while and then took a cab. I was eager to show her my apartment and get suggestions on what more I should do with it. When we arrived, I described in great detail the desk that Sybil had designed. Madhu saw the container of Eros Concentrated Bodyglide by my bed and picked it up. She held it up for me to see with a question mark on her eyebrows. I nodded.

We chatted for a while and then got into bed. She needed to leave for Newark early the next morning to fly to D.C., so I set my alarm for six. We lay together and hugged. She held me close to her and touched my face. Then she kissed me. It had a sudden effect on me. Within seconds I was making love to her like I always had, a heterosexual man.

I went to work the next morning whistling. I thought of Nathan only when I reached the office. I realized I hadn't missed him the previous evening. It made me sad and angry at the same time. I wanted my love to be extreme and true, unsubstitutable.

It was Tuesday. I opened my miniplanner. It was blank for the rest of the week. I needed to set my priorities right. I wondered if I should still call Bobby. What was the point? Did there have to be a point? And if there was a point, why should I think I'd know it ahead of time? I called and left a message on his machine. Then I went to Nathan's office. He wasn't in yet, though it was nine-thirty.

I went to the front desk and chatted with Martha. I remembered the morning-after pill, but I didn't want to ask about it. I didn't want to bring up our one-night stand at all. She asked if I wanted to go to a movie later in the week. I said yes.

Then I called Sybil. She asked to meet me that night. I agreed. I e-mailed Nathan immediately and asked if he would spend Wednesday night with me. I also e-mailed Madhu asking her when she'd be in Newark next.

"It was wonderful Madhu, and I'm still carrying the feeling of you," I wrote.

After taking care of my personal life, I called Horfmeister and went over to his thirteenth-floor office with a yellow legal pad to jot down notes on salaries we'd offer candidates. By the time we were done it was lunchtime. I went back to my desk and checked my e-mail.

Madhu had written back, "Me too, André. I'm in town again Friday night and again next week Tuesday." She'd added, "P.S. I haven't come like that in two years."

I wrote back, "Book me for both nights."

Nathan had written back, "Tomorrow night, great! And lunch today?"

I buzzed him and we went to lunch. I told him in the elevator that I had slept with Madhu and that I still had feelings for her. He might have been hurt, but he was very mature about it. He asked me to talk about her and my feelings. He said he understood.

The night with Sybil was very mixed. We joked around more than we usually did. And in jest I even asked her if she had gone on a date after our last conversation when she'd threatened she would.

"Don't look so smug, André. Maybe I did."

"With my boss, Yoshi Kato, I bet. Just to get even with me," I said. I watched her closely. Her face fell a little.

"He has a small dick," she said sullenly.

I couldn't believe my ears. So she had. For real. I wanted to tell her that it was dangerous. She was sleeping with all three people in the chain of command: me, my boss, my boss's boss. Moreover, Yoshi had power and influence beyond his official capacity. He could be Nathan's nemesis, and if Yoshi ever found out about me, then mine as well. I felt like the custodian of important facts. I had to protect Nathan from Yoshi now. If Nathan found out, I wasn't sure what would happen. I wanted to deflect all Yoshi's attentions away from Nathan. Judging by the way Yoshi had stared at Sybil at the office party, I thought he would go to any lengths for her. He'd have us both fired from our jobs. He might even have both of us killed. But then, maybe I was wrong. Maybe Yoshi only wanted Sybil for her beauty and didn't care beyond that. I felt a sense of real danger.

"Is he in love with you?" I asked.

"That's none of your business."

If Sybil was having an affair with anyone else, I might even have been relieved, but she had to choose the one person with whom it was inappropriate. And I couldn't tell Nathan about it, because he'd wonder how I knew.

"Fine," I said. I could feel myself wanting to fight with her. I changed the topic and arranged with her to go together and pick up my designer desk at the end of the week. Then we got into bed and made love. The one thing we did that felt perfect.

I had a lengthy e-mail exchange with Madhu the next day. We sent each other one-liners asking personal questions. We agreed that on Friday when we met I'd take her to a gay and lesbian bookstore and then we'd get dinner in a gay restaurant. I wanted her to see me respond and react to men in tight black Lycra shirts and silver pants. I wanted to see myself torn between Madhu's soft femininity and pants bulging with inches of promise. Somewhere along the line my attraction to Nathan had spread out into a general attraction to men. I couldn't remember a discrete moment when that had happened but it reminded me of the time I had first fallen for Madhu. After a few weeks, I had started noticing Indian women in a way I had never done before. Brown skin and black hair got my juices flowing just like a favorite piece of music did. All Indian women had a little bit of Madhu in them. And now all men had some Nathan.

At work I was flooded with phone calls from programmers. I also had to interview a couple of people based on internal recommendations, people who'd been interviewed before and made it to a final cut. They were always the first ones called in when a new position became available. I had an appointment to interview some Jake Turner at two in the afternoon. I had a heavy Mexican lunch and was ready to sleep after it. He showed up at the dot of two.

"Jake Turner," he said, putting his hand out.

We sat at the conference room table, and I went over his résumé, asking him specific questions about his skill set. His voice was flat and toneless. It made it difficult for me to pay any attention to him. I had to keep taking notes to stay awake. There was a knock on the conference room door.

"Come in," I said.

Martha walked in. She said that Nathan needed me immediately. I left Martha with Jake, asking her to tell him more about the office environment, and almost ran to Nathan's office. My first thought was that Sybil had told him about Yoshi, or me—or both of us.

His door was half shut. I barged into his office without knocking.

"Are you all right?"

He was grinning. He looked mischievous.

"I'm fine."

"I was worried. What's going on?"

"I was missing you."

I was taken aback.

"Just that?"

"I feel like I've hardly seen you all day."

I leaned across his desk and touched his hand.

"I'll see you soon, Nathan. I was interviewing this guy," I said.

Nathan needed to get out. He was too intelligent to spend time being bored. I also had a sense of the larger picture. There was very little time for things to sort themselves out. We were living with a time bomb. It was all a question of when Nathan would find out about Yoshi and Sybil and me and Sybil, when Madhu's marriage would break up, when Nathan would leave or be fired, when Sybil would find out about Nathan and me, when Yoshi would find out about me. There was no doubt in my mind that all these things would happen. It was as if we were all on a sinking ship and I was the only one who knew. I only wished I knew whether it was going to be in one day or one year. Time meant everything in this case.

When I got back into the conference room, it was obvious that Martha and Jake Turner had been having a good conversation. I thanked Martha and resumed the interview. At the end of the interview I asked him if he had any questions.

"Does Martha have a boyfriend?" he asked.

"I don't know, ask her," I replied.

After I had shown him to the door I wrote, "Did not make first cut this time." I put the résumé in an interdepartmental envelope and tossed it on Martha's table to send to Horfmeister.

"Was he that bad?" Horfmeister called later that afternoon and asked.

"He was a turd."

"Incompetent?"

"Yes, and he has no idea what is appropriate. Wouldn't fit in around here."

"Why?"

"He had only one question for me," I said.

"What?"

"If Martha had a boyfriend." I could imagine Horfmeister's reaction. He had a crush on Martha and would be enraged.

"Turd," Horfmeister said and hung up.

I tried to figure out if I was a small time jerk who could not stand any infringement on what I considered my territory, in this case Martha, or whether I had some real feelings for her. I concluded I was a brat who always had to outshine everyone else. Martha had seemed to get along with him. And some part of me was threatened by that.

Nathan announced in the evening that he was going to start painting regularly. The Ringolds, friends of his, had a house in the country, and he had stored his old paintings there. He wanted to drive up to the country with them on Friday night and bring everything back.

"I would really like you to come, André. But they know Sybil really well, and the two of us are going up."

"Nathan, that's fine. Madhu will be here on Friday, anyway."

He looked relieved. As if he were glad he didn't need to feel bad about not spending time with me.

"André, I heard you tell Martha at the office party that your dad was going to visit."

"Yes, he is."

"Will I get to meet him?"

"Of course, I was planning on having Sybil and you over for dinner. He's a great cook."

"I'd like to cook for you one day," Nathan said.

"I bought some spices."

I showed him all the things I had in my kitchen. He offered to cook me dinner. We went to the supermarket nearby and bought vegetables. Then Nathan said he wanted me out of his hair, so I listened to some chamber music and reread the article on dreams while he cooked Pad Thai.

Thursday was chock-a-block with interviews. Sybil managed to catch me at my desk in the morning before I disappeared into the conference room. She wanted to meet at night. We decided to meet at a movie theater in Sutton Place, and I wrote "S" in my miniplanner. Then I rushed to the conference room. I had four interviews lined up back to back before lunch. It was exhausting asking one graduate student after another the same set of questions about database systems, object-oriented technology, and encryption. Not one of them was good-looking. Moreover, they were all very dull. They wore boring striped ties and gray suits. No one had any personality or spunk. By lunchtime I was exhausted. I ordered a sandwich from the coffee shop downstairs and decided to eat at my computer so that I could catch up on my e-mails.

Madhu had written that she couldn't wait to see me. She'd filled the e-mail with symbols of smiling faces.

Nathan had sent me an e-mail titled "Over." It read, "Sybil slept with Yoshi. This is the beginning of the end."

The e-mail was clear. I didn't get a sense of Nathan being upset from it. I sat still and forced myself to imagine it. It registered this time. When Sybil had told me, I had heard but not really thought about it. It was good Nathan knew. I could imagine him sitting at his desk and typing it without feeling. I walked to his office.

"I go your e-mail. What are you going to do?"

"Nothing. There is nothing to do."

He had taken the news with a calmness and indifference I hadn't expected.

"You're not upset."

"It's going to create more professional problems than personal ones," he said matter-of-factly.

"I know what you mean," I said.

For a moment I wanted to tell him about Sybil and myself. He might as well face the music (now a whole orchestra) at the same time. But they were totally different issues. He didn't need to deal with me in the same way. I wasn't a Japanese scion.

"After I get my paintings from the country, I'm going to spend some time thinking about my career."

"Yes. I think you should. I have to get back to interview those people."

"How is it going?"

"I will like this job so much less if you aren't around, Nathan," I said.

"I know. I don't know how much longer I can last. The only thing that sees me through it right now is my ambition for you."

The afternoon interviews were less grueling. I was so tired that I noticed less. I made less effort to concentrate on the drone of voices. I also found one candidate who was exceptional. He was young and earnest and bright. His name was Ruskin. I was sure we'd hire him. I scheduled him for a second-round interview the next week and then went back to my cubicle. Martha came by my desk and asked me if I wanted to watch a movie Friday night. I apologized, saying I had other plans.

"Maybe later in the weekend?" I suggested.

I didn't want to commit. I wanted to keep my options open so that depending on my mood I could take it up. Or not.

"Call me," Martha said.

I left shortly after that and met Sybil. We watched a comedy starring Gerard Depardieu. It made me laugh. After that we went to dinner. It was a warm evening, and we dined at a restaurant where we could sit on the sidewalk by their open full-length door-like windows. I felt on top of the world eating pasta with shiitake mushrooms as the world went by. It struck me again how much I loved Manhattan.

"Have you seen Yoshi again?" I asked as casually as I could.

"No. But he's after me. He calls every day."

"So, you don't like him very much?"

"He'd be okay if he wasn't so damn proprietary."

"Is he in love with you?"

"Yes."

"Did he say anything about the two of us dancing together?"

"Yes. He said that if I ever got involved with you he'd have you fired. I think he was joking."

"Does he want you to leave Nathan?" I asked her.

"Yes."

"What did you tell him?"

"I told him he could forget about it."

Sybil looked delightful that night. She was wearing tiny red earrings and matching lipstick.

"Sybil, have you ever wanted to sleep with a woman?"

"No. I like sex with men. One of my friends, Sally, was a lesbian. She told me that women can ejaculate like men if they are fisted."

"You're kidding!"

"No. She had some manual she showed me that described how to do it."

"Did you ever try?"

"She did it to me, and though I wasn't excited in the beginning, I got excited because of the sheer mechanics of it. And then I did ejaculate. Then Nathan and I tried it. But his hands are too wide."

"You have to have a certain kind of hand?"

"Well, flexible and narrow is good."

I put mine in front of her. She gripped my knuckles and squeezed them to see how narrow they could get.

"It may work," she replied.

"Let's try."

"I think we need the manual. It's not easy."

"We'll go get it," I said.

"Now?"

"Yeah, we'll stop at a bookstore on the way home," I said. New York was the only city in the world where you could go to a bookstore at eleven-thirty at night and buy an instruction manual for lesbians.

Before we left the restaurant I excused myself to use the restroom, which was in the interior. I walked inside and saw Nathan at a table with a couple. I almost did a double-take. My heart started beating very fast. He waved at me. I went up to him.

"Meet my friends Rob and Rita Ringold," he said.

They were the couple he was going to spend the weekend in the country with. I was shit scared. If Sybil decided to use the restroom now and walked indoors, I'd be done for. I hastily excused myself and went straight back to Sybil.

On the way out to the sidewalk table I handed the waitress my credit card and asked her to process the bill "pronto."

"Sybil, we have to leave," I said as soon as I got to the table.

"Let me go to the bathroom."

"Not now."

"I need to pee, André."

"Your husband is inside," I said quietly. Calling Nathan her husband made me feel miles away from him.

"Shit."

"Let's separate. Just walk away to the end of the block and wait for me."

She was sharp and moved fast. I waited for the waitress to return and prayed Nathan wouldn't come my way to say hi. It would be difficult to explain what I was doing in the restaurant all alone. And if he kissed me on a whim, then what would I tell Sybil, who'd be watching from the end of the street?

It was my lucky day. The waitress came with my receipt, and I signed and left. We went to Barnes & Noble, and Sybil used the restroom while I picked up the book. Neither of us talked about the close shave we'd just had.

When we got home, I washed my hands and dipped them in lube. I flicked the pages of the book while Sybil lay naked on my bed with her legs spread out. I tried to make my way in slowly finger by finger while she guided me. After half an hour I had managed to put my whole fist in and open it inside her like a flower. Sybil's reaction was extraordinary. I felt as if I were witnessing a miracle, something like the birth of a baby.

In the bright sunshine streaming through my window the

next morning I remembered it again with wonder. In my mind's spreadsheet I wrote "Time with Sybil last night = Time with Nathan."

"Not too many men could do that to a woman and not feel castrated by the experience," Sybil said over our morning coffee.

"Castrated? Why should anyone feel castrated?"

"André, most men would hate the idea that a woman could have her best orgasms without their precious penises."

"I see."

"You are so damn gay. So is Nathan. Don't you ever see it?"

"Of course I'm gay," I said.

"So you do see it."

"Yes I see it."

"Have you slept with a man, André?"

"Of course I've slept with a man," I replied, trying to sound funny, as if I were joking.

She looked at me perplexed.

I winked and tried looking funny again and said, "Come on, it's time to go to work."

All the way down the passageway to the elevator and on the ride down, she shook her head and muttered to herself. Then she said, "You are fucking exactly like Nathan."

"Come on Sybil, can't you take a joke?" I said. I was kicking myself for not having lied.

She shook her head, dismissing me.

"Why do I have to fall in love with men like you? I need someone like Yoshi. A real man."

"Hey, this is ridiculous. If a guy doesn't want to fist you he's weak and insecure—if he does, then he's gay. This is ridiculous." I was angry.

"I can't believe this. My life sucks," Sybil muttered to herself and flagged a cab on the street, ignoring me completely.

I flagged another cab and got in. "Little shit, this is the last time I'm fisting you," I said to her in my head. I opened my mind's spreadsheet again and scratched out the equal sign between Nathan and Sybil. Experiences could change after they had happened. Sustainability was important too, not just the moment. Then I remembered how she had climaxed, and I hoped Madhu would let me try it on her that night. I wanted to compensate her for having had to sleep with her stuffy husband for two years. I felt an utterly selfless fondness and affection for Madhu.

Friday was another crazy day at the office. It was impossible to wind down for the weekend. I had to interview six other programmers. Two of them seemed competent, and I asked them to come in for a second-round interview the following week. At lunchtime, when I was on my way to Nathan's office to say hi to him, I ran into Yoshi in the corridor. I hadn't seen him in the past few days. I pretended everything was normal and chatted with him.

"Had fun at the party?" he asked me.

This was my chance. I could tell him I was gay and get him off my back. It wouldn't be very cool, but it would be better than if he really suspected anything between Sybil and me.

"Yeah, great. Remember the band?"

"Yes. They were good."

"I have a date with the saxophone player this weekend."

"But he's a man," Yoshi said, looking absolutely confused.

"Yes," I nodded.

"You're gay?" he said.

"Yes," I said.

"But then why did you dance with Nathan's wife?" he asked. I was surprised by his bluntness.

"Because she wanted to. She knows I'm gay, so I guess she was very comfortable with me."

"Yes. Yes. I get it. But she didn't tell me," he said.

"You talked to her? Asked her about me? When?"

"Yes. Later."

"I had told her not to tell anyone," I replied.

I was beginning to feel ill. I had liked Yoshi Kato. But his conduct was abominable, and he was rapidly diminishing in my eyes. He was taking me down with him. I abhorred myself. I ended the conversation and went to Nathan. I wanted to talk to him about it, but I couldn't, since it would sow seeds of doubt in Nathan's mind about Sybil and me. I remembered that I was seeing Madhu this evening. I could tell her everything. She was removed from this incestuous circle. It was a relief to know that I'd be able to talk about it.

Nathan and I got soup from the shop in the lobby and sat outside on the steps in front of our building to eat it. The weather was not as warm as the night before, and we had to keep our jackets on as we ate.

"Can I see your paintings when you bring them back?" I asked Nathan. I sounded fake to myself. I had already been to his house and seen some of his paintings. I knew that he liked to splash paint carelessly. Colorfully.

"Of course. I think I'm going to start painting again and also maybe have an exhibition."

"That's a good idea. I want to see you happy in what you're doing."

"Do you enjoy working here, André?"

"I think I do."

After lunch, when I resumed interviewing programmers, I would remember with a startle every half an hour or so my episode with Yoshi.

"Shit, I've come out at work," I'd keep telling myself again and again.

I had neglected to let Sybil know. It would be a disaster if Yoshi called her and she didn't corroborate.

I made the next candidate wait and went to my cubicle. Then I decided that using my phone wasn't the safest thing to do. So I took the elevator down to the lobby and used a pay phone.

"Sybil, I told Yoshi I'm gay. Please don't contradict me if he asks."

"Have you gone mad?"

"Sybil, please, please. I can't get fired from here. Just please do this one thing for me."

There was a long pause. Then she said, "Okay."

"Thanks, Sybil."

"You're such a faggot, André," she said and hung up.

Sybil was disgusted by my lack of masculinity. I had an epiphany by the pay phone. Man likes being penetrated, has a papa complex, falls in love with man in an authoritative position, doesn't want to face danger in professional life—true and total wimp, I thought, summing myself up.

I went back up to the conference room and completed the interview. After that I had two more. Then I left for the bookstore in Chelsea where I had arranged to meet Madhu.

She was already there waiting for me and looking at gay magazines.

"Having fun?"

"These men are so hot," she said.

I looked over her shoulder and agreed.

"They serve coffee at the other end. Want to get a cup of coffee and check out a few more?"

"Sure."

We sat at the table and went through a few magazines. We compared notes on who we found hot. Our tastes overlapped half the time. I noticed that Madhu had a penchant for hairy men. I couldn't believe it. I pointed it out to her.

"But I also like hairless men with light hair," she said, ruffling my hair.

"And long schlongs?" I asked.

"Yours is a good size."

"I want you to ejaculate. Can I fist you?"

"What are you talking about?"

"Come, I'll show you," I said.

We walked over to the Sexuality section and I pulled out the manual. I flipped the pages and pointed out the section on ejaculation. I opened the last page with the drawing of the hand opening out.

"Wow! It'll hurt."

"Babies come out of there. It won't hurt," I said.

"It hurts when babies come out of there!"

"Hmm." I felt foolish. I could be so clueless sometimes, I wondered if the rest of the world thought I was dumb.

"Have you done it before?"

"Yes," I said and thought to myself, not too long ago, either.

"Okay, then we can. As long as you know what you're doing."

In Madhu's presence I felt like a schoolboy embarking on an adventure. I cherished it. We left the bookstore and went to dinner. I told her about all the office developments since I'd last seen her. I shared my anxiety about Nathan finding out about Sybil and me.

Our short-haired waiter was wearing tight clothes and a dog collar with a small metal plate that said, "I'm gay." He smiled a lot at Madhu, who clearly enjoyed his attention and smiled back as much. She flirted with him.

"Now, don't get too friendly with him," I said at one point.

"I'm only trying to be your pimp."

"In that case, continue."

When we were leaving she scribbled on the bill, "You're so cute, I want you to call my friend."

"What are you doing?"

"He'll call you," she said.

"No, he will not."

"What's your number?"

I gave it to her and said, "He will not call me."

"Yes he will—you watch."

I was touched by her gesture.

We left the waiter a big tip and went home.

"Madhu, time is such a weird thing. I slept with you three nights ago, and before that two years ago, but right now it doesn't feel as if the gap between those two events was all that long. Time is imaginary."

"No, it feels like it's imaginary, but it isn't. It deceives. People need glasses after the age of forty, most girls hit puberty within fourteen years, a hard-boiled egg takes ten minutes to cook, and babies are born in nine months. Time is inevitable, and without it there's nothing."

"But some periods of time feel shorter and others longer. Why is that? I don't think that's a function of being bored or entertained."

"I don't know why it is. When we made love earlier this week it was entirely different from having sex with Srini. With him it feels like a long fifteen minutes, and with you it felt like a terribly short forty-five."

Madhu had a sparkling intelligence that lived and breathed from every pore of her skin. When she spoke, her eyes glinted like mirrors. I was happy I'd found her again.

We got ready for bed. I asked her to lie down with her legs spread apart, and I put lube on my hand. I wondered if I should feel bad in any way. Twenty-four hours ago I'd been in the same spot doing the same thing to Sybil. It felt entirely different, though. Just like Srini and I felt differently for Madhu, I thought. The consciousness that this was Madhu permeated my whole being. But a certain part of me was sad. It shouldn't be possible to do something with deep feeling and do the same thing again with a different deep feeling.

In the morning I gave Madhu the article I'd read on dreams. I knew it would make her think like it had made me think. Then I walked her to the PATH station on Thirty-fourth Street. On the way we passed a protest march. Six monks in long gray robes stood outside a building called The Nottingham with posters of mangled babies.

"No baby should die by choice," the poster said.

A group of old women were also standing with the monks. They all had cottony hair and held rosaries in their hands.

"I've been trying to have a child, André," Madhu said, touching my arm as we passed them.

"Since when?"

"For a year. Something is wrong."

"Do you know what?"

"I may be barren." She flinched when she said the word.

"Did the doctor say that?" I asked, getting angry.

"No. We're going to a doctor if nothing happens in another month. One of us is infertile."

"Do you really want to have a child with Srini? You're so uncertain about the marriage—it may not be a good idea."

"You're right. I started thinking of it myself after I saw you on Tuesday."

I dropped Madhu off and wandered down from Thirty-fourth Street to the farmer's market on Union Square. The day was almost balmy, and the market was swarming with people. Roller-bladers bought raspberry-apple cider from an ancient woman in a green army hat. A band played music. As soon as a handful of people had gathered, the band stopped playing and one of the musicians walked from person to person trying to sell a CD and a tape. No one was interested, and the crowd started drifting away. It was such a beautiful day, I thought it would be a crime against God if people were unhappy. The CD and tape were both the same album, called *Music from the Andes*. I bought both a CD and a tape and slipped them into the pocket of the canvas coat I was wearing.

I drifted past a large caravan selling flowers and bought a bunch of irises. A young man carrying a little child in a baby seat strapped on his front bought sunflowers. The baby played with his hair. I looked at the man and smiled. He was beautiful and reminded me of Nathan. I could imagine Nathan carrying a baby like that. I daydreamed that we'd go to farmer's markets on Saturdays and live like a couple. The beautiful man turned around, waved his sunflowers, and said, "Dad, I bought these, should I buy the freesias too?"

I looked in the direction in which he was speaking. A handsome and distinguished man with a rugged-looking face smiled and came toward him. He touched his grandchild's cheek and then spoke to his son. I had a second daydream of walking around the farmer's market on a Saturday with my dad and Nathan. I felt wistful and depressed. I walked away from the father and son and went toward a cart selling iced tea and gingerbread. I drank a cup and walked around some more. A man with a huge dog stood in the center of the road, blocking everyone's way. He was holding a bottle of water in the dog's mouth. The bottle had a nozzle for sucking the water, and the dog was drinking from it exactly as a human being would. People were stopping and admiring the dog and the man. The man looked at the crowd around him and smiled like a proud father. I walked away and went to a section with postcards. I flipped through several postcards and then bought a few. When I walked back, the man was still giving his dog a drink of water. The man with the baby and his father were standing and watching the dog. The young father was pointing the dog out to his baby and saying, "Look, doggy." Then he turned around to look behind him to a woman approaching him and said, "Ellen, did you see this dog?" Ellen must have been his wife. All four of them stood and watched the dog, and then Ellen turned around and asked her husband, "Should we buy a dog?"

I realized it must be obvious that I was staring at them and eavesdropping on their conversation. I walked away. Back home, I put the irises in the vase Nathan had given me. Sybil had left me a message that she wouldn't be able to go with me to bring my desk back, since Nathan had decided to extend their trip in the country by another day. She apologized. I called the furniture store and made arrangements to go in and look at the desk right away. It looked and felt exactly like Nathan's furniture in the office and their home. The toffee-colored wood was neither matte nor glossy in its finish. I loved it. The saleswoman said they could deliver it to my place in the afternoon or I could take it with me. I paid them for delivery and then went to a bookstore. I bought a cookbook and went back home.

At home, I cooked rice and a simple vegetable dish following the instructions in the cookbook. I used my Thai green curry sauce and the coconut milk. It smelled good. I set the table for myself, put on some music, and sat and ate my lunch with a book. The food had turned out well. It made me happy.

After the desk was delivered, I spent the rest of the afternoon fussing over it. Sybil had designed it for a specific corner, but I moved it around the apartment nonetheless to see how it would look in other places. Then I put it where it belonged and placed the vase with irises on it. I wanted every item on the surface of the desk to look perfect. Beside the vase I put an antique knife that my father had given me as a high school graduation present.

Nathan called me in the afternoon saying that he would not get back from the country till late at night on Sunday. He had been inspired to start painting and had also been able to talk easily to Sybil for the first time in weeks. We arranged to meet on Monday night. After I spoke to him, I opened my miniplanner and put him in for Monday. I was to meet Madhu again on Tuesday. That meant I couldn't see Sybil till Wednesday. As soon as I'd shut my miniplanner the phone rang again. This time it was Sybil.

"André, I'm not coming back into the city till Sunday night."

"I'm busy on Monday and Tuesday. Can we meet on Wednesday?"

"That's so far away."

"I know—I was hoping to see you this weekend."

"Yeah. Nathan just wants to stay on. I guess I can come back on my own. Take a bus down or something."

"No. No. Stay with him," I said. He'd sounded happy to have her with him. I didn't want to be the cause of him losing his happiness.

"If you want me to come, I'll come."

"I don't want to take you away from him, Sybil."

"I guess I should stay. He really wants me to."

"Then you should."

"For a change, he wants me to," she said bitterly.

"I got the desk. It's beautiful. I can't wait for you to see it," I said, changing the topic.

The conversation with Sybs left me with the same feeling that seeing the happy family in Union Square had. Everyone else belonged to a unit. People lived together and had each other. I felt alone and isolated. Hooking up with different lovers and becoming one with them several times a week was just not the same as having a dull routine life with a family. I wanted my own family, at least at that moment.

Nathan was with Sybil painting yellow abstractions on canvas. She was probably taking a walk around the garden and waving to him occasionally. Madhu had probably just gotten home to Srini. He was asking her about her weekend, and though she was thinking of me in the back of her head and missing me, she was also talking to him. Yoshi was pining for Sybil. Martha was probably hanging by her couch waiting for me to call for a movie. That was one person who I knew needed me. I wasn't interested in her, but at that point she was the only option that made sense.

I called Martha. She wasn't home, so I left her a message asking if she wanted to go to a movie. Then I put on some Brahms and lay down on my bed, closed my eyes, and listened to his piano trio till I was no longer alone.

I must have fallen asleep. When the phone rang, it was six already. It was Martha, saying she'd like to go to a movie. We arranged to meet at the Quad in half an hour.

Tickets for the French flick we wanted to see were sold out for the seven o'clock show. We bought tickets for the next show at nine and wandered around to find a restaurant. Martha was lively and interesting. The last few times I had been with her, I had forgotten what I had liked about her. Now I appreciated her again.

The movie was one of those films that make you wonder, "What was that about?" We walked out of the theater complaining in agreement. Sometimes, all one wanted from life was to be negative and express disdain for other people and their ideas. Martha made me feel pedestrian. I had needed to feel that way.

We went back to my apartment. I wanted to ask her if she had been fisted. I wondered if her labia piercing would make it more difficult. But watching Sybil and Madhu climax had made me feel awestruck. I didn't want to react the same way to Martha, whom I really didn't care much for. The rake in me felt unjust and unfair: it was a crime to deny a woman a climax like that. After all, it was unlikely that any other man would do it for her. But I managed to stop myself. We just had normal sex. Man on top.

The next morning was Sunday. I woke up and saw my new desk. I felt like going out in the sunshine and buying things for my apartment. I wanted to be alone. Martha was sound asleep on my bed. I made cappuccino so that the noise of the milk steamer would wake her up. I shook her awake and gave her coffee.

"What are your plans for today, André?" she asked sleepily.

"Got some stuff to do."

"I have to be somewhere at three in the afternoon. Do you want to walk around the park and go to brunch?" she asked.

I wanted very much to go to the park and then eat brunch, but I wanted to be doing it with Nathan, Madhu, or Sybil. Maybe even Bobby. I resented Martha for not being one of them.

"Can't do it, Martha. I have to take care of a few things. My father is coming next weekend."

"That's right. Okay, then, I guess I'll just go," she said.

She was waiting for me to protest or to say that I really didn't want her to leave but I had all this work. I didn't apologize and did nothing to show my regret. I thought to myself that I was what women called a jerk.

I smiled in response.

She got dressed and went to my bathroom to wash her face. Then she left. My apartment and my unmade bed suddenly felt oppressive. I pulled out my sheets and opened my windows. I threw my sheets into the laundry bag and got clean bed linen from the cupboard and made my bed. Then I took a quick shower and walked to Central Park.

The day passed remarkably easily and well. I listened to Mozart's *Divertimenti* again and again. And I walked. The sunshine and the green made the walking joyous. I missed nobody and did nothing all day. The rocks by the lake in Central Park were isolated, and I lay down on them and watched the world go by. I slowly made my way home, walking down Fifth Avenue for most of the way. I had had enough of a respite from people. I wanted to be social again. I decided to go to a café in the village. I purposely avoided Chelsea; a gay café would mean trouble. I didn't want to flirt. I was afraid of myself. Afraid that I had eyes for everybody, was incorrigible, incurable, and a compulsive male nymphomaniac. I was afraid I was radiating some strange pheromone like the guy in the radio show had mentioned. That's why people were wanting to bed me all the time. I had always been good-looking, so that couldn't be the cause of this sudden attention.

I went to Le Poeme on Prince Street and ordered a little salad for myself. Then I pulled out Kafka's short stories and started reading "The Metamorphosis." There was only one other customer in the café, a young girl with a travel backpack. She was speaking to the proprietor of the café in French. She had a huge New York guidebook. They discussed something urgently, and I tried listening in. After some discussion the young tourist came up to me and said with a strong French accent, "Excuse me, would you know where this is?" and pointed to her map.

She was looking for an art gallery on the Lower East Side. The address was scribbled in pencil beside a subway map. I figured that it was only several blocks away and tried explaining to her. I asked her what the exhibition was about. She said it was a collection of photographs. She had met a photographer in a bookstore who had said he was having an exhibition in this gallery. I said I'd go with her to the gallery. I hadn't been to a photo exhibition in ages. She looked very young and was friendly. I finished my salad and we left Le Poeme. I offered to carry her backpack but she declined. It felt odd walking unencumbered side by side with a girl who was lugging twenty or thirty pounds of weight.

Her name was Justine, and she was traveling to Boston the next day. She said she'd be back in New York after a week and then she'd leave for Paris.

"My father is coming to visit me in New York next week. He was born in France. It will make him happy to see you. Will you come to my house for dinner?" I spoke to her slowly because she found it hard to follow. Eventually, I made myself understood and she agreed. We settled on having dinner the next Sunday.

The exhibition was crap. There were urban landscape pictures, usually a tree or cactus plant or bonsai juxtaposed next to one of New York's buildings. The photographer had managed to make my favorite buildings, the Flatiron and the Empire State, look ugly and mundane. On the Empire State building he had done a double image of a rubber plant and on the Flatiron a magnolia tree. I hated magnolias after that.

"Did you like it?" I asked her after we'd stepped out.

"Beautiful. Very beautiful," she said. She opened her eyes wide and raised her eyebrows to emphasize herself.

"Did you really like it, or are you being polite? I thought it was pretentious."

She slowly said, "Pree-tentio—us?"

She was pulling out her dictionary to look up the word.

"Never mind," I said. I couldn't have a subtle conversation with her, and it wasn't important.

We walked up to Astor Place, and then I asked her where she was staying.

"Youth hostel. I don't know," she said raising up her shoulders and turning down the corners of her mouth. Her face was expressive.

"You want to come with me to my house?" I asked.

"Your house," she said, pointing to me.

"Yes."

"Ça va. Okay," she said, laughing at her slip.

I hailed a cab and we got in. Once we reached my place, I got her out of her backpack and offered her some orange juice. She started fiddling with my CD collection and put on some Bjork. Her presence made my apartment colorful and youthful. She was wearing a bright tie-dyed T-shirt under her sweatshirt and orange jeans. She started dancing to the music. It was natural to join her. We hopped around the apartment for a while till there was a knock. My neighbor from the floor below was at the door.

"You're making a tremendous racket. It sounds like the hoofs of stampeding animals," he said.

I apologized and told Justine we couldn't do it anymore. She smiled at me and then went to my desk and admired it. She knelt on the floor and began with the legs, touching them with the tips of her fingers and then her whole hands. Looking at her touching the desk was sensual and made me want to make love to her. After she was done examining the desk, she gestured to my bathroom and asked if she could take a shower. I gave her a towel.

In five minutes she came out smelling of my musk soap and wrapped in my towel. It had been a hot day, and I decided to take a shower as well. When I stepped out of the bathroom, I found her lying on my bed completely naked. I was in my boxers and a T-shirt. She called me toward her.

I took off my clothes and lay down next to her. Her skin was delicate and warm and smelled of my soap. Justine had a light touch and gave me tender kisses on my mouth, my chest, my balls. She was tiny and her back was perfect. At night I dreamt of her wheeling my baby in a pram as we strolled around the farmer's market.

In the morning I woke her up and offered her coffee. She shook her head no and kissed me sleepily. Then she pointed to her backpack. I brought it to the bed. She pulled out her dictionary and after looking at several pages, she said, "Can I sleep here some more and then leave?"

Since I had married her in my sleep (even though it was triggered by chemicals and not a reflection of truths I was running away from), I trusted her completely. I said yes. She kissed me again and went to sleep. I left her a note saying not to forget to come to dinner the next week. I wrote my name and phone numbers on the paper and also my home address. Then I left for work.

I was almost startled to see Nathan on Monday morning because I hadn't seen him in so long. It felt like years. He looked fresh and rested. We made a date for lunch. I didn't want to wait till the evening to find out what had happened over the weekend in the country with his paintings and with Sybil.

Four of the guys I had interviewed were coming in for second-round interviews in the afternoon. Nathan was supposed to come in and talk to them. I also had three first rounds to do by myself in the morning. I checked my e-mail before I disappeared into the meeting room for the rest of the day. Madhu had written, "Friday night was explosive. Can't wait for the things you'll do on Tuesday." I felt a pang of fear that my repertoire had been exhausted.

I went to the conference room and asked the first guy in. Between interviews I would remember that Justine was sleeping on my bed at home. It sent a warm and delicious feeling through my body. At noon when I was done with the three, I buzzed Nathan and asked him to lunch. Instead of sitting on the steps and getting a sandwich, we went to a real restaurant for a change.

"So, tell me about your weekend."

"A lot has happened."

"What's going on?"

"Sybil says she's half in love with another man, and she says it affects her feelings toward me."

"Are you upset?"

"No. We talked a lot and I feel closer to her. I feel like we are friends again. And she said she slept with Yoshi only because she was having problems with her guy."

"What's going to happen?"

"She knows I'm having an affair."

"You told her?"

"Yes, there was no point in her feeling bad or guilty. Now we're on an even footing."

"I guess so."

"I need a favor, André."

"What?"

"Sybil and I think it will be a lot better if we can be open about our lovers, and we'd like to all get together."

"So you think we're all going to be one big happy family?" I asked incredulously. My heart was thudding.

"We could be. I told her that you might feel odd meeting us alone, so she agreed to ask her lover as well. We can all four eat brunch. No one will feel they are under scrutiny then. "

"You haven't told her it's me, have you?"

"No. Not yet."

"Don't tell her."

"So, will you meet with us?"

"I'll think about it. When do you want to do it?"

"This weekend."

"My father is coming this weekend. Let me think, Nathan."

"Yes."

Back in the office I had trouble stopping my hands from shaking. My throat was dry, and even four glasses of water did not help. I was up shit creek. I could refuse to do it. But if they were both thinking along these lines, then they might one day give in and trade the names of their lovers. Then I'd have no control over the situation. If I agreed to meet them, I'd be prepared. And I'd be more prepared than they would be. A little part of me also wanted a clean break from the duplicitous life I was leading. It was exhausting having to be on guard and watch myself all the time. Now I could choose when I wanted the bomb to blow up in my face. Sunday brunch would be ideal. If things went badly, I could come home to Dad and Justine for dinner. I would have an escape plan.

Nathan and I interviewed the second-round candidates jointly. I had a hard time focusing. My head played dissonant modern music—first Dave Brubeck and then Nine Inch Nails sounded an infuriating din in my inner ear. My internal film studio saw me like a ball in smooth motion that had suddenly started to spin, a top that was wobbling. I wanted to press my hand to my ears to stop the music and close my eyes to get rid of the image, but everything was being generated internally, and simply shutting off the external sensory organs wasn't going to work.

When I passed my desk on my way to the men's room, I saw my voicemail light flashing. Sybil had called. I called her back.

"I told Nathan I have a lover. He wants to meet you," she said.

"Interesting."

"Will you meet him?"

"No," I said.

"Please."

"We have to talk about this. Let's talk on Wednesday night," I said.

"Okay. He has a lover, too, and we can all meet."

"I have a condition," I added.

"What?"

"You won't tell him it's me before we meet."

"Okay."

As soon as I'd hung up on Sybil, Martha stopped by my desk and asked me if I wanted to hang out over the weekend.

"Dad's going to be here. I don't think I can."

She shook her head and went back to her table at the glass doors in the reception area.

Nathan had wrapped up one interview and was on to the next one. I joined in half-heartedly. It occurred to me that I might lose Nathan altogether. Next week at this time he might be my sworn enemy. Life sucked the big one.

In the evening I suggested to Nathan that we go to a movie. I didn't want to think about the upcoming confrontation.

When Nathan and I stepped out of the theater after the movie, it was pouring. We waited under the awning of the Angelika for a good five minutes before a vacant cab drove by. We darted across the street and got into it. The few seconds it had taken us to dash across had left us thoroughly wet. We shivered in the cab and hung on to each other. As soon as we got into the apartment, my only thought was to make us both some hot tea. Maybe take a hot shower. I took our jackets and hung them on the shower curtain in the bathroom.

"That's pretty," Nathan said.

"I beg your pardon," I said, walking out of the bathroom.

He pointed to my bed. There was an iris on my bed. Justine must have left it. My heart felt exactly the same way my mouth would feel when I was eating a liqueur-filled chocolate. Justine's warmth was like liquid gold, and it flowed right inside my heart. But in a second I had realized what must have been obvious to Nathan by now: someone had slept in my bed.

"Oh! That's nice," I said and picked it up from my bed. I could feel my face get hot.

Nathan looked away. I went to my kitchen and put the iris in the vase Nathan had given me. For a second I missed Justine. Then I returned to the moment, to guilt and the next step to appease Nathan. We didn't say anything about it. I knew no language to make up with him except for the offering of my physical self. I aroused him and bent over. Then I aroused him and bent over again. After that we talked. But not about Justine. We talked about different things, about the upcoming meeting with Sybil and her lover.

He brushed his palm on my back and played with my neck. He said he had never hoped for this before, but now maybe he could hope that I'd move in with him one day. He had forgiven me for the flower on my bed and the intimacy it spoke of. I wanted to hope for a life together too, but I was sure I'd be toast as soon as he knew the whole story.

"Will you accept anything at all from me, Nathan?" I asked.

"I'd accept anything as long as you loved me."

I told him about my jaunt through the farmer's market, the father, son, and baby. I wanted to soften him up as much as I could before the event.

"It made me want to marry you, Nathan," I said.

"Maybe Sybil can have two kids—one for herself and one for us."

I didn't respond. Instead I asked, "Nathan, can we get the brunch over with this Sunday?"

"Yeah, let me check with Sybil to see if her guy can make it, too."

"Okay. Let me know. And can we not talk about this again?"

"All right, André. Is something the matter?"

"No, Nathan. I love you. Remember, whatever happens, I love you."

"It'll be good, don't you see? I am so hopeful about this."

I had to keep silent again. This was just death. I wanted it to be Sunday soon. I couldn't stand the torture anymore. Nathan fell asleep after that. I couldn't sleep till several hours later.

I woke up in the morning feeling unrested and exhausted and spent all day Tuesday in a stupor at work. When I met Madhu in the evening, I was a wreck. She saw me walk into the restaurant where we had arranged to meet and said, "You look terrible."

"I'm done for and so tired I'll collapse."

"Then what are we doing in a restaurant?"

She got a cab and shepherded me home. She looked at my take-out menus and ordered a delivery of Indian food. Then she ran the bath and told me to get in. It revived me.

"Now, tell me what's going on," she said, drying my hair.

I gave her a blow-by-blow account of everything that had happened since I'd last seen her. There had been a time when I would sit with John in college and give him such updates about Madhu.

"So I am most likely going to see them on Sunday for brunch."

She let out a whistle.

"I'll be praying for you."

If I'd hoped for consolation, creative ideas, and a way out from Madhu, but none of these were coming. She didn't make it easier for me.

"You'll just have to face the consequences," she said.

"Tell me he won't be mad."

"I don't know Nathan—I can't guess what he'll do,"

The delivery guy buzzed my apartment and Madhu went down to get the food. She set the table and we ate. I decided it was pointless thinking anymore about it. I had to make the most of the few days I had before it happened. With Sybil on Wednesday and maybe Nathan on Thursday. On Friday, Dad would arrive, and on Sunday I'd take the plunge. I felt like a man with limited time. A man who could do anything because he knew it was all going to be over in a few days. Then I remembered that "over" meant my job could be over, too.

"Madhu, what if he fires me?"

"You should be sending résumés out, sweetheart."

"I should. I'll get them ready tomorrow."

She came over to me and patted my head.

"Poor André, got himself into a spot of trouble," she said. I could see myself complaining about it to Madhu the rest of the night. My view of myself got unappealing. I resolved not to talk anymore. Focus on the night ahead, I told myself. After dinner we talked for a little while about John and some of our other friends. I was physically exhausted and wanted to sleep. But then I thought that we didn't get this sort of opportunity every day, remembered this mug that Madhu had in college that said "Carpe Diem," and energized myself into performing.

I was so depleted at work on Wednesday that I could hardly get any work done. Horfmeister sent contracts to the candidates who'd made it past Nathan. I tried sketching out an orientation program for them for their first day. I'd brief them on the project so that they could start programming on the second day. The hours at work hung above my head like stolid August weather, humid and uncomfortably hot. I didn't even feel the urge to run to Nathan's office. Life had become utterly devoid of joy. In the evening when Sybil came over, it was impossible to make the most of it or live in the moment. I was a stress case.

"André, please do this for me."

"You're the one who never wanted him to know, Sybil," I said.

"I know, I know. But everything has changed."

"How?"

"My feelings for him have changed. I think I may want to leave Nathan one day."

"So?"

"He's having an affair, he told me. Both Nathan and I are involved with other people. What sense is there in being married and tied down? I think it's just mature for us all to meet and talk like adults."

"Yeah, but how is it going to help to bring other people in?" I cringed. There was only me, and she'd know in two days that I had been lying.

"It's our life, André, it's me and you."

"I don't want anything more out of us, Sybil. I am perfectly happy as things are." I admired my own honesty with her for a second.

"I know, André. But it costs you nothing to do this for me. Nathan likes you already."

She hadn't understood me.

"Precisely, and my professional life, which is just fine right now, will be placed in jeopardy," I said.

"What if I promise you that your professional life won't be affected?"

"How can you promise me something like that?"

"I can. Nathan will listen to me if I ask him."

Getting Sybil to be reasonable was useless. Especially since I had already figured out her part of the deal. She was hoping that she would fall more in love with me and less in love with Nathan. As long as she could ride both boats for a while, she'd succeed in emerging from this mess with a new lover and no hurt feelings. She'd move in with me and Nathan could then move on with his life. Of course, none of it would work out this way. Unless life turned out like a French movie, in which case we'd all three live together and Sybil would have our children. Nathan would sit home and paint and take care of them.

I broke out of my reverie.

"Sybil, I'll do it. But you can't breathe a word of who I am till the meeting."

"Do you think you can do it on Sunday morning?"

"Yes, I said. I had thought for a moment that I should pretend to check my calendar, but I changed my mind. This wasn't funny.

She wanted to make love after that, but I fell asleep. In the morning I went to work dreading the idea of having to do things. The programmers would start next week on Wednesday. I had to make schedules for everyone. In a way it was good that I was past the proposal stage. I could cruise for a couple of weeks at work, giving instructions to the new recruits and managing them instead of having to perform at full horsepower.

Thursday flew by. I decided to keep myself Nathan-and-Sybil-free till Sunday. My only contact with them was a confirmation of where to meet. Sybil had suggested a café in a quiet part of the far West Village near their brownstone.

I was afraid of letting them spend three nights in a row with each other, but I was too nervous to see either of them again. Moreover, Dad was arriving Friday night and I needed to spend Thursday making sure my kitchen was stocked. My father loved to cook for me. He would be thrilled that I wanted to learn.

Friday passed quickly. I e-mailed Madhu that I was really nervous, and she called me back in the afternoon with a few soothing words. I was glad she was sticking by me through this. My father's flight was arriving at eight-thirty in the evening. I wanted to call and tell him to take a cab to my apartment. But I thought of him struggling with his luggage and worrying about Manhattan taxi drivers. I felt like a selfish twerp for even having thought of it. I went over to Martha's desk to ask her the easiest way to JFK.

"You can take a Carey bus from Forty-second Street near Grand Central."

"Great. How long should I give myself?"

"Around an hour. Really depends on the traffic."

I left work at six-thirty and walked to Grand Central and took the bus. I watched the sun set over the most dismal and decaying areas of Queens. Man was born alone and was going to die alone. And the fact that this was happening to man in littered streets, around scrap metal yards and gutted buildings, was somehow worse than it happening to him in mountains or by a spring stream.

The florescent lobby of the arrival terminal at JFK was full of people. There was a Muslim family with several women in veils standing around. A young Asian girl was waiting with her father. She was holding a bouquet of flowers. Car service drivers were holding placards that said, "Mr. Wheeler" and "Miss Waters." I played the *Jupiter* Symphony in my head. It filled me with delight as I waited for Dad. I wished I had brought my Walkman so that the sounds outside my head could resonate the ones within. Now my Jupiter Symphony was adulterated with people speaking Arabic and Russian. There was nothing to do but walk up and down and wait. There was not a single good-looking man or woman out of the hundred and fifty people in the lobby.

Finally they announced the arrival of the flight from Raleigh. I stood in a corner near the entrance and looked out for Dad. The door would open periodically and I would watch various people walking from the baggage area toward the doors in the lobby. I caught sight of my father when he was still in the baggage claim section. He had brought too many bags and was struggling. He was finding it hard to wheel the cart with his suitcase in a straight line and balance his duffel bag with the other. A young man noticed and offered to help him. When my father shook his head, the man insisted and simply took over. As soon as they both emerged into the arrival lobby, I waved at Dad. My father pointed me out to the young man, and they came over to me. I shook the young man's hand and introduced myself. His name was Vincent. We were sep-arated by a metal divider, and they had to make their way down the passageway before I could start wheeling Dad's cart. I asked Vincent where he was going.

"The New York University medical campus. Thirty-fourth Street and First Avenue," he replied in a strong southern accent. I hadn't lived in one place long enough to acquire an accent.

"It's right by where I live. Let's take you there," I said.

We got out of the building and got a cab. I put my father in the backseat and the two of us loaded the trunk. We grabbed the suitcases together and threw them in.

"Is this your first time here?"

"Yes."

"You're a handsome man," I said.

He blushed. He was virginal. Innocent. From the South.

On the cab ride home, I asked my father if he'd had a comfortable flight. I asked Vincent if he was going to medical school. He was here to stay. He was in a five-year program.

We dropped him off at his student housing. I helped him unload his suitcase and then handed him my business card. I asked him his last name.

"Martin."

"Call me, okay?" I said and patted his elbow.

Then I got back in the taxi.

"He's very nice," my father said.

"Yes."

Dad was limping a little. It was worrisome. We sat at the table and talked and then went to bed. I got into bed with him. In the morning he woke up well before me and tiptoed around the house. I slept lightly and was aware of his movements. He checked things out. He sat by the desk for a long time. When I opened my eyes and got up, he was holding the vase Nathan had given me and feeling its surface. It hadn't occurred to me before that my father was a sensuous man.

"What do you want to do today, Papa?" I asked him.

"It doesn't matter much, André."

"Would you like to go to the Empire State Building or go to the park?"

"Whatever you feel like doing."

I made him cappuccino in my coffeemaker. It was the first time I had made him anything. He drank a sip and said it was very good.

"This is very beautiful," he said, making a sweeping gesture around my studio.

"Thank you."

"Shirley would like it."

I was jealous for a second. When I was growing up, whenever I made him proud he would say that it would have made my mother happy. Now he only talked about Shirley.

We went walking down to the farmer's market, since it was a Saturday. I had to keep reminding myself to walk slowly so that he could keep up. I asked him to teach me how to choose vegetables. He taught me to feel beets and tomatoes, to get the ones that were neither overripe nor raw. He snapped the ends of green beans to show how you could tell the best from the average. Then we walked to the seafood section and he chose monkfish. I told him I had invited Justine for dinner on Sunday.

"I want to learn how to cook," I said.

"Fish is good then, better than chicken," he said.

"I want to learn to cook vegetarian food."

"Vegetarian?" he asked.

"Yes."

"Why?"

"It's more healthy," I murmured.

After buying fresh produce we dropped it off at home. Then I took him to the top deck of the Empire State Building.

"Do you like it?" I asked him.

"It's all right. You can see many tall buildings."

"Isn't it impressive? What mankind has achieved?"

"Man's heart has not changed. It's as black as it used to be before these buildings were made."

We came back home at four in the afternoon. Dad said he was tired and went to sleep. I read at my desk. At six I woke him up and took him to dinner to an Italian restaurant next door. I listened to Dad snore through the night. I tried thinking about what I would say to Nathan and Sybil in the morning. I couldn't think. I tried playing Satie in my head and couldn't. I counted his snores. I didn't sleep a wink. At seven I slipped out of my studio and went to a coffee shop across the street. I bought two croissants and came back and brewed some coffee. Dad said he would stay home and prepare for dinner while I was gone. He said he'd do the real cooking when I got back.

I took an hour to dress. I wore a dress shirt and a tie, though it was Sunday. I wanted to be crisp and clear. I wanted both Nathan and Sybil to desire me when I walked through the door. It might help them forgive me afterward.

I got to the café twenty minutes late. I wanted them to be waiting for me. I wanted them to see me at the same time when I walked in. I had decided that there should be some humor in the situation. I brought the tape and CD I had bought at the farmer's market from the band that had been playing there.

I asked the cab to stop a few blocks away from the café and walked. I played my favorite bits of Mozart's *Prague* on the way, to bolster my soul.

Sybil and Nathan were sitting at a round table outside in the sun by the French windows. There were two vacant chairs across from them. I played with the tape and CD in both pockets of my cotton jacket. We all saw each other at the same time.

"Hi, folks," I said.

They both stood up.

I turned to Sybil and said, "Hello, Sybil." And handed her the tape.

"Thank you, André," she said, leaning forward to kiss me. I kissed her on the cheek. She was beaming. Proud that her lover was me.

"And for you, Nathan," I said, pulling out the CD.

We all sat down. They still hadn't got it. Each thought that I was there for them and that the other was merely playing it cool.

I looked at them both and said, "So, I'm here. Aren't you both going to shoot me?"

Nathan understood. He glanced at the CD I had given him and then at the tape in front of Sybil. He understood it hadn't been a gesture to appease my lover's wife. He looked rattled.

Sybil laughed nervously and said, "Why should we shoot you, André?"

I got up and lifted the vacant chair next to mine. I pushed it away from our table, looked at her, and said, "There is nobody else joining us."

Nathan was glowering. I wanted to tell him a million things—how much I loved him, how sorry I was, how he could punish me. But I was tongue-tied.

It finally hit Sybil. The color of her face visibly changed. She looked at Nathan and then at me and then again at Nathan. Nathan nodded his head when she looked at him for the second time.

"You fucking faggots," she spat.

Nathan was not glowering any more. He was stony. Cold and chilling. In the space of a minute or two, he had gone from being shocked to being angry to writing me off. I was aghast. I wanted to stop him before it was too late. I felt as if my arms and limbs had been cut off.

I suddenly didn't care what Sybil thought.

Neither of them was making any effort to talk. Since I was responsible for the situation, I had to say something.

"Well, is there any point in us all staring at each other?"

No response.

"Doesn't look like it? My father is alone at home, folks. I'm going to leave if you have nothing to say."

"How could you, André?" Sybil hissed.

"I fell in love with him before I met you," I answered, looking at her. I wanted to be truthful and make up for all the secrets I had been lugging around.

"Why my wife?" Nathan said. His face was no longer expressionless. It looked hurt now.

"Because she kissed me. I liked her. She's beautiful."

"That's it—you liked me?" Sybil said raising her voice.

"Yes—didn't you like me?"

"You cheat." Sybil was on the verge of tears now.

"Who did I cheat? You're the one sleeping with everyone on the Risk Management desk at Kenji Japan Bank."

Nathan looked at me and then at Sybil. He seemed to look down on our squabbling.

"First I fall for Nathan, and he's inaccessible. Then I fall for you, but you're in love with Nathan. This sucks," Sybil said.

"Maybe you need a real man like Yoshi," I said, quoting her. I suddenly felt very bitter.

The waiter came to our table to take our orders. Nathan told him to get three coffees, without even asking us. Sybil looked at the waiter and pointedly said, "Can you make mine an iced tea, please?" Then she looked at Nathan, her eyes full of hate.

I looked at the waiter and said, "Can you make mine a hot tea, please?"

"Sure," he said and looked in Nathan's direction slyly.

I felt bad. I hadn't changed my order to contradict Nathan. I just didn't want another coffee. I said to no one in particular, "I'm coffeed-out today." The waiter had left our table and didn't hear me say it.

Nathan had zoned out. His eyes were unfocused, he looked old.

"I can't believe the two of you. I just can't believe this." Sybil's mood had changed to combative and belligerent.

"Sybil, I'm tired of you," Nathan suddenly said. I didn't think he had been listening.

She turned and stared at him dumbly.

"Did you hear that? Did you hear that? My faggot of a husband telling me he's tired of me." she was hysterical again. She looked at me when she spoke. As if I was supposed to second her. "I would be, too, if I were him," I said. I was angry with her. It would take me years to mend the fence with Nathan, and this woman was to blame.

"You're both alike. No wonder I fell for you," she said, looking at me.

"We're not that alike," Nathan said softly.

"I'm leaving," Sybil said and got up. She picked up her purse and looked down at both of us uncertainly.

I didn't say anything. Nor did Nathan. She started walking away. Then she came back and threw the tape I had given her on the table.

"You can keep that as a souvenir," she said.

We both watched her recede.

The waiter came with our coffees and teas. He placed our orders in front of us.

"Iced tea for the lady," he said, with an unwarranted flourish.

"Just put it down," I said.

Nathan was quiet. He wasn't talking to me anymore. And without the excuse of a conversation with Sybil, I could say nothing to fill the void. I drank my tea silently and played with Sybil's iced tea. I put salt and pepper in it, and sugar and ketchup. I stirred it. Eventually I even tasted it.

"Yeeuw," I said.

Nathan didn't even look up. I tried playing music in my head. My internal Walkman, the one in my head, had broken. Silence was death.

When he was done with his coffee, Nathan said, "Excuse me."

He disappeared into the restaurant. I asked the waiter for the check and paid him.

When Nathan got back I stood up and said, "I'm leaving."

We both walked away. At the first crossroads on Seventh Avenue South, I said, "Nathan, I'm sorry."

He didn't respond.

"Bye," I said.

I walked away in the opposite direction from him, even though I had to go the same way for a while. I felt nonexistent. I walked like a zombie till I eventually reached home. It was all over.

"André, are you okay?" my father said, opening the door.

"Yes."

"You look ill."

"I'm fine."

"Do you have parchment? Unbleached is better."

"I don't know what you are talking about, Papa."

"For the monkfish fillet."

"Oh yes."

"We need to get some things from the market. I made a list."

"Great," I said, my mouth, throat, and chest all feeling very hollow.

"I saw that you don't have all the herbs."

"Can we go in ten minutes, Papa?" I said.

"Of course. Are you okay?"

"I'll be fine," I said. I put an Albinoni CD in my stereo and lay down and closed my eyes. Very, very slowly, my head started playing what my ears heard. I got up.

"We can go now," I said.

My father sat down on the bed to put on his shoes. He had trouble bending his knee. I went to where he was sitting and sat on the floor. I picked up his shoes and put them on for him. He was touched and looked like he would cry. Papa, I'm dying of pain, I wanted to say to him. I tried smiling back.

We went to Lord Portnoy & Company, a gourmet store in my neighborhood, and got everything he needed. Watching his old gnarled hands examine jars of foodstuffs on the shelves was strangely soothing. It brought me back to the present. I was fascinated by the sheets of parchment and wondered what we'd do with them. He picked up a bottle of vermouth.

"I think Justine will prefer wine," I said.

"This isn't for drinking. It's for the fish."

"Oh!"

"What's for drinking?"

"Let's see."

We walked over to the wine rack and he picked up two bottles of white wine and two of red.

"You should have a stock," he said.

When we came back I checked my voicemail to see if Nathan or Sybil had called. I had only one message. It was from Martha. As soon as I heard her voice I pressed 2 to save the message. I couldn't be bothered hearing what she had to say.

My father scraped potatoes and cut artichokes. He asked me to wash the asparagus we had bought. He talked nonstop as he worked. He asked me to set the table. I put out napkins and plates and wineglasses with blue stems. He admired them.

I reflected on how ironic it was that now that I could learn to cook from Papa, I was no longer talking to Nathan. Just as well that I was going to learn to cook monkfish fillet. There was no longer a point in learning to cook vegetables. My father buttered the parchment and placed a monkfish in one corner, then carefully wrapped the parchment around it as if it were an envelope.

"Remember, André, the sauce and side dishes are always important."

I nodded.

"Two spoons of crème fraîche, a dash of vermouth, and slivers of garlic in this case," he said.

It sounded like art. And made me smile.

"And asparagus, artichokes, potatoes go best on the side with it," he continued.

My mouth was watering.

We set the fish in the oven at four hundred degrees.

"How long does one bake it?" I asked.

"Ten minutes."

"Can I take a quick shower?" I asked.

"Yes. Your lesson is over."

When I got out of the shower, Justine was already in my apartment, laughing with my dad. They were both talking in French. My father's parents had moved from Paris when he was still young, so his French was broken and rusty, but I could tell he really enjoyed trying. I felt redundant. Justine waved and smiled at me, and my father did the same. But they were wrapped up in their own world. They were happy.

We sat down to eat. My father insisted on getting the fish out of the oven himself. He put it on the table and opened the parchment with a great flourish. A heavenly aroma filled the room, and Justine clapped her hands and jumped up and down with schoolgirl delight. In a perfectly natural gesture, my father reached out to her and kissed her cheek. I went numb.

We started eating. They kept talking and Dad told her stories. I got more and more upset. I had wanted them both to fuss over me and make me feel better. They were hardly aware of me.

I ate quietly. After a while, my dad noticed and said something to Justine in French and they both laughed.

"You were like this even as a child, André," my father said, tweaking my cheek. I was embarrassed. What would Justine think? He was treating me like a boy.

After we were done with dinner, I got up to clear the table. Justine insisted that my father sit down and relax. She helped me rinse my dishes. She kissed me on the mouth and said in her halting way, "Are you feeling alone?"

"No."

"I am leaving for Paris tomorrow."

"I know. I'll miss you."

"We will meet again," she said.

I made espresso, and the three of us sat down together and drank it. I brought out a pack of cards, and we played rummy till eleven-thirty. Then Justine left. I saw her out to the front of my building and kissed her on the lips. Then I went back up the steps. The Nathan-Sybil confrontation from the morning wasn't burning as much in my stomach. Dad was ready to go to bed, and we called it a night. I was exhausted and felt as if I had nothing more to lose. I told myself that I would face whatever happened. I slept.

In the morning I woke up with a sick emptiness in my stomach. As soon as I opened my eyes I remembered that Nathan was no longer with me. I skipped drinking coffee in the morning because I knew it would make me more ill. I drank a glass of water and showered. When I got out, I made my father some coffee. He said he would go for a walk and then have lunch at home.

I kissed him good-bye. Then I picked up my Walkman and checked the tape in it. It was Haydn. I removed it and put in my favorite Mozart instead: *Jupiter* on Side A and *Prague* on the other. I left for work. For a few minutes I was oblivious to the music bellowing in my ear, but then Mozart took over. I was soon smiling to Amadeus. When I got off at Grand Central, I decided to walk to my office on the West Side instead of taking a shuttle to Times Square. My hands, as usual, insisted on pretending they were conducting an orchestra. I had to keep them in my pockets to prevent them from flailing around with the music. A seven-year-old boy from seventeenth-century Vienna made me whole in a way that only the most immediate and intense love could make me whole. Happiness wasn't something to be waited around for. And it wasn't rare. It was in my Walkman and in my head, it could be played at will, dependent only on two double-A batteries and a spool of tape that wasn't broken. If I listened to music all day and all night, then I would heal and live without Nathan. I felt strong.

"Did you get my message yesterday?" Martha said, looking up coldly from her desk when I walked through the glass doors on my floor the next day.

"Yes," I said and continued to walk to my desk. I immediately picked up my phone and checked my home voicemail where I had saved the message. I should have listened to it before coming to work. I had twelve saved messages. I'd saved every message Nathan had left me. I wanted to erase them now, but I realized that that might be all I had left of Nathan. The thought left me cold. I had to resave each one before I could get to Martha's message from the night before.

I finally reached the last message. I brought the phone closer to my ear.

"This is Martha. I'm pregnant."

I gripped the handset tighter.

"To hear this message again, press 1," the synthetic instructions on the voicemail service said. I pressed 1.

"This is Martha. I'm pregnant."

I banged the receiver down.

I sat down at my desk and stared blankly. It wasn't possible. I wanted to scream, "Someone help me!"

The rubber had burst, she had conceived, termination would take half a day. I didn't need this right now. I made myself think quietly for a few seconds. I buzzed her.

"Can we have lunch today?" I said.

"Yes."

I booted up my computer and tried to work. After a few minutes, my thoughts returned to the crisis. When it rains it pours, I thought. The only small consolation was that Dad was in town. The person on earth who most loved me was right by my side through all this drama, though he didn't know and I couldn't tell him. He'd be appalled that I was sleeping with a husband and wife. He'd want me to marry Martha and have the child.

I visited the men's room constantly all morning. I wrote Madhu useless e-mails saying I had bad news but couldn't send it over e-mail. I felt as if I were in a prison where people were flashing bright lights into my eyes every minute, not letting me rest or sleep.

In the men's room in front of the mirror I said to myself, "You are paying the price for every single thing you ever did. Pay up."

With a pregnancy hanging over my head, I missed Nathan even more. Music could not talk back, it could not counsel. Not even Mozart's. It could make me dance and it could light a fire, but it couldn't solve my problem. I kept telling myself if only Nathan were with me, everything would be okay. I broke down and wrote Nathan an e-mail that said, "Will you talk to me?"

At twelve I asked Martha if we could go to lunch. It was a very warm day and she'd worn loose white cotton pants and a loose white shirt. She looked as if she'd walked out of the Sahara. We went to a restaurant that had tables on the sidewalk and ordered soup.

"Are you sure about this?" I asked.

"Yeah. I waited for a week, hoping my period was just late. Then I did a pregnancy test. I repeated it."

I wanted to ask her how she knew it was mine. But then I stopped myself, thinking she might get offended.

"So?" I said. I didn't want to name anything. I was afraid.

"So? Are you asking me so?"

I didn't want to be the one to say it. To ask crudely if she'd get an abortion.

"When are you seeing a doctor?" I asked.

"For what, André?" she said. She was pushing me to say it, suggest it.

"To make sure everything is all right," I said ambiguously.

"I'm keeping it, André," she said forcefully and loudly enough for people at the next table to turn and look at us.

"You're what?"

"I'm having this child. Your child." The waiter who had just put our soups on the table looked at me sympathetically.

I took a few spoons of my soup. Was this woman going to have my child? I couldn't just let her go away and have this child. I had to get her to get rid of it. If it was born I couldn't go about life knowing my own flesh and blood was around somewhere. Tell her she can't, a part of me said. But how can you tell her to kill your own child? another part of me screamed. André Bernard, be practical and act quickly or you're ruined, another voice screamed.

"Why? Did you want to have a child?" I asked as calmly as I could.

"No. But now since I'm carrying one, I'm going to have it."

"What am I supposed to do?" I asked stupidly.

"You can do whatever you like," she said.

"But it was an accident," I said, defending myself. I was angry with her. I hadn't been reckless in my desire for her. It wasn't my fault that the latex had given way.

She shrugged.

"Would you marry me?" I asked, thinking far ahead of myself and shrewdly. An idea had occurred to me.

"Yes," she replied, her eyes shining.

I needed to think some more. It was plausible, though unlikely, that having this baby was a ploy to get me.

"But if I were married to you right now, I still wouldn't want a child."

"You wouldn't?"

"No, I couldn't afford it, for one thing. I've just embarked on a career. I have loans. Can you afford a child?" I asked.

She didn't respond immediately. I had to play my cards very close to my chest. One false step and she might change her mind. I could see that she hadn't thought about raising a child—her reaction had been emotional. Then her face hardened.

"You don't afford children. I am having this one because I'm pregnant."

"Yeah, but wouldn't you want to give your child the best? Wouldn't you want to be settled in life? After all, how old are you?"

"Twenty-nine."

"There you go. You have plenty of time."

Then I sat back and said nothing more. I drank my soup and wore a mask on my face. I had to pretend that I was capable of handling all outcomes. She had to hand herself over to me and trust me. I wanted her to think I wasn't scared of anything that might happen, that I'd be happy to marry her if she had the kid except that I didn't think it was a smart idea. If she thought that way, then I thought I could persuade her to end the pregnancy.

She started saying something about wanting to be a mother. It was the kind of thing all women said, so I didn't pay attention to her. I nodded a lot, but inside I was thinking if she really had this kid, I would actually have to marry her. I couldn't cope with the idea of a child born on the wrong side of the blanket. My son, a bastard. My son, going to some lousy public school with a secretary for a mother. I'd be paying for this for the rest of my life.

Living my life with Martha. I would have affairs, I decided. I didn't owe her anything. I only owed the kid.

"How far do you think you are into this pregnancy?" I asked and then felt dumb. I knew when the condom had burst. It was the night of the office party.

"A couple of weeks. I'm going to the doctor this week."

"Just for a checkup?"

"Yeah, just a checkup."

"You should think some more about what I said. Do you really want a baby now?"

"I'll think."

I paid for lunch and we left the restaurant. On the walk back to the office, she put her arm in mine. I wanted to remove it. I was not ready to walk around linked with this woman in broad daylight. But I had no choice. She was nurturing my gametes, and that gave her the offensive right to touch me like this. In a familiar fashion, as if I belonged to her, not Nathan. It was like slavery.

"I haven't seen Nathan all day—have you?" I asked her.

"He called in to say he was taking the day off."

So he hadn't received my e-mail. I wondered if I was supposed to go with Martha to the doctor. I decided I should offer. I was sure that if I feigned concern, I was much more likely to be able to manipulate her into terminating the pregnancy.

"When is your doctor's appointment?"

"At four in the afternoon on Wednesday."

"Would you like me to come?"

"Would you?"

"Yes, of course."

Martha was a parasite, a leech. She wanted to marry one of the guys in the bank. Have a cushy life. You're a jerk for thinking like this, André Bernard, she's carrying your offspring, another part of me said.

We had reached the offices. She had resolutely clung to me till we reached the glass doors on our floor. I gently unlinked my arm and made my way to my cubicle. I surfed the Internet to find out how late we could wait before the procedure. I needed to know exactly how much time I had. Down to the last day. I opened my miniplanner. There was nothing written in it for the future except "Dad leaves" under Saturday.

This was it, then. No more "N," or "S," or "Sweet Justine." Now there would be a three-month stretch of time, interminable and full of anguish—at the end of which I wrote "D-Day." If Martha didn't go in for the procedure by D-Day, then I was in for the long haul.

I was unable to get an honest bit of work done the rest of the day. I sat around clicking open programs on my computer like Paint and Object Packager and drawing tulips on my screen. Time was dragging. It was only three-thirty. I opened my "Time warp" spreadsheet and wrote "Nine months in Martha's womb" = "André Bernard Junior." I started shaking uncontrollably.

I went to the bathroom in the hope that I would throw up. But I wasn't sick and I didn't throw up. My body quivered and quivered. I came back to my cubicle. I hoped nobody had noticed. I was like a rattlesnake. Tad started talking to me without provocation. He told me he was going to propose to his girlfriend in a year. I breathed deeply and tried to listen to him in the hope that it would calm me. I decided to leave at five-thirty that day. As I was getting ready to leave, my phone rang. It was Nathan.

"Do you have a few minutes to meet tonight?" he asked.

From his tone I couldn't tell if he had forgiven me. But the very fact that he had called was forgiveness in one way.

"Yes," I replied.

"When can you do it?"

"Now?"

"Okay. There's an Irish pub on Third Avenue near where you live. I think it's called O'Shea's. Do you know what I'm talking about?"

"Yes."

"I'll see you there in about half an hour."

I left my cubicle. On the way out, I passed Martha, who raised her head from her desk and looked at me expectantly.

"I'll call you," I said and continued walking out. My stomach had been in knots all day. The row from my spreadsheet where I had written "André Bernard Junior" kept flashing my head. Madhu's voice started echoing in my head as well. She'd said, "Babies are born in nine months."

I got to O'Shea's before Nathan. I ordered myself a whiskey and sat at the bar. I ordered another whiskey and another till the crisis felt dimmer and duller. Nathan walked in fifteen minutes late and sat down on the stool beside me. He looked as if he hadn't slept. He'd aged years.

"I had to sleep at a friend's. Sybil wouldn't let me in at home."

"I'm sorry."

He looked into my eyes for the first time since my revelation. He was searching. I looked back into his. I silently implored him to listen.

"How have you been?" he asked.

"Martha is pregnant with my child and is insisting on having it," I blurted. I hadn't had any intention of telling Nathan about it. That was the last thing he needed to know. I should be plying him with apologies for having slept with his wife.

He had expected me to say anything but that. He shook his head. He looked at me with disbelief.

"Shit's hit the fan. Your André has landed himself in a lot of trouble," I said, continuing to talk. It was easier for me to talk about myself as another person. It was easier for me to be honest that way.

"I'm cursed. I'm jinxed. Things that happen to people over years have happened to me in a month. I was sleeping with my boss and his wife. I got the secretary pregnant. I'm going to be a father." I was getting hysterical.

Nathan's eyes narrowed. He was alarmed at my lack of composure. He patted my back and said, "Calm down."

I was overwhelmed by the gesture. He cared. His heart hadn't turned to stone.

"I'm paying for the mess, Nathan."

We were silent for a few seconds. I touched his lips with my finger. The bartender saw me and looked away.

"Nathan, I'd still follow you to hell and back. Nothing's changed for me." I was doing all the talking. It was necessary.

He stared at my face and my eyes. A part of him believed me in spite of what had happened. A part of him still had faith.

"I'm still letting it all sink in, André."

I nodded and said a silent prayer in my head. I had imagined worse than this.

"So tell me the full story with Martha," he said.

I told him what had happened earlier in the day. I told him all the things I'd felt. I asked him if he had any suggestions.

"I don't know. I haven't dealt with this before. Sybil might have an idea or two, but at this point she's not going to share it with us."

"Should we talk about it? About yesterday?" I asked.

"Unless you have something you want to tell me, I don't see the point."

"You're right. There's no point," I said, then continued anyway. "I did it partially to get closer to you, though that's no excuse. I've been drifting. I've been going along with whatever comes my way. I didn't have a reason not to. You were a married man."

"I know, but she was my wife," he said between clenched teeth.

"It's wrong. It's wrong. Punish me."

"I've been doing a lot of thinking since yesterday. I've been thinking about Sybil and you."

I flinched when he said "Sybil and you," making us one unit.

"Hmm, hmm," I said.

"I've thought about myself as a result. I need to tell you something, André," he said.

I waited.

"About eight years ago when I was living in London I saw a bum on the street. It was a wet night. He was a young and good-looking guy, though you could easily have missed it under his stench and torn clothes. I took him home with me. I ordered some take-out and ran a hot bath for him. When he was done, I threw away his tattered clothes and gave him some of mine. After he had eaten I made him drop his pants and bend over. When I was done with him, I handed him an old overcoat and drove him nine miles away from where I lived and left him on the street. He opened the car door and said, 'Thanks for the meal and these clothes.' I drove off."

I didn't know what to say. I didn't know what I was expected to say. I didn't say anything.

"I'm going to leave Sybil. I would like to live my life with you, André. We'll need to work a lot of things out. Think about the story I just told you and tell me if you'll take me for a partner. Don't decide today. Take your time."

"Right," I said, utterly numb. The little grasp I had on life was slipping away from me. I had tried getting used to the idea of Nathan leaving me forever, then I had to get used to the idea that I'd impregnated the secretary, and now I had to consider getting married to Nathan. An image of myself in a white wedding gown flashed in my head. We'd marry in a park. I shook myself out of it.

"Can we go to your place? This bar is rather impersonal," Nathan said.

"My father is visiting."

"I know that. Let's take him to dinner."

"All right."

We took my father to a Thai restaurant in the village. I couldn't get the image of Nathan and the bum out of my head. I imagined the bum as particularly destitute and suffering. I imagined Nathan cruel and even more good-looking than he was now. I drank two glasses of white wine rapidly. The whiskey and wine had helped in facing all the hell that had broken loose in my life. I was happy when I was drunk. Nathan and my dad did most of the talking. My father assumed that New York was a small town and that everybody knew one another. He asked Nathan if he'd met Justine through me. Nathan said he hadn't.

"Very nice girl. She was here alone from France. Very brave."

Nathan looked at me. I knew what he was wondering. I looked down at the floor in confirmation. He might as well know everything I'd been up to and everyone I'd been in to. In love there could be no shame, I decided.

The night was pleasant and we walked back home. Nathan walked us back to my place. He walked between my father and me and lightly touched my hand every now and then. We had not been on talking terms for only a day, but it had felt like an eternity. Talking to him again felt like returning home from a long and dangerous journey. I was incredibly optimistic now, walking with the two men on earth I most loved. A sudden image of Martha feeling her womb at night intruded into my brain. It took over all my emotions. My chest constricted, and the muscles of my stomach tightened. No, I thought, she's not going to get in the way of my whole life.

By the time my father and I went to bed, the alcohol had worn off. I could clearly think of Nathan again. I had haunting dreams of him all night. I dreamt of him wandering around ghettoes and bringing back young men to his house, feeding them and stripping them. Then I dreamt of him going to hell and suffering from a plague. Beside him in hell there was a woman with a large stomach. She was touching the area below her navel, and the skin there had creases. I put my hand on it and felt little feet kicking. My child was being born in plague and in hell, and I had to get him out of there at the cost of my life. I caught the plague and woke up from my nightmare furiously scratching the skin on my neck and chest.

"Mother-fucking serotonin and brain stem," I said loudly to the room when I got up. My skin was still itchy. I took a shower and put on a CD. I played Wagner, but my father slept right through the din.

I wondered why when most men proposed on their knees with a gold ring, Nathan had proposed to me with this sordid tale. Why was he testing my love? I had loved him because he was good, and now he wasn't. And I still loved him.

When he woke, my father asked me for directions to the Met. I wanted to take the day off and take him, but there was too much work. I gave him a subway map and drew directions on it.

At work I did things without being aware of doing them. The world around me was going on like a spool of film; it didn't affect me. I was living in my own world contained in my head. I needed sound advice. From a woman. To hell with discretion. I e-mailed Madhu. I wrote, "I got someone pregnant. Now she's insistent on going ahead with it. What should I do?"

After I clicked the Send button on my screen I remembered what Madhu had told me about not being able to have kids. Here I was trying to get rid of mine. I felt low and cruel, a cad. All you're interested in is your own measly happiness, André Bernard, I said to myself.

I had an e-mail back in seconds from her saying, "Shit."

I wrote back, "Did I neglect to mention yesterday that I had my confrontation date with him and his wife?"

Madhu called me.

"André, what is going on with you?"

"Everything. They know now. She's not talking to either of us."

"And he?"

I looked around the room. Tad was absent as usual. There was nobody around.

"I think he'll be okay. Thank God."

"Who did you get pregnant?"

"The secretary."

"What?"

"Yes."

She was silent. I could imagine her bright black eyes judging me.

"What are you going to do?"

"Marry her," I said. I didn't mean it, but I wasn't joking. I wanted Madhu to come up with a solution.

"You're not serious."

"Do I have a choice?"

"Have you tried reasoning with her?"

"It's not working. Any suggestions?"

"Let me think, André."

"Thanks."

"By the way, I'm coming into town tomorrow."

"Let's meet for dinner. My dad is with me."

"Okay. I'd love to see him. How is he?"

"He's well. Getting old. It scares me."

We made arrangements. I told her we'd meet her at her hotel in Newark and then go to a restaurant nearby. I took out my mini-planner and wrote "dinner M" under Wednesday. In the afternoon there was the doctor's appointment, so I wrote "M." They were both "M," so I changed the initials to "Mu" and "Ma." It was Tuesday and my day was blank.

I buzzed Martha and asked her if she would meet me for a quick drink after work. I wanted to appease her and keep her soft. I felt like the slimiest man on earth. An insect.

"I'm not drinking anymore. It's not good for the baby," she said.

I thought quickly. "Of course—I meant juice," I said.

"I can do that," she said.

I wrote "Ma" in my miniplanner under Tuesday evening, and I filled in Monday night with "N and Dad," just for the record. I could feel my health coming back.

When I got to my desk I had e-mail from Nathan saying that Sybil had gone off to Yoshi's. Rocks formed in my throat. This was it. If she told him about me, he'd have me fired. It was a matter of days, I was sure. He wouldn't need to even come up with an excuse if he didn't want to. I started working on my résumé. I sent an e-mail to the headhunter who had found me the job, asking him to keep a lookout for me. I told him I was beginning to look around.

The threat of losing my job came as a great relief. It got my mind off Martha, the child, and Nathan's evil story. You can't keep calling it a child, it's barely a fetus, I thought, reprimanding myself. No, a glob of tissue, undifferentiated in form and gender.

At five-thirty, when it was just about decent to leave, I asked Martha to leave with me. I told her I didn't want to keep my dad waiting at home too long.

"I'd love to meet your father."

"He's not doing terribly well. We had a couple of strenuous evenings, and he needs rest now."

"Maybe some other night," she suggested.

"Yeah. Yeah, that would be nice," I said.

We went to the nearest Au Bon Pain and parked ourselves. I wanted to ask her if she'd thought about it again. But I didn't want to push her—it wouldn't go down well. I wanted to threaten her. I won't pay a penny, I wanted to say, let's see your secretarial job get him a decent standard of living.

"Martha, I've been thinking of nothing but this. This is really not the right time to have a baby," I finally let out after we had got our drinks.

"It's the right time for me. That's why I conceived."

"It was a mistake, Martha."

"It was a sign from God. We even used a prophylactic. It was meant to happen."

I was seething inside. The idiot thought that this was divine intervention, fate. She actually believed that her happiness and her pathetic desire to have a kid were important enough for God to play a part in this. She thought that her life mattered to the heavens. Up there, they didn't even give two bits about entire cities burning down in fires. They didn't care about a whole nation of Bosnians or about widespread diseases like AIDS, so why would they care about getting her pregnant? She wanted to make her life more palatable by fooling herself into believing someone cared, someone no less than God. But I couldn't explain any of this to her. She was not on the same wavelength as me, she wouldn't understand. Nathan would have understood. Even Sybil. And Madhu, of course. And my friend John in Seattle. This was going to be my new litmus test in life. People who had a particular sensibility and could appreciate certain ways of thought. These people were my community.

"Martha, by saying that it was fated to happen, you're giving up all responsibility for life. You're saying you're no longer a free person. You're saying you didn't have a choice."

"I was never for choice except in the case of rape or danger to the mother's health," she replied.

"That's not the choice I was talking about," I said quietly.

I wanted to shake her up. How could she think it was a good idea to raise a child without a father, or a reluctant father? How could she insist on having my child against my wishes? And if the kid did badly and dropped out of school, did drugs, what was she going to tell him? That it was all fated to happen? I wouldn't let it. If he were born, then I was going to take all responsibility. I needed to get a lawyer and find out the legal ramifications of things. I imagined there would be some. They might not give me custody, but I wanted rights. In another city they might discriminate against me because I was gay, but this was New York. Men could marry men here, and women women—even if it wasn't a legal marriage. A man could even turn himself into a woman and then marry a man, or a woman.

"So, are we still going to the doctor tomorrow?" I asked.

"Yes."

"Okay."

I got out of my chair and helped her with her jacket. Then I put her in a cab and walked home to meet my dad. On my walk back home, my heart swished and swooshed loudly inside me. If she had the baby, I wouldn't want him (I assumed it would be a son) to grow up under her influence. I'd take him to the woods and teach him how to play sports. I'd talk to him about things in this world that really mattered. I knew Nathan would be a good influence on the little guy. He'd teach him how to paint. We'd both teach him math. Martha could do whatever the hell she wanted. I hoped he didn't get her brains. Or look like her. I wanted him to be in my image. I would name him Camille. He could then decide if he would be a boy Camille or a girl Camille. If Martha wanted to name him something else, then he would have two names. I wouldn't give in to living with her. This was New York at the beginning of the new millennium. The kid wouldn't be ostracized for not being the son of married parents. He wouldn't be teased because his father was a fag. No one would really call him a bastard. All the other kids would probably think he was really hip for having a name like Camille and having a gay dad.

I could feel lumps in my throat as I imagined him grow up a little and ask me why his mother and I weren't married.

"Why are you living with Uncle Nathan?" he'd ask.

He wouldn't ask me all this because he wanted me to be married—he would ask me this to know why I had been inconsistent. I would have to explain how I got a woman pregnant if I really liked men. It might confuse him, and Martha would add to his confusion. She might even tell him about Sybil (it would probably be in the public domain by then), and he would be disappointed by his father's lack of restraint. He'd want to hero worship and respect his dad, but he would have to reconcile everything he knew about his father into a cohesive story, and it would prove to be a strain.

How could a child ever understand that his father was only a child himself when he became a father?

Camille would end up a head case, and he'd need therapy at the age of seven. I wanted to lie down on the road and let a speeding car drive over me on Park and Thirty-third.

I knew this was unhealthy. I was getting attached to the life growing in Martha's womb. It would cloud my judgment and prevent me from convincing her thoroughly to put a cruel and necessary end to things. I also had to make my intentions known to Martha. Since being nice hadn't helped any, I might as well resort to open threat and unscrupulous manipulation.

I thought of Martha screaming in the delivery room. I wondered whether she'd need to remove her labia ring when she delivered. How could a woman with a mouse tattoo and a nipple ring be the mother of my child?

By the time I got back home, in less than twenty minutes, I had changed from an irresponsible rake who never meant badly toward anyone into a scheming scoundrel. Now I was not beyond any kind of mind game that I could possibly play with her.

That evening I took my father to watch a 3-D movie at the IMAX theater. I wanted to see my father being a boy. It was necessary. I couldn't stop thinking of Camille. In my mind, I called him Kid. Sometimes I had conversations with him in my head. I'd say, "Hey, Kid, did you know that Papa was a very bad boy till you were born?"

I dreamt of hell again that night. This time it looked remarkably like heaven. It was clean and antiseptic. I was in a chamber with a steel maze of some sort, and all the various joints, hoops, and walls of the maze were clicking shut with a locking kind of noise. Martha, Madhu, me. Nathan, me, Sybil. Sybil, Yoshi, me. An airtight compartment in which I was trapped.

Everything was beyond my control. I was a puppet, and in my dream all these people had formulated some grand scheme so that no matter how far I thought I'd gone, I found myself facing the same locked walls of the maze. I threw myself into a corner of the maze and sat down ready to accept anything: starvation, death, a life without sleep. I became perfectly apathetic toward myself. Then I caught sight of Camille in a stroller. He was outside the maze. I had to get out immediately. I had to escape and embrace him. He was mine. He alone was mine. But the maze was locked firmly shut. Its steel hoops formed a closed circle from which there was no out. Eternity, repetition, and sameness were the only possibilities in the world of the maze. I could not break the cycle. I shot myself in my dream. I let out a cry in my sleep. It woke me up. And Dad.

"Are you all right, son?" he mumbled.

"Yes," I said patting his head.

"Who is Nathan?" He asked.

"Who?" I asked stunned.

"Nathan."

"Nobody," I said.

He went back to sleep. He had met Nathan—had he forgotten? I wasn't going to remind him. Dad had met the most important person in my life and not realized it. I sat upright. My mind was playing tricks on me. I was sure I had dreamt of Camille, the images were vivid. But between the time I dreamt of Camille and the time I dreamt of shooting myself, I had cried "Nathan." I could not remember that part of the dream. Maybe Camille and Nathan were one. My whole universe was like a black hole in my heart. It swallowed everyone I was close to—my father, Nathan, and Camille. I had to separate them all over again from one another. I would never be able to shoot myself in real life if Camille was around. I would live because I had a son. No torture would be too much to go through if I knew I was going to see him again. I could never lose hope. My son would be my sun, my light. I was shaking. I had to stop doing this. I already loved Camille more than everything else in the world put together. Real life was going to be nothing like this. He'd be a mediocre and disappointing son. He might even be slightly dull, or even dim. He might never love me. And even if he did, he'd just go about his own life eventually. Call me occasionally and check in on me. Give me grandchildren who were vaguely disrespectful or just distracted. It would be the Year of Our Lord 2035 and I would die. But even thinking like this did not help me detach myself from Camille. I had no perspective.

I eased myself back into a horizontal position and managed to sleep again.

In the morning I gave my father a kiss on the cheek before I left for work. I said, "I love you, Dad."

I hadn't talked to Nathan since Monday night. As soon as I got to work, I asked if he'd eat lunch with me. I wanted to talk to him before taking Martha to the doctor. I was taking a half day so that I could go home after the appointment. Dad and I were going to Newark to meet Madhu for dinner.

I was able to concentrate on work again. If Martha decided to keep the child, then she could. I could live with it. The pressure was off. I had not consciously reached the decision. But I just knew it. Nathan and I sat on a bench in Bryant Park during lunch. I told him about my talk with her the previous evening.

"She's not yielding," I said. At this point I was merely reporting. My brain was tired. I didn't know that I wanted her to yield.

"Damn. Why couldn't you have gotten Sybil pregnant instead if you had to? She's going off with Yoshi, I think."

"Yoshi will fire me if he finds out about Sybil and me."

"No, he won't."

"Of course he will."

"Yoshi isn't that kind of guy, André."

I raised one eyebrow questioningly.

"Yes. And I'm sure."

"We're going to the doctor in a few hours," I said. I didn't feel much relief at hearing that my job was safe.

"I think she'll come around, André. She'll terminate."

I felt a sharp pain in my stomach. I imagined that Camille would have straight sandy hair like mine, and it would flap around when he walked.

"He's my son, Nathan—I can't let my son die," I said.

Nathan grabbed me by the shoulder and shook me hard.

"André, it's a fetus. A fetus. It doesn't even have feet and hands yet. It has no thought. It's a bunch of cells just like a lot of other cells in your body or mine or Martha's."

I stared back at him. It was too late. I couldn't give my child up.

"Nathan, he's my son, Camille. Even if he's a girl, he can be Camille. I'm not crazy. I've thought about him too much."

Nathan's shoulders fell. His entire face surrendered to me. He knew what I was talking about, and he understood that nothing could be done about it.

"Martha's dumb, Nathan. My son is going to be dumb," I said, lightening up and laughing.

"Martha is nice in a lot of ways. She's not brilliant, but she's bright in her own way. He'll be all right."

"You'll teach him things, won't you, Nathan?"

"I'll teach him everything I know, André. He's yours."

I knew then that Nathan was of my flesh and blood and bones and heart. He was my other half. He completed me and made me whole. The world was suddenly clear like a crystal, hard and shining. My father, Nathan, and Camille. Everything else was noise.

"Nathan, can we live the rest of our lives together?"

"Yes."

We got up from the bench and walked to the office. We didn't say anything to each other. We didn't need to.

I worked for another hour and then took Martha to the doctor. I didn't need to act with her any more. I would tell her in due course that I was gay and I was going to live with Nathan. We'd support her in every way. Once upon a time I had been attracted to something in her. So had Nathan. We'd open up our friendship to her again.

As I flipped through *Vanity Fair* in the doctor's office, I felt at peace for the first time in weeks. A mother and her little child were next in line after Martha. The child must have been around ten. I started talking to him. I showed him photographs of cars from *Vanity Fair* and made noises of machines. I asked him what he liked to study. I made faces so that he laughed. It was simple to make him happy. It was simple to be happy. Even with a complicated life.

Then Martha walked out of the office. I got up and walked toward her. I put my arm behind her shoulder as we went out into the street.

"Everything in order?"

"Yes. The doctor says I should come back in a few weeks."

"Can we call the child Camille?"

"That's a nice name," she said, looking at me and smiling.

"Martha, we need to talk. I can't marry you."

"I didn't think so."

I had expected a scene. I hadn't thought she'd let go so easily. She was radiant and happy. She held her stomach lightly as we walked along. I knew she loved Camille—she was carrying him.

"Had you already given it a name?" I asked.

"No, I wanted to see the doctor first."

"So Camille is really okay?"

"Yes, it is." She was smiling again. I felt warmly toward her. She was carrying my child. I might even be willing to let her live with me while she's pregnant, I thought. And maybe even later. It would be best for Camille to have a single home. And Nathan wouldn't mind. I was sure.

"I'd like to be completely involved in every way," I said.

"With what?"

We were standing on the corner of Park and Seventy-ninth Street. I gripped her shoulder more firmly and placed my other hand on her stomach.

"I love him already, Martha. More than anything else in this world."

She touched my face and gave me a kiss on the lips.

"That makes two of us," she said.

"So can I be involved?"

"I'll think about it," she said.

I walked her home, since she lived in the area. Then I stopped at the Barnes & Noble near her apartment and went to the Child Care section. I bought two books, one called *Do's and Don'ts During Pregnancy* and another called *Even in the Womb Your Child Can Appreciate Classical Music*. Then I took the subway home. We would play Mozart at home during the later days of the pregnancy. Camille would appreciate little Amadeus more than some boring forty-year-old composer.

My father and I went to meet Madhu. They had met once before during Junior Parent's weekend when my father had visited me. They chatted like old friends. He told her he had seen Indian miniature paintings at the Met that day and had liked them. Every once in a while she discreetly squeezed my hand.

The next day I decided to go in to the office to wrap up some crucial things and then take the rest of the day off to hang out with my father. I got home by noon, and we went to Coney Island. I had not seen much of New York myself, and it gave me an opportunity to do things with him. I toyed with the idea of telling him about Camille, but then decided I would cross that bridge when I got there.

The rest of the week passed uneventfully. On Friday, Nathan, my father, and I went to see an Italian mobster movie that made us all laugh. Saturday came quickly, and it was time to take my father to the airport. I called Martha after that to see if she wanted to get dinner. She agreed. I spent the rest of the day reading about pregnancy and childbirth. I thought of suggesting prenatal yoga classes so that Martha could deliver in a squatting position.

We would live in harmony, Nathan, Martha, and I. I would sound Nathan on my ideas. But I was sure he would agree. Martha was already in love with me, and she'd slept with Nathan before, so she must have liked him. I was almost looking forward to seeing her by the time we met. We had arranged to meet on the Upper West Side. We went to a Greek restaurant.

Once we were seated, I got to the point right away. There was no time to waste—we had to get started on the plan.

"I am glad you agreed to name him Camille."

"I like the name," she said matter-of-factly.

"Do you want a boy or a girl?" I asked. I wanted a boy.

"I'd prefer a girl. But I wouldn't mind a boy."

"Martha."

"Yes."

"I'm gay. I'm in love with Nathan."

"Nathan."

"Yeah."

"Good God." I was relieved by her coolness. Things were going to work my way.

"Look, Martha, I've thought a lot about this. I think we should live together."

"You just said you were in love with Nathan," she said.

"I mean all of us. You, me, Nathan, and Camille."

"I'm not going to live with Nathan. And I'm going to live with you only if you marry me and are truly my husband."

"Why? You like Nathan—you've even slept with him. I'll be a good father. Nathan will be a good role model. You'll have your freedom and two nannies in the house."

"And what if I meet a man who loves me and wants to marry me?"

"You'll marry him," I said, as if it were not a problem.

"Will Camille come with me, or will he stay?"

"He can stay. Or he can split time with both of us."

"So I stay with you guys and we all live together. You don't marry me but you take on the role of the child's father. Then if I find someone, I can leave and you and Nathan will raise him. And I can see the baby on the weekends?"

I nodded. She was coming around to the idea. She played for a few seconds with the stem of her water glass. Beads of precipitation had formed on the glass, and she rubbed her finger on it. Then she spoke. At first slowly, then with gathering momentum.

"Fuck you, André. You think I have nothing better to do than hang around as your fag hag? My baby and I are not going to accommodate ourselves to your life with Nathan. It was bad enough that I fell in love with a jerk like you, but you're truly the most selfish pig I've ever seen. I've had enough. I was crazy about you, so I didn't get out of your life fast enough when I saw the signs that you weren't in love with me. But I'll be damned if I'm putting myself through any more of this. The baby is mine, and you're going to have nothing more to do with it." She had been speaking so rapidly she was out of breath. She held the edge of the dinner table and stood up.

"Martha," I said. I was afraid of her. Afraid she'd leave. Leave with my Camille.

"I am going, André. And don't call me or get in touch till you've figured out why you're an asshole," she said.

The hostess came to our table to take our order. Martha got up abruptly and walked past the hostess.

"Is everything okay?" the hostess asked, looking at me.

"No," I said.

"Well, would you like something to eat?" she asked in a curt voice, reminding me that they were running a business.

"Actually, I'm sorry, I have to go," I said. I fumbled through my pocket and pulled out a five-dollar bill, which I left on the table. My first instinct as I stepped out onto the sidewalk was to rush to Martha's home and talk to her. But I held back.

No one had said such harsh things to me before. Or if they had, I hadn't listened, because it wasn't important. Martha was still not important. But Camille was. I had to be careful. I walked down Broadway. It was chilly, and my canvas coat was not quite enough, but being physically uncomfortable reminded me of the discomfort I was feeling within myself. I trudged slowly. Memories of my childhood floated in and out of my head, along with images of Nathan and Sybil. I wished suddenly that I could see Sybil, just smile with her and have some of the old moments back. She had been lovely. Why had things changed?

It had been only a day since I had seen Nathan. But ever since I had married him in my own mind I felt incomplete without him. I felt as if I should return to him. I hadn't made plans to see him. I passed a pay phone and stopped. I fumbled through the six pockets of my coat looking for a quarter and eventually found one. I picked up the handset and put the coin in. But then I hesitated. What was I doing? I had to think by myself. I couldn't keep running away from facing the consequences of everything I had done by burying myself in activities. I had affected three people's lives profoundly. I had broken a marriage, made a baby, hurt a woman's heart. In order to live with myself, I had to atone. Or come to terms in some other way. A lot of the damage was irretrievable, but I had to patch up what I could. I put down the handset and rotated the coin return wheel. It jingled down. I put my finger in the slot and took out the quarter and put it back in my pocket. I started walking again.

I had already reached the theater district. There were crowds everywhere. Between the Pepsi Cola sign on one building and the Ramen Noodle sign on another building on Times Square, there was a world all its own. An imaginary world of Broadway shows and the Marriott Marquis. The Morgan Stanley building flashed with electronic news. Tourists on the street were posing for photographs, oblivious to the frenzied pace of New York. A man in a purple apron stuck a postcard in my hand. I looked at it absent-mindedly. It said "Flash Dancers. Only $5." I threw it in the street. A small cell in my brain said, "You littered." I ignored it and walked faster. The crowds were getting on my nerves. They were busy forgetting themselves. They had come to New York to have a good time, leave their troubles behind. I wanted to return to a part of New York that belonged to me. To the natives. A neighborhood bar where the local drag queen was unwinding or a coffee shop where students wrote their term papers.

I turned onto one of the side streets and walked east. It was immediately calmer. My hands had gotten cold, so I put them in my pockets. I played with the stuff in my pockets. My little miniplanner was in one of them. I pulled it out and opened it. Each page had three days on it. The part I had opened had "S, N, Mu, Ma, N, S" written on the two pages that stared back at me. I couldn't even imagine how I had embarked on such a voyage of excess. Was it possible that it was just my biology? Faced with something to screw, I screwed. A man with a need to fuck everything, I said to myself. I rode with the idea for a while.

I walked crosstown on Forty-fourth Street past Sixth Avenue and then Fifth thinking about this. It was a fantasy. It wasn't true. I had been quite involved with some of the people I had fucked. I still loved Madhu. I had liked Sybil and been attracted to her. I was in love with Nathan. I had used Martha. It was shameful and bad, but that hardly made it only about sex. The random anonymous guy in the club was just that: a random anonymous guy in a club. Maybe I'd done him for the record. Or out of loneliness. He and Martha had been out of loneliness. The rest I'd cared about. I couldn't come up with any neat theories about my own actions. I had reached Park Avenue. I stood at the corner of Park and Forty-fourth for a second, debating if I should walk onto the little pedestrian pathway under the Helmsley Building and into the MetLife building and down Park or if I should walk down Lexington. I'd had my epiphany about Camille on Park. I decided to walk east till Lex, and then downtown.

By the time I reached home, I felt incredibly sad but calm. The past few months had felt as if I were living with a sort of gay abandon, in many senses of the word. I had been free. I had acted on the spur of the moment. If I felt like doing something, I had done it. My emotions for Nathan, Sybil, and Madhu had all been distinct, different. In some sense they couldn't be compared. But time was limited and you could be with only one person at a time, so you had to choose between them. I hadn't had to choose because of the way things were set up. The three of them were married. But it had still gotten out of hand. I remembered Sybil at brunch. Her face crushed, the corners of her mouth bitter and battered at the same time. She had loved me. And, at that moment, I had really known how much. But I'd let her get up and leave. I'd hurt her by being close, open, accessible and then suddenly letting her go. I felt as if I'd betrayed her. She'd been disappointed in me. I felt disappointed in myself. My heart was a faulty, unreliable instrument.

As soon as I got home, I opened the windows, though it was not warm inside. I let some air into my apartment, got my shoes and socks off, and sat at my desk. It reminded me of Sybil. No matter what happened, this beautiful physical object would always be there to remind me of her standing outside the furniture store in her red clothes, her perfume blowing in the air. I pulled out my miniplanner and got out a plain white sheet of paper and laid both on the desk. I had no way to solve problems except by reducing them to equations or columns in spreadsheets. Reducing human relationships along a time factor axis had helped initially in deciding what was important, but now I was in desperate need of some tools to set my life straight or not-so-straight.

I wrote "Sybil" and "André" at the top and made two arrows, one in each direction. Then I crossed mine out. She loved me. I didn't love her back as much. I wrote "Madhu" and made two arrows. We were on an even footing. I cared, she cared. I wrote "Martha" and crossed out the arrow going from me to her twice. I wrote "Nathan" and left the arrows intact. But what if I loved him more than he did me? I wrote a question mark in the direction going from him to me.

I called Sybil's work number late at night. I rehearsed what I'd say. I didn't know if the days that had gone by were enough for Sybil's anger to cool off. But I had to try. When the voicemail tone went off, I spoke into the mouthpiece, "This is to beseech you for an audience. I know I've been a jerk. I won't make excuses for myself. But we had something going, and I'd like to make amends."

Though it was past midnight, I wasn't sleepy. I opened a book of math problems that contained puzzles a professor at my university had put together for the graduate students. None of the solutions required much formal training. In a one-page preface to the booklet he had written, "The idea is to come up with a simple and elegant solution." I played for a while, then slept. Math was the only thing left that was perfect, clean. When I was ill as a child I would eat nothing but pizza. Math was like that for me now. It was an intellectual comfort food.

The next morning when I was busy typing up the final instructions for the new programmers we had hired, my phone rang.

The call had come through on an external line that went through Martha at the reception desk.

"Your boyfriend's wife," Martha said by way of introduction.

"André Bernard," I said.

"You called," Sybil said.

"Can we meet?" I asked.

"Tonight, same café where we first met, at seven."

"Thanks. I'll see you."

I returned to my typing with a feeling that air bubbles had burst in my head.

The café was close to work. I arrived early and sat down. I pulled out a piece of paper and worked on a triangle problem from the puzzle book that I'd gotten stuck on the previous night. I drew parallel lines and extended the interior angles of the triangle. I imagined it was a big house, the steeple of a church. Sybil would enjoy it. With her mathematician's mind and her interior designer's vision, she would solve it more quickly than me. That would cast a poor light on me. I could only give her a problem that I had already solved. I chuckled. My vanity was amusing even to me. I pulled out another sheet of paper from my briefcase and tried to remember another problem from the puzzle book. She came in without my noticing.

"Hello, André," she said.

I looked up. She wasn't smiling. She looked cold. I forced a smile.

"Nice to see you, Sybil," I said. She sat on the chair across from me without a word. I pushed the sheet of paper in front of her. She looked at the round coins I had drawn without much interest.

"It's a sweet problem. The solution is so beautiful it's like a poem," I said. She stared at the paper. I needed to draw her in. This was going to be difficult enough as it was.

"Look, Sybil," I said, forcing enthusiasm into my voice. I pointed to the coins and explained the problem. When I was done, I knew she had listened.

"But you don't know the number of coins," she said.

"No. Nor the exact shape of the table. Any regular shape will do," I said.

"Hmmm."

"Can I keep that paper?" she asked.

"Sure," I said and handed it to her. She folded it into two and slipped it into her purse.

"I'll call you tomorrow with the answer," she said. I smiled. We'd at least keep talking this way.

"Thank you for granting me an audience, Madame," I said, faking formality. I wanted to lighten the mood. She didn't smile.

"Sybil, seriously, I am sorry," I said. I felt lame. I was apologizing for something I didn't really want to change. So how could I be sorry? I was afraid she would turn her humid sarcasm on me now. But she kept silent. The lines of her lips drooped down as her smile faded.

"Sybil, I didn't mean to hurt you. I didn't mean any of this. It was impulse at the beginning, but then it was all beyond my control."

"You fell in love with Nathan," she said grimly. I nodded.

"It's okay. I mean, it's not okay. But," she paused, then said, "whatever."

"No it's not okay, and I should never have started anything with you, since I was already involved with Nathan," I said. She shook her head for a few seconds.

"It had to happen," she said.

"How so?"

"He spoke of you so highly that I knew I'd like you when I met you. He must have done the same with you. It would be a lot worse if he wasn't my husband, wasn't your boss. Do you see?"

A part of me, the inner brute that watched out for André, was relieved that she was talking this way, but the rest of me was perplexed.

"I don't see," I said.

"It's sort of within the family this way. It's like three people who were close and just didn't draw boundaries. You know how your friends' friends are your own friends, too. There's an instant bond," she said.

I stared dumbly. Within the family? Family meant Camille. Camille wasn't born. Camille was Martha's. Martha was not family.

"What's the matter, André?" she asked.

"I got a woman pregnant," I said. She had barely adjusted to the situation with Nathan. This would be too much. Her jaw tightened again. Her face got harder. I could anticipate her lips turning into a cruel, cold shape. But everything—the café, Sybil, even I—was receding away into a distance.

A huge white cloud imploded in my head. In silver, glittering letters it said "Camille."

Her face changed its shape again. She had grabbed my hand and was shaking it. "André, talk to me. Do you need an ambulance?"

"Huh?"

"André."

I blinked. My vision had gotten blurry for a moment, but now my eyes came back into focus.

"Sorry," I said.

"What happened?"

"I think I got dizzy."

"Are you all right?"

"It's the child," I said. I felt pins and needles in my head, as if it had fallen asleep. It took a minute to go away. Maybe it was I who was pregnant.

"Who is she?"

"Martha, the secretary. I had no feelings for her whatsoever. It was the night of the office party. I was depressed that neither of you could come home with me," I said.

"You're not like any man I know. You're an even bigger sissy than Nathan."

"I'm weak," I said. I lowered my eyes. I was aware that I was manipulating her. And mildly aware that it was necessary. With Camille around, especially a still-to-be-born Camille, I felt anything but weak. I felt immune to everybody. Emotionally invulnerable. Because almost all of me was vulnerable only to Camille. But when someone thinks you are weak, they forgive you.

"You are weak," she agreed.

"I called to say I want to be friends," I said.

"Friends?"

"There's been a lot of water under the bridge, I know."

The waiter interrupted us with my cappuccino.

"Would you like something?" he asked Sybil.

"Same," she said, pointing to my cup. He inclined his head and left.

"Sybil, we got involved because there was an instant bond," I said, repeating her words, then added, "that's still there."

"You have never used my name as many times before as you have in this one conversation," she said.

I shrugged.

"I have to think about it," she said. She said it the same way as Martha had said it at the doctor's. A chill ran down my spine. We sat in silence. I emptied three packets of sugar into my coffee and stirred it. I pulled out the spoon and licked the froth.

"How's Yoshi?" I asked. It was hard to say his name. Her eyes flickered a little. I felt the hair on my neck rise. I felt like I was at war and he was my enemy. I was jealous of him. It made no sense.

"He's all right. He's good for me right now," she said. I sensed that something else was on her mind. For a second I felt a different sort of affection for her. Something akin to the kind of concern I would have felt for John or my dad if they weren't well.

"Are you okay, Sybil?" I asked. It was the first genuine selfless moment I had had in days.

"I'll be all right. I need to see a shrink," she said. Her cappuccino arrived. She smiled at the waiter when he put her drink down in front of her. He smiled back. They had a moment. I looked away.

"I need to figure out why I keep falling for fags. Nathan was not the first one," she said.

"He wasn't?"

"Jason was bisexual, and Rich turned out to be a flaming queen later."

I'd never heard of these people. "I'm sorry," I said.

But she didn't hear me. She wasn't listening. Her eyes were looking far ahead, and she spoke as though I wasn't there.

"Is it something about me, or is it something about them?" she said.

We sipped our cappuccinos. I played with a packet of sugar. She was running her fingers on her cup. I saw that she had removed her wedding ring. After a while she said, "Yoshi and I are going away."

"Vacation?"

"Yes. To Hawaii. He says it will do me good."

I was silent. Who was Yoshi to barge into all of this overnight and decide what was good for her?

"He's helped me accept this," she said.

A part of me wanted to know how. But asking questions meant investing in the answers. I had to let go. There was a vestige of emotion—visceral emotion, irrational, jealous—left in me for her. I let it go. I said, "I'm glad."

We chatted for a little while about work, and then Sybil looked at her watch and said, "I have to go."

We paid and got out. On the sidewalk as we waited for a cab I said to her, "I hope you'll consider being friends."

"Maybe I'll call you when I come back, André."

Then she patted her purse and said, "Unless I solve your coin problem before that."

A taxi stopped in front of us, and I opened the door for her. She closed the door and the yellow cab receded into the traffic on Sixth Avenue and was lost in seconds.

I went home. I remembered a scene from a movie in which some characters were spat out of the stomach of a cockroach and emerged covered in a thick layer of slime. I felt as if that layer of slime were within me, somewhere between my body and my soul. All the people I'd been with who were associated with one another were touched by it. Nathan, Sybil, Martha. A little bit of me felt sick at the thought of the overlapping conjugation: Nathan-Sybil, Nathan-Martha, Nathan-Me. I felt a lot worse than I had felt face to face with them at the round table at the office party. Even confronting Nathan and Sybil at brunch had made me feel nervous, but not sick in this way. I could not understand it. It was almost as if the concept of it was far worse than the reality of it. Madhu and Justine were clean in my mind. I was grateful for having Camille. Even if he was only in my head.

If I could associate Nathan with a sick feeling in my stomach, I could associate anyone with a sick feeling in my stomach. It corrupted the love a little, it made life less wholesome. Only Camille was pure. He would never make me feel ill at my own humanity. If I still ended up with Nathan, I knew that something in our life would always be tainted. I, by myself, was already impure, tainted. But a partner who wasn't tainted in my eyes could heal me of everything. A life with someone who was tainted would mean a tainted life. Was I willing to have that? I did love him, but within my own fucked-up mind I had now seen him, briefly, coated with this slime that made me sick. Could love overcome that?

I felt like retching. I went to the bathroom. I hadn't eaten all day. Nothing came out. I brushed my teeth and then sat on my bed. My belt was still on. I pulled it off and then undressed. I sat back on the bed in my boxer shorts. I looked down at my chest. I checked to see if I had a paunch. I didn't. I got up and padded to the mirror at the end of the room and looked at myself. I stood with my side to the mirror and checked out my body. I had good skin without too much hair. My butt was round. I could see why Nathan had decided to pick me up. My shoulders were round and my pecs were strong. I could see why Sybil always placed her head on my arm. My glasses made me look intellectual, and my eyes were a hazel brown under them. Madhu had fallen for that. She had told me that my eyes looked luminous. Especially in the fading light of day. Even if life sucked, I looked good. It would never be tough to get laid. I thanked God for his small mercies. If only I could clutch at the things people liked about me, I could love myself again.

The more I tried being objective, the harder it was. I had to give myself a break. I needed to feel better. I could call Madhu. Or Justine. I rummaged through my drawer for the scrap of paper on which I'd written her number in Toulouse. It was around one in the morning there. I called.

"Allo," she answered. Underground dub music was playing in the background.

"Allo," I said, cutting off my "h." I continued, "Je suis André." It was all the French I could remember.

"André! 'Appy, I am 'appy," she said.

I couldn't do this. I could communicate nothing to this girl over a transatlantic phone line. I closed my eyes and remembered the colors of her clothes, the delicacy of her nose, the fine hair on her face.

"André, you come to Toulouse for 'oliday," she said.

"One day, one day."

It would be easier to write. She could find a translator. I felt sadness creeping in on me; the slime was dissolving in a brackish wave of hopelessness.

"I write," I said.

"Okay."

"Au revoir."

"Au revoir."

I hung up and was about to slump back in bed. I debated whether I should call Madhu. Her husband would probably be home. But since I hadn't done it before and would anyway be discussing my own problems, he shouldn't mind. But it felt like a crutch. I had to get out of this funk without running away. I hadn't been facing myself all these months—I'd taken refuge in whomever came my way. I padded back to the mirror and peered at myself.

"André Bernard, you're alone. Just the way your dad is alone even though he has you. And you'll be alone after Camille comes. But you'll love him in a more noble way than you've loved anyone else. You'll be alone even if you live with Nathan. But it's not that bad, because you've always been alone. Since the day you were born. Even if you didn't know it. Everyone else is alone, too. So it's not bad at all. And it's not a revelation. Just chill out, go to work, earn money, take a holiday to Greece, bring up your kid well, and relax. If you screw around forever, that's okay. And if you don't, that's okay. What happened was unfortunate, but you'll pay the price and then it will have been paid. It's good you'll take responsibility for your son. And for the first few months when he can't even bring his own hand to his own face, you'll feel something you have never felt before or will ever again feel. You'll talk Martha out of cutting you off from Camille, and if you can't convince her, the lawyers will figure out a way."

Saying these things to myself loudly calmed me down. My voice had filled the room and made me feel as if there were two me's: myself and I. We would help each other to smooth things out as best as possible.

The next morning I felt a new sense of purpose as I knotted my tie and dressed for work. I chose my yellow tie with kittens. Yellow was the color of sunshine and freedom. Of cheerfulness.

Martha was at her desk and seemed in a good mood. She smiled at me. I was amazed she'd found it in her to smile. I felt like she had a big heart.

"Martha, I'm sorry about the other day. I'd like to get together with you and have a chat. Can we have dinner sometime?"

She looked at me suspiciously. As if this was another trick I was trying to pull out of my sleeve. I couldn't blame her. But I was eager to come clean. My new life would be clean.

"I'm not trying to push any agenda. I'm really sorry about the way I've handled things."

"When do you want to meet?" she said.

"Whenever is good for you," I said. There was no need to do things immediately—that style of impulsive living had to end. I had to learn patience.

"Maybe this weekend?"

"Is Friday better, or Saturday?"

"Friday."

"Friday then. We have a date," I said. I felt determined to make things better. I smiled.

She didn't smile back.

I popped by Nathan's office on the way to my cubicle. He was reading the Wall Street Journal. I couldn't read his mood.

"Hi. How are you?"

"All right."

"Is Sybil talking to you?" I asked softly. Yoshi's office was the next one. I didn't know if he was in or had left for his vacation with Sybil.

"She is. She's not as angry anymore. She called me yesterday to arrange picking up some of her things. It was an amiable talk. She told me she saw you."

I nodded.

"Do you want to have lunch?"

"I can't. I have an appointment."

I waited for him to suggest an alternative, but he didn't. There was an awkward silence.

"Back to work," I said and waved him good-bye. He waved back. As I walked to my cubicle, I could feel my back getting tense. It was early morning and I was already upset by Nathan. As my computer booted and information about it flashed on my screen, I took a few deep breaths. I checked my voicemail. No one had called. There were no personal e-mails for me either. Only reports from the guys working on the risk management system. I had fallen back on some of the personal deadlines I'd set for myself on the project. I made a quick list of some of the things I had to do that day and plunged into work.

At three in the afternoon my stomach rumbled and I decided to run down for some lunch. I printed out the latest copy of the specs for the program and started reading it in the elevator. On the tenth floor, Botolph got in.

"How's it going, man?" he asked.

"Good. You?""

"How's that secretary chick on your floor?"

"Do you mean Martha? She's all right," I said.

"I heard you got it on with her?"

"Where did you hear that?"

"She told the secretary on our floor."

I regretted having told Martha about Nathan. Now everyone would know that, too.

"What else did she say?" I asked in a neutral tone.

"She says she's going to have your kid."

"She is," I said, in a way that could be interpreted as either a question mark or a statement.

"Man, you have to be careful around here. Some secretary hooks up with you and the next thing you're paying for her drug habits and some child you didn't want," he said. His eyes were gleaming. He was pretending to counsel, but his manners were sly.

I felt anger rise up to my head, and my nose and ears and face filled with blood. I wanted to hit him.

"That's my problem, dude," I said. A part of me noticed how cold I sounded, though I was ready to bust his face.

"Sure is your problem," he chuckled. The elevator came to a halt and opened. I walked out rapidly and got out of the building.

He'd gotten under my skin. I played baroque music in my head. First Corelli, then Vivaldi. I ate a sandwich sitting on the steps of the office building. A lot of people usually ate lunch there, but it was past lunchtime so it was quiet. I could hear water pouring from the fountain in front. Every time the wind blew, a spray of mist would hit my glasses. I liked it. It occurred to me that my own perception of myself had changed since I was young. I'd grown up in a relatively homogenous white community and had felt like everyone else. When I went to college I embraced the diversity around me and immediately felt comfortable in it. When I dated Madhu I quickly forgot the differences between us and noticed only the similarities. With my gay friend John and his friends, I laughed. The usual points of difference, the things that typically alienate people, like race and sexuality and economic status, had left little or no mark on me. Now I felt like an outsider to myself, a man on the fringe of society. Lots of people screwed around and screwed in the same circle—it wasn't that. It wasn't that my miniplanner was cluttered. The alienation was within. I finished my chicken parmigiana sandwich and walked back to the building.

I flashed my ID to the guard at the elevator bank. The ID was a security blanket. I felt emotional about the bank, its solidity, the identity it gave me. I waited for the elevator feeling ridiculous. Getting sentimental about a Japanese bank, a capitalist machine, was a clear indication I needed help.

Out of the corner of my eye I saw Yoshi showing his ID to the guard. I prayed the elevator doors would open and swallow me in. But that did not happen.

"Hi," he said curtly, coming up to me and looking at the wall. I turned around to face him and smiled.

"Hello, Yoshi, how are you?" I said.

"All right," he replied. I could read nothing from his small eyes, his shiny, smooth forehead.

"I saw Sybil last night. She speaks highly of you," I said.

He didn't respond. I felt committed to getting a reaction from him, turning him my way. He was with Sybil. My sweet Sybil, my ex-lover and friend. I needed him to like me. That way my friendship with Sybil would be smoother. We must have something in common if we had been with the same woman.

"Are you mad at me? You can punish me if you like," I said. Trying to be flippant and at the same time direct.

"Sorry, don't swing that way," he said and winked. I felt instant relief.

"I didn't mean it that way," I said.

"Sybil and I are going to Hawaii. I'll teach her to windsurf."

"I and me are going to roast in hell," I said.

The elevator beeped loudly. It was an express elevator to the tenth floor, after which it beeped at every floor. We still had seven more to go. Yoshi looked at me for a second and then said, "One has relationships. It's inevitable somebody gets hurt. So long as you don't kill anyone, you're not going to roast."

I remembered the antiabortion propaganda that Madhu and I had walked past. Fetuses in trash cans. My whole body broke into gooseflesh.

"Sybil told me about Martha," he said. Everyone in the bank knew.

He grabbed my shoulder and said, "Momentous things happen. Big wars, plagues, the institutional perpetration of crime.

Accept your human slips and be calm. Just try to be your best, and don't take everything so seriously."

The elevator let out a final beep and opened its doors. We walked quietly past Martha's desk. Was he imparting some Japanese philosophy? Or a windsurfer's delight in catching a wave and coasting? It seemed as though he felt so bad for me that he couldn't even disapprove. We reached his office.

"Thanks, Yoshi," I said.

"See you later," he said.

He'd talked to me like some old uncle. I could imagine Yoshi and Sybil having a conversation about how badly I'd screwed everything up. I felt as if I'd actually been there when Yoshi shook his head slowly and said "poor boy" before he poured himself a small cup of sake. In a way maybe it was good I'd made such a mess. It was easier to forgive someone who had erred so completely.

Back at my desk I pulled up my e-mail and started to write to John, "I've been a drama queen, but those days are over..."

It is the miracle of e-mail that small discrete packets of thought are transferred across the world in seconds. Tiny observations and huge emotions that one might never otherwise communicate are sent with a click to someone far away. John called me in seconds on my office line.

"André, honey," he said as soon as I picked up.

"John! I just sent you an e-mail."

"I just got it. I have something to say."

"What?"

"You've been with four women recently: Madhu, Sybil, Martha, Justine. And only one man."

"Actually, two. I didn't mention the other. One-night stand."

"Honey, are you sure you're gay?" he asked.

"Of course."

"When I started sleeping with men I stopped sleeping with women," John declared.

I didn't know what to say. I liked women.

"You could be bi, you know," he said. His voice was like almond paste—smooth, scented. He was not speaking in his usual excited style.

I didn't think of myself as bisexual. I bristled at the thought of it. It sounded like I didn't know what the hell was going on. As if I couldn't tell dick from not-dick.

"I'm not," I said, looking around the office to see if anyone was listening. Tad was not there, as usual.

"It's okay to be. It doesn't have to mean you're not monogamous."

"John, stop it. I know exactly what I am," I said, and I glanced behind my shoulder before saying, "And I'm not bi."

"All right, all right."

"What's it to you?" I said, suddenly getting irritated. Was it that he didn't want to accept me into that special circle—into the gay community? I was on the fringe of everything. Marriage, fatherhood, homosexuality. On the fringe, yet completely trapped.

"André, it's hard sometimes to accept that in oneself. I just wanted you to know that no matter who you sleep with or what you call yourself, you're my friend and I'll love you." I had hurt him.

"Are you all right?" I asked.

"I'm okay. Usual love problems."

"Tell me."

"Guy I was sleeping with has stopped returning my calls. I think he's seeing someone else."

"Oh, baby! Do you want to come visit me?"

"Hmmm." I could hear him thinking.

"It'll be a break," I said.

"I'll come."

"Check on tickets and let me know. Anytime is good."

"Can I meet Martha?" he asked.

"Sure," I said. It was odd he'd mentioned Martha over Nathan. I remembered the blow job he had given Nathan. I got utterly still on the phone. The silence was telling. He remembered it, too.

"Well, Nathan, too," he said. I heard a rush in his voice, an unnatural tension. Then he added, "But Martha is the mother of your child."

"We think it's mine," I said.

After all this, if Camille ended up looking like Horfmeister or Botolph or something, then we'd know he wasn't mine. I'd love him anyway, I decided. I liked the idea of being his father. He'd solve the coin problem I'd given Sybil by the time he was seven or eight years old.

"I'll go then. And call you back with dates," John said. We hung up.

Something in my chest lifted up after the talk with John. Or it might have been that I got more adjusted to the new crazy world. It was a less crazy world in some ways. I didn't need my miniplanner to keep track of whom I was seeing.

I worked some more on the specs and called Nathan in his office as the day drew to an end. Why had he hesitated in the morning when I had invited him to lunch? A sixth sense told me something was on his mind. I asked him flat out if he wanted to meet. After a moment's hesitation, he said he did.

We picked up pizza on the way to my house and ate at home. I put on a Beethoven CD and opened a bottle of white wine.

"André, I guess I'm not quite over the shock of everything," he said. His voice was even, unemotional. I stared at his face without saying anything. Sometimes it was hard to know what he was thinking or feeling. I could see a shiny fluid coating his eyes as he looked fixedly at something behind my left shoulder. He wasn't making eye contact.

I put my plate down and went beside him. I kissed his cheek.

"Are you all right?" I asked.

"I'll be fine," he said, continuing to stare at the point in deep space. A small part of me was desperate to have him back. Another part was a little less selfish—it was more concerned for him.

I knelt beside his chair and put my head in his lap.

"Talk to me, please. Yell. Shout. Beat me. Do whatever you have to," I pleaded.

"I'm just getting over it. I mean, I did love her. She was my wife. I'll miss her. And then, I felt betrayed."

He stopped. I had been rubbing his knee lightly. I kept rubbing it.

"I guess I feel like a total fool," he said quietly.

I was speechless. He was right.

Finally I said, "I was thoughtless. That much at least you should know. I didn't do it to make a fool of her or you or anyone else. And I've only made a fool of myself."

"I still love you, André. I'll get over it," he said.

We were quiet, and then I put away the food and we went to bed. He lay down and didn't turn around to spoon me as he usually did. I felt disconnected from him. I moved closer and hugged him. He put his hand on mine, but it was limp. It lacked the force that one needs to push through boundaries.

I couldn't sleep, so I lay still, my hand heavy on Nathan's stomach as I imagined the future. Camille would grow up and leave home. Nathan would be much, much older than me. At that time our age gap would be more obvious. I'd still be young and youthful. He'd have all white hair, and his skin would sag. He might even be in a wheelchair. I'd have to take care of him. Did I love him enough for that? Did I have enough strength? I didn't know.

On Friday evening after work, Martha and I went down to the Village. The night was damp and cold. She said she wanted a grilled cheese to cheer her up. It was hard to find a restaurant that wasn't ethnic—one that served regular American food but was not a diner. Eventually we found one on Thompson Street.

We chatted about work. I told her what had happened in the elevator with Botolph. I tried to tell her without attacking her for having told the other secretary.

"I told her not to tell anyone else," she said, looking upset.

I shrugged. "People talk. It's all right."

"It's not all right for me," she snapped at me.

"Well, then you shouldn't have spread the word," I said, getting irritated.

Now things had to be repaired again. I sighed. If anything was oppressive, this was. I was forced into conversations I didn't want to have. I couldn't get up and leave. This woman and I had to raise a baby together. I had to make it work—there was no choice.

"Martha," I said softly. I reached out and placed my hand on hers. I could feel a muscle in her hand trying to draw back. Not consciously, just by reflex. But she let her hand stay.

"I want to say that I realize what a jerk I was. And I'm not going to ply you with verbal apologies. You'll see that I'll be different. I care about the baby and what happens to you and me and us. We can't be together, but I want the baby to have us both. I want to be there when you need me. I hope you'll let me."

"So, what's the plan?"

"There's no plan. We'll see what happens. After the baby is born, you can decide. My house will always be open to you."

"You can get involved as long as you don't expect anything," she said.

"I want to be legally acknowledged as his father. I expect nothing else," I said.

"He should have a father. That's acceptable," she said.

"Thank you." I felt grateful. Even though he was mine. Mine by blood and DNA and right. She was still carrying him. And he was hers. No matter how hard that was for me, I had to respect it. "You're welcome," she said and smiled. It was her first full smile since she had told me about the pregnancy. It reminded me of one of our first dates.

After dinner we walked around the Village. Martha bought a pair of yellow sunglasses from a shop on St. Mark's Place. Then we took the uptown subway and I got off at Twenty-eighth Street. She rode it up.

On my home voicemail there was a message from Madhu to call her back. Her voice, usually calm and sweet, sounded full of panic. Her husband answered when I called.

"This is André. Is Madhu there?" I asked. I felt protective of her. I had an awful feeling he'd hurt her.

"Hold on," he said.

When she came to the phone, I could tell she had been crying.

"Madhu, is everything all right?" I asked.

"No."

"Tell me."

"My father died."

"I'm sorry." I didn't know what to say or ask. I wished I could be with her and hold her till she had cried herself out.

"His car just spun out of control on the highway. They rushed him to hospital, but he'd lost too much blood."

"Are you going to Texas?"

"Yes, the first flight out is tomorrow morning."

"Your mother?"

"She's been sedated. She was hysterical. The neighbors brought her to their home and gave her sleeping pills."

"Madhu, I love you. I'll always love you," I said all of a sudden. I wanted to be with her. I didn't want her to feel alone or lonely at a time like this.

She was crying uncontrollably again.

"When are you and Srini going there?" I asked.

"Srini can't come. He's got to go to a meeting."

I couldn't believe he wasn't going with her at a time like this.

"Should I fly down?" I asked.

"To Texas?"

"Yes. Tomorrow."

"That would mean a lot, André."

"I'll come. Give me the details."

After hanging up on Madhu, I left a message on Martha's work voicemail saying I had to go out of town because of a family emergency. I called Nathan at home. He didn't answer, so I left a message. Then I called my father. My heart started beating loudly as I dialed his number. I had spoken to him only once since he'd left. I was a horrible son.

It was not yet eleven. There was no answer. He was still at the restaurant. Or was he not at the restaurant? My heart filled with anxiety. I called the restaurant. After several rings, he picked up. His voice was raspy.

"Papa, it's me."

"André. What a surprise! Are you all right?"

"I'm fine. Are you keeping well? What's wrong with your throat?"

"Just a little cough. Everything is fine."

"I just wanted to chat."

"I'm still working. And after this I'm going for a walk with Shirley"

"I'm traveling tomorrow. I'll call you when I get back."

"God bless."

I sat down on the edge of my bed. I had broken into a sweat and was now feeling cold. I set the alarm for five in the morning and went to sleep.

My plane to Houston got in at the same time as Madhu's. We met at as we had arranged and took a cab to the hospital morgue. It was a forty-minute ride. She buried her face in my shoulder and cried. Her dark Indian face had gotten darker with all the crying. Big black circles hung from her eyes.

"I'm leaving him," she said between her sobs.

"Your husband?"

"Yes. He was awful when I heard about my father. He was unsupportive."

"Bastard."

"One marries for companionship if nothing else. If he can't stick with me through this, I'm not putting up with anything more."

I patted her hair. I knew that deep inside she was blinded by grief for her dad. This was incidental. There was nothing to say that could drive that grief away. Nothing anyone could do. I held her tighter in my arms. Her body convulsed as she cried, and I could feel tremors from her pass into me. It was like absorbing a current because I was grounded. I massaged whatever parts of her were accessible to my hands. In my mind I thought to myself, Madhu, I'm with you. And hoped that something inside her would hear it and draw strength from it.

We reached the hospital and went through the procedure for getting the body. Her mother would soon come with their neighbors. They were going to go through some Hindu rites at the electric crematorium. I was so busy running from hospital to Hindu temple to crematorium that I registered very little. Madhu and her mother were unable to stop crying. They were almost glazed over. I took care of all the logistics with one of the neighbors. I was mad at Srini for not being there for Madhu. I knew Nathan would have been there for me. In the end, the things that counted were things like this.

A priest from the temple came with us to the crematorium. He was wearing a thin white cloth that went between his legs and was tied at the waist. His chest was bare. A single white thread ran diagonally across it. He had so much chest hair that the thread sat on his hair and not on his skin. He muttered chants.

"Please step forward," I heard him say.

No one stepped forward. I looked around to see whom he was talking to.

"Please step forward," he said again.

I pointed to myself questioningly.

He nodded.

I looked at Madhu.

"In the absence of a son, the son-in-law should do the rites," he said.

I didn't know what to do. If no one else was going to do it, I would. But I didn't want to offend anyone. I looked over at Madhu again. She recovered from her state and realized what was going on. She nodded her head in affirmation.

I stepped forward. The priest brought my palms in front of him and placed some things in my hands. He asked me to bring the offerings to my head and press my forehead to my hand. I did as he instructed. Then he chanted some more.

"Your name?" he asked.

"André Bernard."

"Father's name?"

"François Bernard."

He prayed and in between his foreign words I heard "André Bernard" repeated a few times. "François Bernard" was repeated only once.

Then the rites were over.

"Don't tell my mother about that," Madhu whispered to me.
"Where's your mother?" I asked. We had all gone in to the room with the priest: Madhu, her mother, the neighbor and his wife, and another neighbor.

"She left as soon as it started. She couldn't take it."
I hadn't noticed her leave.

I had become her father's son-in-law in death. I had been Madhu's husband for a day, just before she separated from her real husband and filed for a divorce.

With all the running around, I had not eaten or drunk anything all day. I felt I was about to faint. I leaned closer to Madhu and on her.

"Thank you, André," she said.

I put my arm around her small shoulders and squeezed them.

"I need something to drink."

"The neighbors always have some Coke in their trunk," she said.

We stood outside the crematorium in silence. Everyone had already paid their condolences. Madhu brought me a Coke. I drank it while everyone stood in a small circle. I was the only one making any movement of any sort. Everyone was deadly still. I was gulping large quantities of the sweet fluid from the can. It was awkward.

"I'm going to stay on with my mom for a few days," Madhu said, addressing me.

It was odd being spoken to directly when so many people were standing with us.

"Yes," I said. Then, after a second, I said, "I'll get a cab to the airport."

"We'll drop you, Mr. Bernard," one of the neighbors said formally. He was older than me but younger than my father.

"Thank you," I said, inclining my head.

No one had mentioned the fact that I had played son-in-law at the funeral. I presumed they'd all been to Madhu's wedding and knew she'd married an Indian. I felt guilty, like an usurper, though I'd done nothing wrong.

We broke up the circle. One set of neighbors drove Madhu and her mother home. The other drove me to the airport. On the way in the car, the man asked me for investment tips. He was a doctor and invested a lot of money in the stock market. I was in no mood to chat about such things, but I answered his questions as best I could. Something was gnawing inside me, and this man wasn't letting me focus and put my finger on it.

From the airport I checked my voicemail at work and at home. Nathan had called both to say he was thinking of me. He said he was thinking of Madhu. I felt strongly bonded with him. The difficult times we'd had made me feel even closer to him.

The wait in the airport lounge was a relief after the ride. There were children in squeaky shoes and young couples making out. Amid the harsh fluorescent light and the big windows, looking out on the tarmac I wondered why everything had happened. I'd always rejected the idea that things happen for a reason. I still rejected the idea. But the incident with Madhu's father's death was beyond random. For a day I had left my life and all my issues and spent it in a crematorium, a morgue, a Hindu ceremony in the Lone Star state becoming the husband of a woman I had once wanted to marry and whom I still loved. It was like some sort of coded message from the gods. No amount of knowledge of notational systems from my math years was helping decode it. It was as if something greater than me and my life had given me a quick glimpse of itself and vanished. I'd have to spend the rest of my life seeking an answer.

I puzzled over it all the way back to New York. At La Guardia I reset my watch. It was nine in the evening. It felt as if an eternity had gone by. At the first pay phone I saw, I called Nathan. He asked me how Madhu was, how I was.

"Can I see you later?" I asked.

"Of course. Do you want to come to my place?"

"Yes. I'll come. I have something to take care of—then I'll be there."

"I'll be waiting," he said and made a kiss over the phone before hanging up.

I called Martha.

"It's André. I got back from Texas. How're you doing?"

"Not great. I have a slight fever."

"Are you all right? Have you been to the doctor?" I was concerned.

"I'm fine, it's nothing to worry about."

"Have you eaten?"

"I didn't feel like it."

"You should be eating properly. And drinking milk."

"That's all I drink. There's nothing else at home. I don't want to bother."

"I'll bring something over," I said.

"Now?"

"Yes."

"All right. Can you get more milk?"

"Of course. Anything else? Toilet paper? Candy?"

"No nothing," she said, laughing.

I hung up and got out of the automatic revolving door at the airport and hopped into a cab. I got off a block from her house where I saw an organic market. I bought regular milk and a couple of cartons of soy milk, which would keep longer, for days when she ran out. I bought a vegetable protein sandwich. The guy at the register put everything in two plastic bags for me.

The bags were white with thick red lines showing Manhattan's skyline. They said "I Love New York." I carried them in one hand. I walked across the street and up the block to Martha's apartment and rang the buzzer. She buzzed me in. There were candles all over her apartment. The smell of incense infused the air.

"Hello, André," she said, kissing me on the lips.

I kissed her back weakly and excused myself to her kitchen to put the stuff I was carrying in the fridge.

"I got a sandwich if you feel like it," I said.

"No, not now."

"Okay, I'll put it in the fridge as well."

I stepped back into the living room and noticed the clock on her wall. It was already a quarter to ten. I wanted to go to Nathan.

"Well, then," I said, looking at her. She was sitting on her couch with one foot up on her side.

"Come sit. I was daydreaming about her," she said, rubbing her tummy.

"Him," I said, smiling.

"Let's talk about how we'll raise her," she said. Her face was glowing. The familiarity of the situation, the candles, her attitude felt oppressive. Camille was mine. I wanted to escape from the idea that Martha had any say about how he would be raised. I couldn't bear the idea of sitting on her couch and dreaming of a future with her. It made me remember the family in Union Square, the father, his son, his grandson. I could only include Nathan in something like that.

"Unfortunately, I have to go," I said.

"You'll always have to go. Do you think someone who's always leaving will make a good father?"

I was strapped for words. Leaving Martha was not the same as leaving my son. It infuriated me that just because she was bearing him she thought she could have the expectations of me that he could have. She didn't deserve what he deserved. For me she was a vessel. A bearer. I couldn't say that.

"Sorry, Martha. I just came back from a funeral that shook me up. Now is not the best time. I'll call you tomorrow."

"Oh! I'm sorry. I forgot," she said. She genuinely meant it. I felt bad at having used an excuse, but I felt justified.

"Don't get up. I'll close the door behind me," I said as I bent down to her and gave her a quick hug. Then I turned on my heels and walked out quickly.

Stepping out on the sidewalk in front of her apartment made me feel free again. There was something inevitable about meeting Martha. And inevitability was death. Nothing before in my life had felt that permanent. It was like walking around with a huge block of lead hanging down from my shoulders. As I hailed a cab to Nathan's, I opened my miniplanner and pulled out my pen. I wrote "N" under all the days for ten full pages. Each page held six days. Then I flipped the pages and saw the "Ns" I had just written under them whiz by me quickly. Two whole months of "N." It suddenly felt permanent. That was its own kind of inevitability.

As the cab made its way down Fifth Avenue I tore out the two months' worth of "Ns" I had written. I flipped the pages. Now there was nothing except Camille's birth someday in the future. The pages were clean and white—only thin gold lines separated the six days on each page. A whole world of possibilities opened in the two months I had torn out of my miniplanner. Maybe possibilities not as good as Nathan. In which case, I'd surely reject them. I felt better, anyway.

About the Author

Abha Dawesar lives in New York. She is a graduate of Harvard University and the recipient of a New York Foundation for the Arts Writer's fellowship.